PENGUIN MODERN CLASSICS

THE ASPERN PAPERS AND OTHER STORIES

Henry James was born in 1843 in Washington Place, New York, of Scottish and Irish ancestry. His father was a prominent theologian and philosopher and his elder brother, William, was also famous as a philosopher. He attended schools in New York and later in London, Paris and Geneva, entering the Law School at Harvard in 1862. In 1865 he began to contribute reviews and short stories to American journals. In 1875, after two prior visits to Europe, he settled for a year in Paris, where he met Flaubert, Turgenev, and other literary figures. However, the next year he moved to London, where he became such an inveterate diner-out that in the winter of 1878–9 he confessed to accepting 107 invitations. In 1898 he left London and went to live at Lamb House, Rye, Sussex. Henry James became naturalized in 1915, was awarded the O.M., and died early in 1916.

In addition to many short stories, plays, books of criticism, autobiography, and travel he wrote some twenty novels, the first published being *Roderick Hudson* (1875). They include *The Europeans, The Portrait of a Lady, The Spoils of Poynton, Washington Square, The Bostonians, What Maisie Knew, The Golden Bowl, The Wings of the Dove, The Turn of the Screw and other Stories* and *The Princess Casamassima.*

HENRY JAMES

The Aspern Papers and Other Stories

INTRODUCED AND SELECTED BY
S. GORLEY PUTT

PENGUIN BOOKS

Penguin Books Ltd, Harmondsworth, Middlesex, England
Penguin Books, 625 Madison Avenue, New York, New York 10022, U.S.A.
Penguin Books Australia Ltd, Ringwood, Victoria, Australia
Penguin Books Canada Ltd, 41 Steelcase Road West, Markham, Ontario, Canada
Penguin Books (N.Z.) Ltd, 182–190 Wairau Road, Auckland 10, New Zealand

'The Aspern Papers' first published 1888
'The Real Thing' first published 1892
'The Papers' first published 1903
Published in Penguin Books 1976
This selection copyright © Penguin Books Ltd, 1976
Introduction copyright © S. Gorley Putt, 1976

Made and printed in Great Britain by
Richard Clay (The Chaucer Press) Ltd
Bungay, Suffolk
Set in Monotype Times

CONTENTS

Introduction   7

The Aspern Papers   11

The Real Thing   107

The Papers   135

INTRODUCTION

THESE stories were written at a time when fiction, as an entertainment, was still almost exclusively literate. There was therefore some (but not much) justification for the view that readers of stories might be interested in the professional problems of the authors who produced them. Nowadays, a sizable proportion of the offerings on film, television, radio, even long-playing records, assumes in the listener or viewer a keen personal interest in the private lives, taken as entertainment in themselves, of the people who are seen and heard. *The Jolson Story* set out to be an entertainment as fascinating as the original film *The Singing Fool* in which Al Jolson had merely been an actor in the story. Later, we were all supposed to be entertained when one wireless comedian imitated another wireless comedian performing in a programme we had not heard. Later still, television brings us a host of 'personalities' – authors, song-writers, producers, as well as actors and actresses – whose actions and opinions and choice of *Desert Island Discs* are deemed to be as entertaining as the artistic products (often lowly enough) which first brought their names to our attention. To be fair to Henry James as a professional writer at the end of the last century and the beginning of this one, he was making a somewhat similar assumption that stories *about* writers and artists were as acceptable, as raw material, as the tailored products of those writers and artists.

This, I believe, was a mistaken view. It would have had worse consequences had it not been for the unemphasized strength of James's own creative imagination, which ensured that even when his characters were conceived as representative types pointing a literary or artistic moral, they still had so much life in them that they outshone, simply as fictional characters, the creations of most other 'straight' storytellers of his day. It is a paradox that would have given James himself a wry pleasure. In the story *The Next Time* (1895) he invented a novelist who is the master of a subtle and distinguished style, whose books are praised by the critics but do not sell, and who therefore tries hard to produce a vulgar best-seller. Alas, his programme of 'writing down' never comes off. Try as he may, his efforts at saleable vulgarity always emerge as new unsaleable masterpieces. His friends groan over his lack of success: 'The book has extraordinary beauty.' 'Poor duck – after trying so hard!' In much the same way, James's own efforts to interest us in the theoretical problems of authors and artists sometimes fail; but instead we may be delighted by yet another set of splendidly imagined social types who – if we really *do* share the writer's and even his ventriloquist's dummies' love for the art of fiction – interest and amuse us far in excess of the somewhat sterile debating points they were designed to make.

So from the long list of tales in which Henry James treated the plight of the creative artist, these three examples here reprinted have been selected because they are splendid stories in their own right. Many of the other tales have an interest as parables of the writer's life, but lack the vigour which here marks James's work as a social observer rather than as a literary apologist.

The Real Thing (1892) poses 'the perverse and cruel law in virtue of which the real thing could be so much less precious than the unreal'. This problem may well worry a writer; but that James himself solved it even in this present instance is manifest in his vivid portraiture of the Monarchs, who have a 'real' life far beyond that required by the parable. Major and Mrs Monarch, indigent but utterly authentic representatives of 'the upper class', find themselves surpassed as models for graphic illustrations of high-society fiction by a 'lower-class' pair who have no authenticity whatever – except the authenticity of professional *poseurs*, whose acting is therefore far more persuasive. Poor Major Monarch in a splendidly realized figure, the sort of knowing but tongue-tied man of the world whose conversation is confined to 'questions of leather and even of liquor – saddlers and breeches-makers and how to get excellent claret cheap – and matters like "good trains" and the habits of small game'. When it comes to *imitating* people like himself, he is of course hopeless. The fable is amusing, and so are the main actors in it, especially the actor who cannot act.

Henry James's deep concern for private feelings bred in him a corresponding distaste for public sham, for 'non-events'. He would have loathed the fully fledged modern profession of 'public relations'. In his short novel *The Reverberator* (1888) he satirized as a 'recording, slobbering sheet' the sort of gossip-mongering newspaper already prolific in his native America, just as in *The Bostonians* (1886) he had satirized a similar journal as being devoted 'to the great end of preventing the American citizen from attempting clandestine journeys'. By the time he came to write *The Papers* (1903) he broadened his attack to include those inane 'personalities' whose vanity is fed by public reference, such as the egregious Beadel-Muffet, 'universal and ubiquitous, commemorated, under some rank rubric, on every page of every public print every day in every year, and as inveterate a feature of each issue of any self-respecting sheet as the name, the date, the tariffed advertisements'. The reader's sympathy is reserved for a young pair of hard-working journalists who are doomed to prostitute their skills to this squalid trade. They, and the still less privileged London drudges who sustain the world of the Beadel-Muffets, eating at 'greasy white slabs' in tea-shops served by 'little weary ministrants' in cap and apron, constitute the submerged part of the Edwardian social iceberg. James spent much of his working life observing the iceberg above the water-line: but only a very short-sighted reader could imagine that James approved what he saw. An attentive reading of *The Papers* will reveal not only a squeamish distaste for the vulgarities of self-advertisement, but also the deeper indignation of a social critic affronted by the class structure of the England he had adopted as his home.

The Aspern Papers (1888) is one of James's best-known tales; it was often reprinted long before the highly successful stage adaptation by Sir Michael Redgrave in 1959. Its moral conundrum is gripping enough to suggest dramatization, and permanent enough to preserve this story beyond the time when the social backgrounds of James's tales have faded away and taken the point with them. It is simply this: how far, in preserving the truth about the famous dead, are we justified in wounding the feelings of the less famous living? Three years after its publication, an anonymous critic (quoted in Roger Gard's *Henry James: The Critical Heritage*) included *The Aspern Papers* in a group of James's 'delightful stories' characterized by 'wit, humour, pathos, a charming gaiety, acute observation of life and character; but it is the faultless skill with which they are framed, that above all, perhaps, "places" them as consummate works of art'. One is tempted to add the examination-paper suffix ': discuss'. Perhaps the last word may be left with Sir Michael Redgrave who had studied the story for many years before he set about turning it into a play. 'The suspense of James,' he writes in his Preface to the adaptation, 'may be finely drawn and almost invisible, like a high-wire above our heads at the circus, but it is there ... So, for that matter, is situation.' The psychological 'suspense' of *The Aspern Papers* is sustained just by one's feeling that the intruding scholar who had penetrated the 'mystic rites of ennui the Misses Bordereau celebrated in their darkened rooms' is *not* merely a 'publishing scoundrel'. The 'situation' is most poignantly realized in the scene of Miss Tita's near-proposal to the letter-hunter, offering herself in a package-deal on terms of conditional sale. When Dame Flora Robson lowered her embarrassed eyes in this scene, the audience, too, lowered its collective head.

As in Leon Edel's admirable edition of *The Complete Tales of Henry James*, the stories are here printed as they first appeared in book form.

S. GORLEY PUTT

THE ASPERN PAPERS

1

I HAD taken Mrs Prest into my confidence; in truth without her I should have made but little advance, for the fruitful idea in the whole business dropped from her friendly lips. It was she who invented the short cut, who severed the Gordian knot. It is not supposed to be the nature of women to rise as a general thing to the largest and most liberal view – I mean of a practical scheme; but it has struck me that they sometimes throw off a bold conception – such as a man would not have risen to – with singular serenity. 'Simply ask them to take you in on the footing of a lodger' – I don't think that unaided I should have risen to that. I was beating about the bush, trying to be ingenious, wondering by what combination of arts I might become an acquaintance, when she offered this happy suggestion that the way to become an acquaintance was first to become an inmate. Her actual knowledge of the Misses Bordereau was scarcely larger than mine, and indeed I had brought with me from England some definite facts which were new to her. Their name had been mixed up ages before with one of the greatest names of the century, and they lived now in Venice in obscurity, on very small means, unvisited, unapproachable, in a dilapidated old palace on an out-of-the-way canal: this was the substance of my friend's impression of them. She herself had been established in Venice for fifteen years and had done a great deal of good there; but the circle of her benevolence did not include the two shy, mysterious and, as it was somehow supposed, scarcely respectable Americans (they were believed to have lost in their long exile all national quality, besides having had, as their name implied, some French strain in their origin), who asked no favours and desired no attention. In the early years of her residence she had made an attempt to see them, but this had been successful only as regards the little one, as Mrs Prest called the niece; though in reality, as I afterwards learned, she was considerably the bigger of the two. She had heard Miss Bordereau was ill and had a suspicion that she was in want; and she had gone to the house to offer assistance, so that if there were suffering (and American suffering), she should at least not have it on her conscience. The 'little one' received her in the great cold, tarnished Venetian sala, the central hall of the house, paved with marble and roofed with dim cross-beams, and did not even ask her to sit down. This was not encouraging for me, who wished to sit so fast, and I remarked as much to Mrs Prest. She however replied with profundity, 'Ah, but there's all the difference: I went to confer a favour and you will go to ask one. If they are proud you will be on the right side.' And she offered to show me their house to begin with – to row me thither in her gondola. I let her know that I had already been to look at it half a dozen times; but I accepted her invitation, for it charmed me to hover about the place. I had made my way to it the day after my arrival in Venice (it had been described to me in advance by the friend in England to whom I owed definite information as to their possession of the papers), and I had besieged it with my eyes while I considered my plan of campaign. Jeffrey Aspern had never been in it that I knew of; but some note of his voice seemed to abide there by a roundabout implication, a faint reverberation.

Mrs Prest knew nothing about the papers, but she was interested in my curiosity, as she was always interested in the joys and sorrows of her friends. As we went, however, in her gondola, gliding there under the sociable hood with the bright Venetian picture framed on either side by the movable window, I could see that she was amused by my infatuation, the way my interest in the papers had become a fixed idea. 'One would think you expected to find in them the answer to the riddle of the universe,' she said; and I denied the impeachment only by replying that if I had to choose between that precious solution and a bundle of Jeffrey Aspern's letters I knew indeed which would appear to me the greater boon. She pretended to make light of his genius and I took no pains to defend him. One doesn't defend one's god: one's god is in himself a defence. Besides, today, after his long comparative obscuration, he hangs high in the heaven of our literature, for all the world to see; he is a part of the light by which we walk. The most I said was that he was no doubt not a woman's poet: to which she rejoined aptly enough that he had been at least Miss Bordereau's. The strange thing had been for me to discover in England that she was still alive; it was as if I had been told Mrs Siddons was, or Queen Caroline, or the famous Lady Hamilton, for it seemed to me that she belonged to a generation as extinct. 'Why, she must be tremendously old – at least a hundred,' I had said; but on coming to consider dates I saw that it was not strictly necessary that she should have exceeded by very much the common span. None the less she was very far advanced in life and her relations with Jeffrey Aspern had occurred in her early womanhood. 'That is her excuse,' said Mrs Prest, half sententiously and yet also somewhat as if she were ashamed of making a speech so little in the real tone of Venice. As if a woman needed an excuse for having loved the divine poet! He had been not only one of the most brilliant minds of his day (and in those years, when the century was young, there were, as every one knows, many), but one of the most genial men and one of the handsomest.

The niece, according to Mrs Prest, was not so old, and she risked the conjecture that she was only a grand-niece. This was possible; I had nothing but my share in the very limited knowledge of my English fellow-worshipper John Cumnor, who had never seen the couple. The world, as I say, had recognized Jeffrey Aspern, but Cumnor and I had recognized him most. The multitude, today, flocked to his temple, but of that temple he and I regarded ourselves as the ministers. We held, justly, as I think, that we had done more for his memory than anyone else, and we had done it by opening lights into his life. He had nothing to fear from us because he had nothing to fear from the truth, which alone at such a distance of time we could be interested in establishing. His early death had been the only dark spot in his life, unless the papers in Miss Bordereau's hands should perversely bring out others. There had been an impression about 1825 that he had 'treated her badly', just as there had been an impression that he had 'served', as the London populace says, several other ladies in the same way. Each of these cases Cumnor and I had been able to investigate, and we had never failed to acquit him conscientiously of shabby behaviour. I judged him perhaps more indulgently than my friend; certainly, at any rate, it appeared to me that no man could have walked straighter in the given circumstances. These were almost always awkward. Half the women of his time, to speak liberally, had flung themselves at his head, and out of this pernicious fashion many complications, some of them grave, had not failed to arise. He was not a woman's poet, as I had said to Mrs Prest, in the modern phase of his reputation; but the situation had been different when the man's own voice was mingled with his song. That voice, by every testimony, was one of the sweetest ever heard. 'Orpheus and the Mænads!' was the exclamation that rose to my lips when I first turned over his correspondence. Almost all the Mænads were unreasonable and many of them insupportable; it struck me in short that he was kinder, more considerate than, in his place (if I could imagine myself in such a place!) I should have been.

It was certainly strange beyond all strangeness, and I shall not take up space with attempting to explain it, that whereas in all these other lines of research we had to deal with phantoms and dust, the mere echoes of echoes, the one living source of information that had lingered on into our time had been unheeded by us. Every one of Aspern's contemporaries had, according to our belief, passed away; we had not been able to look into a single pair of eyes into which his had looked or to feel a transmitted contact in any aged hand that his had touched. Most dead of all did poor Miss Bordereau appear, and yet she alone had survived. We exhausted in the course of months our wonder that we had not found her out sooner, and the substance of our explanation was that she had kept so quiet. The poor lady on the whole had had reason for doing so. But it was a revelation to us that it was possible to keep so quiet as that in the latter half of the nineteenth century – the age of newspapers and telegrams and photographs and interviewers. And she had taken no great trouble about it either: she had not hidden herself away in an undiscoverable hole; she had boldly settled down in a city of exhibition. The only secret of her safety that we could perceive was that Venice contained so many curiosities that were greater than she. And then accident had somehow favoured her, as was shown for example in the fact that Mrs Prest had never happened to mention her to me, though I had spent three weeks in Venice – under her nose, as it were – five years before. Mrs Prest had not mentioned this much to anyone; she appeared almost to have forgotten she was there. Of course she had not the responsibilities of an editor. It was no explanation of the old woman's having eluded us to say that she lived abroad, for our researches had again and again taken us (not only by correspondence but by personal inquiry) to France, to Germany, to Italy, in which countries, not counting his important stay in England, so many of the too few years of Aspern's career were spent. We were glad to think at least that in all our publishings (some people consider I believe that we have overdone them), we had only touched in passing and in the most discreet manner on Miss Bordereau's connection. Oddly enough, even if we had had the material (and we often wondered what had become of it), it would have been the most difficult episode to handle.

The gondola stopped, the old palace was there; it was a house of the class which in Venice carries even in extreme dilapidation the dignified name. 'How charming! It's grey and pink!' my companion exclaimed; and that is the most comprehensive description of it. It was not particularly old, only two or three centuries; and it had an air not so much of decay as of quiet discouragement, as if it had rather missed its career. But its wide front, with a stone balcony from end to end of the *piano nobile* or most important floor, was architectural enough, with the aid of various pilasters and arches; and the stucco with which in the intervals it had long ago been endued was rosy in the April afternoon. It overlooked a clean, melancholy, unfrequented canal, which had a narrow *riva* or convenient footway on either side. 'I don't know why – there are no brick gables,' said Mrs Prest, 'but this corner has seemed to me before more Dutch than Italian, more like Amsterdam than like Venice. It's perversely clean, for reasons of its own; and though you can pass on foot scarcely anyone ever thinks of doing so. It has the air of a Protestant Sunday. Perhaps the people are afraid of the Misses Bordereau. I dare say they have the reputation of witches.'

I forget what answer I made to this – I was given up to two other reflections. The first of these was that if the old lady lived in such a big, imposing house she could not be in any sort of misery and therefore would not be tempted by a chance to let a couple of rooms. I expressed this idea to Mrs Prest, who gave me a very logical reply. 'If she didn't live in a big house how could it be a question of her having rooms to spare? If she were not amply lodged herself you would lack ground to approach her. Besides, a big house here, and especially in this *quartier perdu*, proves nothing at all: it is perfectly compatible with a state of penury. Dilapidated old palazzi, if you will go out of the way for them, are to be had for five shillings a year. And as for the people who live in them – no, until you have explored Venice socially as much as I have you can form no idea of their domestic desolation. They live on nothing, for they have nothing to live on.' The other idea that had come into my head was connected with a high blank wall which appeared to confine an expanse of ground on one side of the house. Blank I call it, but it was figured over with the patches that please a painter, repaired breaches, crumblings of plaster, extrusions of brick that had turned pink with time; and a few thin trees, with the poles of certain rickety trellises, were visible over the top. The place was a garden and apparently it belonged to the house. It suddenly occurred to me that if it did belong to the house I had my pretext.

I sat looking out on all this with Mrs Prest (it was covered with the golden glow of Venice) from the shade of our *felze*, and she asked me if I would go in then, while she waited for me, or come back another time. At first I could not decide – it was doubtless very weak of me. I wanted still to think I *might* get a footing, and I was afraid to meet failure, for it would leave me, as I remarked to my companion, without another arrow for my bow. 'Why not another?' she inquired, as I sat there hesitating and thinking it over; and she wished to know why even now and before taking the trouble of becoming an inmate (which might be wretchedly uncomfortable after all, even if it succeeded), I had not the resource of simply offering them a sum of money down. In that way I might obtain the documents without bad nights.

'Dearest lady,' I exclaimed, 'excuse the impatience of my tone when I suggest that you must have forgotten the very fact (surely I communicated it to you) which pushed me to throw myself upon your ingenuity. The old woman won't have the documents spoken of; they are personal, delicate, intimate, and she hasn't modern notions, God bless her! If I should sound that note first I should certainly spoil the game. I can arrive at the papers only by putting her off her guard, and I can put her off her guard only by ingrati-ating diplomatic practices. Hypocrisy, duplicity are my only chance. I am sorry for it, but for Jeffrey Aspern's sake I would do worse still. First I must take tea with her; then tackle the main job.' And I told over what had happened to John Cumnor when he wrote to her. No notice whatever had been taken of his first letter, and the second had been answered very sharply, in six lines, by the niece. 'Miss Bordereau requested her to say that she could not imagine what he meant by troubling them. They had none of Mr Aspern's papers, and if they had should never think of show-ing them to any one on any account whatever. She didn't know what he was talking about and begged he would let her alone.' I certainly did not want to be met that way.

'Well,' said Mrs Prest, after a moment, provokingly, 'perhaps after all they haven't any of his things. If they deny it flat how are you sure?'

'John Cumnor is sure, and it would take me long to tell you how his conviction, or his very strong presumption – strong enough to stand against the old lady's not unnatural fib – has built itself up. Besides, he makes much of the internal evidence of the niece's letter.'

'The internal evidence?'

'Her calling him "Mr Aspern".'

'I don't see what that proves.'

'It proves familiarity, and familiarity implies the possession of mementoes, of relics. I can't tell you how that "Mr" touches me – how it bridges over the gulf of time and brings our hero near to me – nor what an edge it gives to my desire to see Juliana. You don't say "Mr" Shakespeare.'

' Would I, any more, if I had a box full of his letters?'

'Yes, if he had been your lover and someone wanted them!' And I added that John Cumnor was so convinced, and so all the more convinced by Miss Bordereau's tone, that he would have come himself to Venice on the business were it not that for him there was the obstacle that it would be difficult to disprove his identity with the person who had written to them, which the old ladies would be sure to suspect in spite of dissimulation and a change of name. If they were to ask him point-blank if he were not their correspondent it would be too awkward for him to lie; whereas I was fortunately not tied in that way. I was a fresh hand and could say no without lying.

'But you will have to change your name,' said Mrs Prest. 'Juliana lives out of the world as much as it is possible to live, but none the less she has probably heard of Mr Aspern's editors; she perhaps possesses what you have published.'

'I have thought of that,' I returned; and I drew out of my pocket-book a visiting-card, neatly engraved with a name that was not my own.

'You are very extravagant; you might have written it,' said my companion.

'This looks more genuine.'

'Certainly, you are prepared to go far! But it will be awkward about your letters; they won't come to you in that mask.'

'My banker will take them in and I will go every day to fetch them. It will give me a little walk.'

'Shall you only depend upon that?' asked Mrs Prest. 'Aren't you coming to see me?'

'Oh, you will have left Venice, for the hot months, long before there are any results. I am prepared to roast all summer – as well as hereafter, perhaps you'll say! Meanwhile, John Cumnor will bombard me with letters addressed, in my feigned name, to the care of the *padrona*.'

'She will recognize his hand,' my companion suggested.

'On the envelope he can disguise it.'

'Well, you're a precious pair! Doesn't it occur to you that even if you are able to say you are not Mr Cumnor in person they may still suspect you of being his emissary?'

'Certainly, and I see only one way to parry that.'

'And what may that be?'

I hesitated a moment. 'To make love to the niece.'

'Ah,' cried Mrs Prest, 'wait till you see her!'

2

'I MUST work the garden – I must work the garden,' I said to myself, five minutes later, as I waited, upstairs, in the long, dusky sala, where the bare scagliola floor gleamed vaguely in a chink of the closed shutters. The place was impressive but it looked cold and cautious. Mrs Prest had floated away, giving me a rendezvous at the end of half an hour by some neighbouring watersteps; and I had been let into the house, after pulling the rusty bell-wire, by a little red-headed, white-faced maid-servant, who was very young and not ugly and wore clicking pattens and a shawl in the fashion of a hood. She had not contented herself with opening the door from above by the usual arrangement of a creaking pulley, though she had looked down at me first from an upper window, dropping the inevitable challenge which in Italy precedes the hospitable act. As a general thing I was irritated by this survival of medieval manners, though as I liked the old I suppose I ought to have liked it; but I was so determined to be genial that I took my false card out of my pocket and held it up to her, smiling as if it were a magic token. It had the effect of one indeed, for it brought her, as I say, all the way down. I begged her to hand it to her mistress, having first written on it in Italian the words, 'Could you very kindly see a gentleman, an American, for a moment?' The little maid was not hostile, and I reflected that even that was perhaps something gained. She coloured, she smiled and looked both frightened and pleased. I could see that my arrival was a great affair, that visits were rare in that house, and that she was a person who would have liked a sociable place. When she pushed forward the heavy door behind me I felt that I had a foot in the citadel. She pattered across the damp, stony lower hall and I followed her up the high staircase – stonier still, as it seemed – without an invitation. I think she had meant I should wait for her below, but such was not my idea, and I took up my station in the sala. She flitted, at the far end of it, into impenetrable regions, and I looked at the place with my heart beating as I had known it to do in the dentist's parlour. It was gloomy and stately, but it owed its character almost entirely to its noble shape and to the fine architectural doors – as high as the doors of houses – which, leading into the various rooms, repeated themselves on either side at intervals. They were surmounted with old faded painted escutcheons, and here and there, in the spaces between them, brown pictures, which I perceived to be bad, in battered frames, were suspended. With the exception of several straw-bottomed chairs with their backs to the wall, the grand obscure vista contained nothing else to minister to effect. It was evidently never used save as a passage, and little even as that. I may add that by the time the door opened again through which the maid-servant had escaped, my eyes had grown used to the want of light.

I had not meant by my private ejaculation that I must myself cultivate the soil of the tangled enclosure which lay beneath the windows, but the lady who came towards me from the distance over the hard, shining floor might have supposed as much from the way in which, as I went rapidly to meet her, I exclaimed, taking care to speak Italian: 'The garden, the garden – do me the pleasure to tell me if it's yours!'

She stopped short, looking at me with wonder; and then, 'Nothing here is mine,' she answered in English, coldly and sadly.

'Oh, you are English; how delightful!' I remarked, ingenuously. 'But surely the garden belongs to the house?'

'Yes, but the house doesn't belong to me.' She was a long, lean, pale person, habited apparently in a dull-coloured dressing-gown, and she spoke with a kind of mild literalness. She did not ask me to sit down, any more than years before (if she were the niece) she had asked Mrs Prest, and we stood face to face in the empty pompous hall.

'Well then, would you kindly tell me to whom I must address myself? I'm afraid you'll think me odiously intrusive, but you know I *must* have a garden – upon my honour I must!'

Her face was not young, but it was simple; it was not fresh, but it was mild. She had large eyes which were not bright, and a great deal of hair which was not 'dressed', and long fine hands which were – possibly not clean. She clasped these members almost convulsively as, with a confused, alarmed look, she broke out, 'Oh, don't take it away from us; we like it ourselves!'

'You have the use of it then?'

'Oh yes. If it wasn't for that!' And she gave a shy, melancholy smile.

'Isn't it a luxury, precisely? That's why, intending to be in Venice some weeks, possibly all summer, and having some literary work, some reading and writing to do, so that I must be quiet, and yet if possible a great deal in the open air – that's why I have felt that a garden is really indispensable. I appeal to your own experience,' I went on, smiling. 'Now can't I look at yours?'

'I don't know, I don't understand,' the poor woman murmured, planted there and letting her embarrassed eyes wander all over my strangeness.

'I mean only from one of those windows – such grand ones as you have here – if you will let me open the shutters.' And I walked towards the back of the house. When I had advanced half-way I stopped and waited, as if I took it for granted she would accompany me. I had been of necessity very abrupt, but I strove at the same time to give her the impression of extreme courtesy. 'I have been looking at furnished rooms all over the place, and it seems impossible to find any with a garden attached. Naturally in a place like Venice gardens are rare. It's absurd if you like, for a man, but I can't live without flowers.'

'There are none to speak of down there.' She came nearer to me, as if, though she mistrusted me, I had drawn her by an invisible thread. I went on again, and she continued as she followed me: 'We have a few, but they are very common. It costs too much to cultivate them; one has to have a man.'

'Why shouldn't I be the man?' I asked. 'I'll work without

21

wages; or rather I'll put in a gardener. You shall have the sweetest flowers in Venice.'

She protested at this, with a queer little sigh which might also have been a gush of rapture at the picture I presented. Then she observed, 'We don't know you – we don't know you.'

'You know me as much as I know you; that is much more, because you know my name. And if you are English I am almost a countryman.'

'We are not English,' said my companion, watching me helplessly while I threw open the shutters of one of the divisions of the wide high window.

'You speak the language so beautifully: might I ask what you are?' Seen from above the garden was certainly shabby; but I perceived at a glance that it had great capabilities. She made no rejoinder, she was so lost in staring at me, and I exclaimed, 'You don't mean to say you are also by chance American?'

'I don't know; we used to be.'

'Used to be? Surely you haven't changed?'

'It's so many years ago – we are nothing.'

'So many years that you have been living here? Well, I don't wonder at that; it's a grand old house. I suppose you all use the garden,' I went on, 'but I assure you I shouldn't be in your way. I would be very quiet and stay in one corner.'

'We all use it?' she repeated after me, vaguely, not coming close to the window but looking at my shoes. She appeared to think me capable of throwing her out.

'I mean all your family, as many as you are.'

'There is only one other; she is very old – she never goes down.'

'Only one other, in all this great house!' I feigned to be not only amazed but almost scandalized. 'Dear lady, you must have space then to spare!'

'To spare?' she repeated, in the same dazed way.

'Why, you surely don't live (two quiet women – I see *you* are quiet, at any rate) in fifty rooms!' Then with a burst of hope and cheer I demanded: 'Couldn't you let me two or three? That would set me up!'

I had now struck the note that translated my purpose and I

need not reproduce the whole of the tune I played. I ended by making my interlocutress believe that I was an honourable person, though of course I did not even attempt to persuade her that I was not an eccentric one. I repeated that I had studies to pursue; that I wanted quiet; that I delighted in a garden and had vainly sought one up and down the city; that I would undertake that before another month was over the dear old house should be smothered in flowers. I think it was the flowers that won my suit, for I afterwards found that Miss Tita (for such the name of this high tremulous spinster proved somewhat incongruously to be) had an insatiable appetite for them. When I speak of my suit as won I mean that before I left her she had promised that she would refer the question to her aunt. I inquired who her aunt might be and she answered, 'Why, Miss Bordereau!' with an air of surprise, as if I might have been expected to know. There were contradictions like this in Tita Bordereau which, as I observed later, contributed to make her an odd and affecting person. It was the study of the two ladies to live so that the world should not touch them, and yet they had never altogether accepted the idea that it never heard of them. In Tita at any rate a grateful susceptibility to human contact had not died out, and contact of a limited order there would be if I should come to live in the house.

'We have never done anything of the sort; we have never had a lodger or any kind of inmate.' So much as this she made a point of saying to me. 'We are very poor, we live very badly. The rooms are very bare – that you might take; they have nothing in them. I don't know how you would sleep, how you would eat.'

'With your permission, I could easily put in a bed and a few tables and chairs. C'est la moindre des choses and the affair of an hour or two. I know a little man from whom I can hire what I should want for a few months, for a trifle, and my gondolier can bring the things round in his boat. Of course in this great house you must have a second kitchen, and my servant, who is a wonderfully handy fellow' (this personage was an evocation of the moment), 'can easily cook me a chop there. My tastes and habits are of the simplest; I live on flowers!' And then I ventured to add that if they were very poor it was all the more reason they should let their rooms. They were bad economists – I had never heard of such a waste of material.

I saw in a moment that the good lady had never before been spoken to in that way, with a kind of humorous firmness which did not exclude sympathy but was on the contrary founded on it. She might easily have told me that my sympathy was impertinent, but this by good fortune did not occur to her. I left her with the understanding that she would consider the matter with her aunt and that I might come back the next day for their decision.

'The aunt will refuse; she will think the whole proceeding very *louche*!' Mrs Prest declared shortly after this, when I had resumed my place in her gondola. She had put the idea into my head and now (so little are women to be counted on) she appeared to take a despondent view of it. Her pessimism provoked me and I pretended to have the best hopes; I went so far as to say that I had a distinct presentiment that I should succeed. Upon this Mrs Prest broke out, 'Oh, I see what's in your head! You fancy you have made such an impression in a quarter of an hour that she is dying for you to come and can be depended upon to bring the old one round. If you do get in you'll count it as a triumph.'

I did count it as a triumph, but only for the editor (in the last analysis), not for the man, who had not the tradition of personal conquest. When I went back on the morrow the little maid-servant conducted me straight through the long sala (it opened there as before in perfect perspective and was lighter now, which I thought a good omen) into the apartment from which the recipient of my former visit had emerged on that occasion. It was a large shabby parlour, with a fine old painted ceiling and a strange figure sitting alone at one of the windows. They come back to me now almost with the palpitation they caused, the successive feelings that accompanied my consciousness that as the door of the room closed behind me I was really face to face with the Juliana of some of Aspern's most exquisite and most renowned lyrics. I grew used to her afterwards, though never completely; but as she sat there before me my heart beat as fast as if the miracle of resurrection had taken place for my benefit. Her presence seemed somehow to contain his, and I felt nearer to him at that first moment of seeing her than I ever had been before or ever have been since. Yes, I remember my emotions in their order, even including a curious little tremor that took me when I saw that the niece was not there. With her, the day before, I had become sufficiently familiar, but it almost exceeded my courage (much as I had longed for the event) to be left alone with such a terrible relic as the aunt. She was too strange, too literally resurgent. Then came a check, with the perception that we were not really face to face, inasmuch as she had over her eyes a horrible green shade which, for her, served almost as a mask. I believed for the instant that she had put it on expressly, so that from underneath it she might scrutinize me without being scrutinized herself. At the same time it increased the presumption that there was a ghastly death's-head lurking behind it. The divine Juliana as a grinning skull – the vision hung there until it passed. Then it came to me that she *was* tremendously old – so old that death might take her at any moment, before I had time to get what I wanted from her. The next thought was a correction to that; it lighted up the situation. She would die next week, she would die tomorrow – then I could seize her papers. Meanwhile she sat there neither moving nor speaking. She was very small and shrunken, bent forward, with her hands in her lap. She was dressed in black and her head was wrapped in a piece of old black lace which showed no hair.

My emotion keeping me silent she spoke first, and the remark she made was exactly the most unexpected.

3

'OUR house is very far from the centre, but the little canal is very *comme il faut*.'

'It's the sweetest corner of Venice and I can imagine nothing more charming,' I hastened to reply. The old lady's voice was very thin and weak, but it had an agreeable, cultivated murmur and there was wonder in the thought that that individual note had been in Jeffrey Aspern's ear.

'Please to sit down there. I hear very well,' she said quietly, as if perhaps I had been shouting at her; and the chair she pointed to was at a certain distance. I took possession of it, telling her that I was perfectly aware that I had intruded, that I had not been properly introduced and could only throw myself upon her indulgence. Perhaps the other lady, the one I had had the honour of seeing the day before, would have explained to her about the garden. That was literally what had given me courage to take a step so unconventional. I had fallen in love at sight with the whole place (she herself probably was so used to it that she did not know the impression it was capable of making on a stranger), and I had felt it was really a case to risk something. Was her own kindness in receiving me a sign that I was not wholly out in my calculation? It would render me extremely happy to think so. I could give her my word of honour that I was a most respectable, inoffensive person and that as an inmate they would be barely conscious of my existence. I would conform to any regulations, any restrictions if they would only let me enjoy the garden. Moreover I should be delighted to give her references, guarantees; they would be of the very best, both in Venice and in England as well as in America.

She listened to me in perfect stillness and I felt that she was looking at me with great attention, though I could see only the lower part of her bleached and shrivelled face. Independently of the refining process of old age it had a delicacy which once must have been great. She had been very fair, she had had a wonderful complexion. She was silent a little after I had ceased speaking; then she inquired, 'If you are so fond of a garden why don't you go to *terra firma*, where there are so many far better than this?'

'Oh, it's the combination!' I answered, smiling; and then, with rather a flight of fancy, 'It's the idea of a garden in the middle of the sea.'

'It's not in the middle of the sea; you can't see the water.'

I stared a moment, wondering whether she wished to convict me of fraud. 'Can't see the water? Why, dear madam, I can come up to the very gate in my boat.'

She appeared inconsequent, for she said vaguely in reply to this, 'Yes, if you have got a boat. I haven't any; it's many years

26

since I have been in one of the gondolas.' She uttered these words as if the gondolas were a curious far-away craft which she knew only by hearsay.

'Let me assure you of the pleasure with which I would put mine at your service!' I exclaimed. I had scarcely said this however before I became aware that the speech was in questionable taste and might also do me the injury of making me appear too eager, too possessed of a hidden motive. But the old woman remained impenetrable and her attitude bothered me by suggesting that she had a fuller vision of me than I had of her. She gave me no thanks for my somewhat extravagant offer but remarked that the lady I had seen the day before was her niece; she would presently come in. She had asked her to stay away a little on purpose, because she herself wished to see me at first alone. She relapsed into silence and I asked myself why she had judged this necessary and what was coming yet; also whether I might venture on some judicious remark in praise of her companion. I went so far as to say that I should be delighted to see her again: she had been so very courteous to me, considering how odd she must have thought me – a declaration which drew from Miss Bordereau another of her whimsical speeches.

'She has very good manners; I bred her up myself!' I was on the point of saying that that accounted for the easy grace of the niece, but I arrested myself in time, and the next moment the old woman went on: 'I don't care who you may be – I don't want to know; it signifies very little today.' This had all the air of being a formula of dismissal, as if her next words would be that I might take myself off now that she had had the amusement of looking on the face of such a monster of indiscretion. Therefore I was all the more surprised when she added, with her soft, venerable quaver, 'You may have as many rooms as you like – if you will pay a good deal of money.'

I hesitated but for a single instant, long enough to ask myself what she meant in particular by this condition. First it struck me that she must have really a large sum in her mind; then I reasoned quickly that her idea of a large sum would probably not correspond to my own. My deliberation, I think, was not so visible as to diminish the promptitude with which I replied, 'I will pay with pleasure and of course in advance whatever you may think it proper to ask me.'

'Well then, a thousand francs a month,' she rejoined instantly, while her baffling green shade continued to cover her attitude.

The figure, as they say, was startling and my logic had been at fault. The sum she had mentioned was, by the Venetian measure of such matters, exceedingly large; there was many an old palace in an out-of-the-way corner that I might on such terms have enjoyed by the year. But so far as my small means allowed I was prepared to spend money, and my decision was quickly taken. I would pay her with a smiling face what she asked, but in that case I would give myself the compensation of extracting the papers from her for nothing. Moreover if she had asked five times as much I should have risen to the occasion; so odious would it have appeared to me to stand chaffering with Aspern's Juliana. It was queer enough to have a question of money with her at all. I assured her that her views perfectly met my own and that on the morrow I should have the pleasure of putting three months' rent into her hand. She received this announcement with serenity and with no apparent sense that after all it would be becoming of her to say that I ought to see the rooms first. This did not occur to her and indeed her serenity was mainly what I wanted. Our little bargain was just concluded when the door opened and the younger lady appeared on the threshold. As soon as Miss Bordereau saw her niece she cried out almost gaily, 'He will give three thousand – three thousand tomorrow!'

Miss Tita stood still, with her patient eyes turning from one of us to the other; then she inquired, scarcely above her breath, 'Do you mean francs?'

'Did you mean francs or dollars?' the old woman asked of me at this.

'I think francs were what you said,' I answered, smiling.

'That is very good,' said Miss Tita, as if she had become conscious that her own question might have looked overreaching.

'What do *you* know? You are ignorant,' Miss Bordereau remarked; not with acerbity but with a strange, soft coldness.

'Yes, of money – certainly of money!' Miss Tita hastened to exclaim.

'I am sure you have your own branches of knowledge,' I took the liberty of saying, genially. There was something painful to me, somehow, in the turn the conversation had taken, in the discussion of the rent.

'She had a very good education when she was young. I looked into that myself,' said Miss Bordereau. Then she added, 'But she has learned nothing since.'

'I have always been with you,' Miss Tita rejoined very mildly, and evidently with no intention of making an epigram.

'Yes, but for that!' her aunt declared, with more satirical force. She evidently meant that but for this her niece would never have got on at all; the point of the observation however being lost on Miss Tita, though she blushed at hearing her history revealed to a stranger. Miss Bordereau went on, addressing herself to me: 'And what time will you come tomorrow with the money?'

'The sooner the better. If it suits you I will come at noon.'

'I am always here but I have my hours,' said the old woman, as if her convenience were not to be taken for granted.

'You mean the times when you receive?'

'I never receive. But I will see you at noon, when you come with the money.'

'Very good, I shall be punctual;' and I added, 'May I shake hands with you, on our contract?' I thought there ought to be some little form, it would make me really feel easier, for I foresaw that there would be no other. Besides, though Miss Bordereau could not today be called personally attractive and there was something even in her wasted antiquity that bade one stand at one's distance, I felt an irresistible desire to hold in my own for a moment the hand that Jeffrey Aspern had pressed.

For a minute she made no answer and I saw that my proposal failed to meet with her approbation. She indulged in no movement of withdrawal, which I half expected; she only said coldly, 'I belong to a time when that was not the custom.'

I felt rather snubbed but I exclaimed good-humouredly to Miss Tita, 'Oh, you will do as well!' I shook hands with her while she replied, with a small flutter, 'Yes, yes, to show it's all arranged!'

'Shall you bring the money in gold?' Miss Bordereau demanded, as I was turning to the door.

I looked at her a moment. 'Aren't you a little afraid, after all, of keeping such a sum as that in the house?' It was not that I was annoyed at her avidity but I was really struck with the disparity between such a treasure and such scanty means of guarding it.

'Whom should I be afraid of if I am not afraid of you?' she asked with her shrunken grimness.

'Ah well,' said I, laughing, 'I shall be in point of fact a protector and I will bring gold if you prefer.'

'Thank you,' the old woman returned with dignity and with an inclination of her head which evidently signified that I might depart. I passed out of the room, reflecting that it would not be easy to circumvent her. As I stood in the sala again I saw that Miss Tita had followed me and I supposed that as her aunt had neglected to suggest that I should take a look at my quarters it was her purpose to repair the omission. But she made no such suggestion; she only stood there with a dim, though not a languid smile, and with an effect of irresponsible, incompetent youth which was almost comically at variance with the faded facts of her person. She was not infirm, like her aunt, but she struck me as still more helpless, because her inefficiency was spiritual, which was not the case with Miss Bordereau's. I waited to see if she would offer to show me the rest of the house, but I did not precipitate the question, inasmuch as my plan was from this moment to spend as much of my time as possible in her society. I only observed at the end of a minute:

'I have had better fortune than I hoped. It was very kind of her to see me. Perhaps you said a good word for me.'

'It was the idea of the money,' said Miss Tita.

'And did you suggest that?'

'I told her that you would perhaps give a good deal.'

'What made you think that?'

'I told her I thought you were rich.'

'And what put that idea into your head?'

'I don't know; the way you talked.'

'Dear me, I must talk differently now,' I declared. 'I'm sorry to say it's not the case.'

'Well,' said Miss Tita, 'I think that in Venice the *forestieri*, in general, often give a great deal for something that after all isn't much.' She appeared to make this remark with a comforting intention, to wish to remind me that if I had been extravagant I was not really foolishly singular. We walked together along the sala, and as I took its magnificent measure I said to her that I was afraid it would not form a part of my *quartiere*. Were my rooms by chance to be among those that opened into it? 'Not if you go above, on the second floor,' she answered with a little startled air, as if she had rather taken for granted I would know my proper place.

'And I infer that that's where your aunt would like me to be.'

'She said your apartments ought to be very distinct.'

'That certainly would be best.' And I listened with respect while she told me that up above I was free to take whatever I liked; that there was another staircase, but only from the floor on which we stood, and that to pass from it to the garden-story or to come up to my lodging I should have in effect to cross the great hall. This was an immense point gained; I foresaw that it would constitute my whole leverage in my relations with the two ladies. When I asked Miss Tita how I was to manage at present to find my way up she replied with an access of that sociable shyness which constantly marked her manner.

'Perhaps you can't. I don't see – unless I should go with you.' She evidently had not thought of this before.

We ascended to the upper floor and visited a long succession of empty rooms. The best of them looked over the garden; some of the others had a view of the blue lagoon, above the opposite rough-tiled housetops. They were all dusty and even a little disfigured with long neglect, but I saw that by spending a few hundred francs I should be able to convert three or four of them into a convenient habitation. My experiment was turning out costly, yet now that I had all but taken possession I ceased to allow this to trouble me. I mentioned to my companion a few of the things that I should put in, but she replied rather more precipitately than usual that I might do exactly what I liked; she seemed to wish to notify me that the Misses Bordereau would take no overt interest in my proceedings. I guessed that her aunt had instructed her to adopt this tone, and I may as well say now that I came afterwards to distinguish perfectly (as I believed) between the speeches she made on her own responsibility and those the old lady imposed upon her. She took no notice of the unswept condition of the rooms and indulged in no explanations nor apologies. I said to myself that this was a sign that Juliana and her niece (disenchanting idea!) were untidy persons, with a low Italian standard; but I afterwards recognized that a lodger who had forced an entrance had no *locus standi* as a critic. We looked out of a good many windows, for there was nothing within the rooms to look at, and still I wanted to linger. I asked her what several different objects in the prospect might be, but in no case did she appear to know. She was evidently not familiar with the view – it was as if she had not looked at it for years – and I presently saw that she was too preoccupied with something else to pretend to care for it. Suddenly she said – the remark was not suggested:

'I don't know whether it will make any difference to you, but the money is for me.'

'The money?'

'The money you are going to bring.'

'Why, you'll make me wish to stay here two or three years.' I spoke as benevolently as possible, though it had begun to act on my nerves that with these women so associated with Aspern the pecuniary question should constantly come back.

'That would be very good for me,' she replied, smiling.

'You put me on my honour!'

She looked as if she failed to understand this, but went on: 'She wants me to have more. She thinks she is going to die.'

'Ah, not soon, I hope!' I exclaimed, with genuine feeling. I had perfectly considered the possibility that she would destroy her papers on the day she should feel her end really approach. I believed that she would cling to them till then and I think I had an idea that she read Aspern's letters over every night or at least pressed them to her withered lips. I would have given a good deal to have a glimpse of the latter spectacle. I asked Miss Tita if the old lady were seriously ill and she replied that she was only very tired – she had lived so very, very long. That was what she said herself – she wanted to die for a change. Besides, all her friends were dead long ago; either they ought to have remained or she ought to have gone. That was another thing her aunt often said – she was not at all content.

'But people don't die when they like, do they?' Miss Tita inquired. I took the liberty of asking why, if there was actually enough money to maintain both of them, there would not be more than enough in case of her being left alone. She considered this difficult problem a moment and then she said, 'Oh, well, you know, she takes care of me. She thinks that when I'm alone I shall be a great fool, I shall not know how to manage.'

'I should have supposed rather that you took care of her. I'm afraid she is very proud.'

'Why, have you discovered that already?' Miss Tita cried, with the glimmer of an illumination in her face.

'I was shut up with her there for a considerable time, and she struck me, she interested me extremely. It didn't take me long to make my discovery. She won't have much to say to me while I'm here.'

'No, I don't think she will,' my companion averred.

'Do you suppose she has some suspicion of me?'

Miss Tita's honest eyes gave me no sign that I had touched a mark. 'I shouldn't think so – letting you in after all so easily.'

'Oh, so easily! she has covered her risk. But where is it that one could take an advantage of her?'

'I oughtn't to tell you if I knew, ought I?' And Miss Tita added, before I had time to reply to this, smiling dolefully, 'Do you think we have any weak points?'

'That's exactly what I'm asking. You would only have to mention them for me to respect them religiously.'

She looked at me, at this, with that air of timid but candid and even gratified curiosity with which she had confronted me from the first; and then she said, 'There is nothing to tell. We are terribly quiet. I don't know how the days pass. We have no life.'

'I wish I might think that I should bring you a little.'

'Oh, we know what we want,' she went on. 'It's all right.'

There were various things I desired to ask her: how in the world they did live; whether they had any friends or visitors, any relations in America or in other countries. But I judged such an inquiry would be premature; I must leave it to a later chance. 'Well, don't *you* be proud,' I contented myself with saying. 'Don't hide from me altogether.'

'Oh, I must stay with my aunt,' she returned, without looking at me. And at the same moment, abruptly, without any ceremony of parting, she quitted me and disappeared, leaving me to make my own way downstairs. I remained a while longer, wandering about the bright desert (the sun was pouring in) of the old house, thinking the situation over on the spot. Not even the pattering little *serva* came to look after me and I reflected that after all this treatment showed confidence.

4

PERHAPS it did, but all the same, six weeks later, towards the middle of June, the moment when Mrs Prest undertook her annual migration, I had made no measurable advance. I was obliged to confess to her that I had no results to speak of. My first step had been unexpectedly rapid, but there was no appearance that it would be followed by a second. I was a thousand miles from taking tea with my hostesses – that privilege of which, as I reminded Mrs Prest, we both had had a vision. She reproached me with wanting boldness and I answered that even to be bold you must have an opportunity: you may push on through a breach but you can't batter down a dead wall. She answered that the breach I had already made was big enough to admit any army and accused me of wasting precious hours in whimpering in her salon when I ought to have been carrying on the struggle in the field. It is true that I went to see her very often, on the theory that it would console me (I freely expressed my discouragement) for my want of success on my own premises. But I began to perceive that it did not console me to be perpetually chaffed for my scruples, especially when I was really so vigilant; and I was rather glad when my derisive friend closed her house for the summer. She had expected to gather amusement from the drama of my intercourse with the Misses Bordereau and she was disappointed that the intercourse, and consequently the drama, had not come off. 'They'll lead you on to your ruin,' she said before she left Venice. 'They'll get all your money without showing you a scrap.' I think I settled down to my business with more concentration after she had gone away.

It was a fact that up to that time I had not, save on a single brief occasion, had even a moment's contact with my queer hostesses. The exception had occurred when I carried them according to my promise the terrible three thousand francs. Then I found Miss Tita waiting for me in the hall, and she took the money from my hand so that I did not see her aunt. The old lady had promised to receive me, but she apparently thought nothing of breaking that vow. The money was contained in a bag of chamois leather, of respectable dimensions, which my banker had given me, and Miss Tita had to make a big fist to receive it. This she did with extreme solemnity, though I tried to treat the affair a little as a joke. It was in no jocular strain, yet it was with simplicity, that she inquired, weighing the money in her two palms: 'Don't you think it's too much?' To which I replied that that would depend upon the amount of pleasure I should get for it. Hereupon she turned away from me quickly, as she had done the day before, murmuring in a tone different from any she had used hitherto: 'Oh, pleasure, pleasure – there's no pleasure in this house!'

After this, for a long time, I never saw her, and I wondered that the common chances of the day should not have helped us to meet. It could only be evident that she was immensely on her guard against them; and in addition to this the house was so big that for each other we were lost in it. I used to look out for her hopefully as I crossed the sala in my comings and goings, but I was not rewarded with a glimpse of the tail of her dress. It was as if she never peeped out of her aunt's apartment. I used to wonder what she did there week after week and year after year. I had never encountered such a violent *parti pris* of seclusion; it was more than keeping quiet – it was like hunted creatures feigning death. The two ladies appeared to have no visitors whatever and no sort of contact with the world. I judged at least that people could not have come to the house and that Miss Tita could not have gone out without my having some observation of it. I did what I disliked myself for doing (reflecting that it was only once in a way): I questioned my servant about their habits and let him divine that I should be interested in any information he could pick up. But he picked up amazingly little for a knowing Venetian; it must be added that where there is a perpetual fast there are very few crumbs on the floor. His cleverness in other ways was sufficient if it was not quite all that I had attributed to him on the occasion of my first interview with Miss Tita. He had helped my gondolier to bring me round a boat-load of furniture; and when these articles had been carried to the top of the palace and distributed according to our associated wisdom he organized my household with such promptitude as was consistent with the fact that it was composed exclusively of himself. He made me in short as comfortable as I could be with my indifferent prospects. I should have been glad if he had fallen in love with Miss Bordereau's maid or, failing this, had taken her in aversion; either event might have brought about some kind of catastrophe and a catastrophe might have led to some parley. It was my idea that she would have been sociable, and I myself on various occasions saw her flit to and fro on domestic errands, so that I was sure she was accessible. But I tasted of no gossip from that fountain, and I afterwards learned that Pasquale's affections were fixed upon an object that made him heedless of other women. This was a young lady with a powdered face, a yellow cotton gown and much leisure, who used often to come to see him. She practised, at her convenience, the art of a stringer of beads (these ornaments are made in Venice, in profusion; she had her pocket full of them and I used to find them on the floor of my apartment), and kept an eye on the maiden in the house. It was not for me of course to make the domestics tattle, and I never said a word to Miss Bordereau's cook.

It seemed to me a proof of the old lady's determination to have nothing to do with me that she should never have sent me a receipt for my three months' rent. For some days I looked out for it and then, when I had given it up, I wasted a good deal of time in wondering what her reason had been for neglecting so indispensable and familiar a form. At first I was tempted to send her a reminder, after which I relinquished the idea (against my judgement as to what was right in the particular case), on the general ground of wishing to keep quiet. If Miss Bordereau suspected me of ulterior aims, she would suspect me less if I should be business-like, and yet I consented not to be so. It was possible she intended her omission as an impertinence, a visible irony, to show how she could overreach people who attempted to overreach her. On that hypothesis it was well to let her see that one did not notice her little tricks. The real reading of the matter, I afterwards perceived, was simply the poor old woman's desire to emphasize the fact that I was in the enjoyment of a favour as rigidly limited as it had been liberally bestowed. She had given me part of her house and now she would not give me even a morsel of paper with her name on it. Let me say that even at first this did not make me too miserable, for the whole episode was essentially delightful to me. I foresaw that I should have a summer after my own literary heart, and the sense of holding my opportunity was much greater than the sense of losing it. There could be no Venetian business without patience, and since I adored the place I was much more in the spirit of it for having laid in a large provision. That spirit kept me perpetual company and seemed to look out at me from the revived immortal face – in which all his genius shone – of the great poet who was my prompter. I had invoked him and he had come; he hovered before me half the time; it was as if his bright ghost had returned to earth to tell me that he regarded the affair as his own no less than mine and that we should see it fraternally, cheerfully to a conclusion. It was as if he had said, 'Poor dear, be easy with her; she has some natural prejudices; only give her time. Strange as it may appear to you she was very attractive in 1820. Meanwhile are we not in Venice together, and what better place is there for the meeting of dear friends? See how it glows with the advancing summer; how the sky and the sea and the rosy air and the marble of the palaces all shimmer and melt together.' My eccentric private errand became a part of the general romance and the general glory – I felt even a mystic companionship, a moral fraternity with all those who in the past had been in the service of art. They had worked for beauty, for a devotion; and what else was I doing? That element was in everything that Jeffrey Aspern had written and I was only bringing it to the light.

I lingered in the sala when I went to and fro; I used to watch – as long as I thought decent – the door that led to Miss Bordereau's part of the house. A person observing me might have supposed I was trying to cast a spell upon it or attempting some odd experiment in hypnotism. But I was only praying it would open or thinking what treasure probably lurked behind it. I hold it singular, as I look back, that I should never have doubted for a moment that the sacred relics were there; never have failed to feel a certain joy at being under the same roof with them. After all they were under my hand – they had not escaped me yet; and they made my life continuous, in a fashion, with the illustrious life they had touched at the other end. I lost myself in this satisfaction to the point of assuming – in my quiet extravagance – that poor Miss Tita also went back, went back, as I used to phrase it. She did indeed, the gentle spinster, but not quite so far as Jeffrey Aspern, who was simple hearsay to her, quite as he was to me. Only she had lived for years with Juliana, she had seen and handled the papers and (even though she was stupid) some esoteric knowledge had rubbed off on her. That was what the old woman represented – esoteric knowledge; and this was the idea with which my editorial heart used to thrill. It literally beat faster often, of an evening, when I had been out, as I stopped with my candle in the re-echoing hall on my way up to bed. It was as if at such a moment as that, in the stillness, after the long contradiction of the day, Miss Bordereau's secrets were in the air, the wonder of her survival more palpable. These were the acute impressions. I had them in another form, with more of a certain sort of reciprocity, during the hours that I sat in the garden looking up over the top of my book at the closed windows of my hostess. In these windows no sign of life ever appeared; it was as if, for fear of my catching a glimpse of them, the two ladies passed their days in the dark. But this only proved to me that they had something to conceal; which was what I had wished to demonstrate. Their motionless shutters became as expressive as eyes consciously closed, and I took comfort in thinking that at all events though invisible themselves they saw me between the lashes.

I made a point of spending as much time as possible in the garden, to justify the picture I had originally given of my horticultural passion. And I not only spent time, but (hang it! as I said) I spent money. As soon as I had got my rooms arranged and could give the proper thought to the matter I surveyed the place with a clever expert and made terms for having it put in order. I was sorry to do this, for personally I liked it better as it was, with its weeds and its wild, rough tangle, its sweet, characteristic Venetian shabbiness. I had to be consistent, to keep my promise that I would smother the house in flowers. Moreover I formed this graceful project that by flowers I would make my way – I would succeed by big nosegays. I would batter the old women with lilies – I would bombard their citadel with roses. Their door would have to yield to the pressure when a mountain of carnations should be piled up against it. The place in truth had been brutally neglected. The Venetian capacity for dawdling is of the largest, and for a good many days unlimited litter was all my gardener had to show for his ministrations. There was a great digging of holes and carting about of earth, and after a while I grew so impatient that I had thoughts of sending for my bouquets to the nearest stand. But I reflected that the ladies would see through the chinks of their shutters that they must have been bought and might make up their minds from this that I was a humbug. So I composed myself and finally, though the delay was long, perceived some appearances of bloom. This encouraged me and I waited serenely enough till they multiplied. Meanwhile the real summer days arrived and began to pass, and as I look back upon them they seem to me almost the happiest of my life. I took more and more care to be in the garden whenever it was not too hot. I had an arbour arranged and a low table and an armchair put into it; and I carried out books and portfolios (I had always some business of writing in hand), and worked and waited and mused and hoped, while the golden hours elapsed and the plants drank in the light and the inscrutable old palace turned pale and then, as the day waned, began to flush in it and my papers rustled in the wandering breeze of the Adriatic.

Considering how little satisfaction I got from it at first it is remarkable that I should not have grown more tired of wondering what mystic rites of ennui the Misses Bordereau celebrated in their darkened rooms; whether this had always been the tenor of their life and how in previous years they had escaped elbowing their neighbours. It was clear that they must have had other habits and other circumstances; that they must once have been young or at least middle-aged. There was no end to the questions it was possible to ask about them and no end to the answers it was not possible to frame. I had known many of my country-people in Europe and was familiar with the strange ways they were liable to take up there; but the Misses Bordereau formed altogether a new type of the American absentee. Indeed it was plain that the American name had ceased to have any application to them – I had seen this in the ten minutes I spent in the old woman's room. You could never have said whence they came, from the appearance of either of them; wherever it was they had long ago dropped the local accent and fashion. There was nothing in them that one recognized, and putting the question of speech aside they might have been Norwegians or Spaniards. Miss Bordereau, after all, had been in Europe nearly threequarters of a century; it appeared by some verses addressed to her by Aspern on the occasion of his own second absence from America – verses of which Cumnor and I had after infinite conjecture established solidly enough the date – that she was even then, as a girl of twenty, on the foreign side of the sea. There was an implication in the poem (I hope not just for the phrase) that he had come back for her sake. We had no real light upon her circumstances at that moment, any more than we had upon her origin, which we be-lieved to be of the sort usually spoken of as modest. Cumnor had a theory that she had been a governess in some family in which the poet visited and that, in consequence of her position, there was from the first something unavowed, or rather something positively clandestine, in their relations. I on the other hand had hatched a little romance according to which she was the daughter of an artist, a painter or a sculptor, who had left the western world when the century was fresh, to study in the ancient schools. It was essential to my hypothesis that this amiable man should have lost his wife, should have been poor and unsuccessful and should have had a second daughter, of a disposition quite different from Juliana's. It was also indispensable that he should have been accompanied to Europe by these young ladies and should have established himself there for the remainder of a struggling, saddened life. There was a further implication that Miss Bordereau had had in her youth a perverse and adventurous, albeit a generous and fascinating character, and that she had passed through some singular vicissitudes. By what passions had she been ravaged, by what sufferings had she been blanched, what store of memories had she laid away for the monotonous future?

I asked myself these things as I sat spinning theories about her in my arbour and the bees droned in the flowers. It was incontestable that, whether for right or for wrong, most readers of certain of Aspern's poems (poems not as ambiguous as the sonnets – scarcely more divine, I think – of Shakespeare) had taken for granted that Juliana had not always adhered to the steep footway of renunciation. There hovered about her name a perfume of reckless passion, an intimation that she had not been exactly as the respectable young person in general. Was this a sign that her singer had betrayed her, had given her away, as we say nowadays, to posterity? Certain it is that it would have been difficult to put one's finger on the passage in which her fair fame suffered an imputation. Moreover was not any fame fair enough that was so sure of duration and was associated with works immortal through their beauty? It was a part of my idea that the young lady had had a foreign lover (and an unedifying tragical rupture) before her meeting with Jeffrey Aspern. She had lived with her father and sister in a queer old-fashioned, expatriated, artistic Bohemia, in the days when the aesthetic was only the academic and the painters who knew the best models for a *contadina* and *pifferaro* wore peaked hats and long hair. It was a society less furnished than the coteries of today (in its ignorance of the wonderful chances, the opportunities of the early bird, with which its path was strewn), with tatters of old stuff and fragments of old crockery; so that Miss Bordereau appeared not to have picked up or have inherited many objects of importance. There was no enviable bric-à-brac, with its provoking legend of cheapness, in the room in which I had seen her. Such a fact as that suggested bareness, but none the less it worked happily into the sentimental interest I had always taken in the early movements of my countrymen as visitors to Europe. When Americans went abroad in 1820 there was something romantic, almost heroic in it, as compared with the perpetual ferryings of the present hour, when photography and other conveniences have annihilated surprise. Miss Bordereau sailed with her family on a tossing brig, in the days of long voyages and sharp differences; she had her emotions on the top of yellow diligences, passed the night at inns where she dreamed of travellers' tales, and was struck, on reaching the eternal city, with the elegance of Roman pearls and scarfs. There was something touching to me in all that and my imagination frequently went back to the period. If Miss Bordereau carried it there of course Jeffrey Aspern at other times had done so a great deal more. It was a much more important fact, if one were looking at his genius critically, that he had lived in the days before the general transfusion. It had happened to me to regret that he had known Europe at all; I should have liked to see what he would have written without that experience, by which he had incontestably been enriched. But as his fate had ordered otherwise I went with him – I tried to judge how the old world would have struck him. It was not only there, however, that I watched him; the relations he had entertained with the new had even a livelier interest. His own country after all had had most of his life, and his muse, as they said at that time, was essentially American. That was originally what I had loved him for: that at a period when our native land was nude and crude and provincial, when the famous 'atmosphere' it is supposed to lack was not even missed, when literature was lonely there and art and form almost impossible, he had found means to live and write like one of the first; to be free and general and not at all afraid; to feel, understand and express everything.

5

I WAS seldom at home in the evening, for when I attempted to occupy myself in my apartments the lamplight brought in a swarm of noxious insects, and it was too hot for closed windows. Accordingly I spent the late hours either on the water (the moonlight of Venice is famous), or in the splendid square which serves as a vast forecourt to the strange old basilica of Saint Mark. I sat in front of Florian's *café*, eating ices, listening to music, talking with acquaintances: the traveller will remember how the immense cluster of tables and little chairs stretches like a promontory into the smooth lake of the Piazza. The whole place, of a summer's evening, under the stars and with all the lamps, all the voices and light footsteps on marble (the only sounds of the arcades that enclose it), is like an open-air saloon dedicated to cooling drinks and to a still finer degustation – that of the exquisite impressions received during the day. When I did not prefer to keep mine to myself there was always a stray tourist, disencumbered of his Bädeker, to discuss them with, or some domesticated painter rejoicing in the return of the season of strong effects. The wonderful church, with its low domes and bristling embroideries, the mystery of its mosaic and sculpture, looked ghostly in the tempered gloom, and the sea-breeze passed between the twin columns of the Piazzetta, the lintels of a door no longer guarded, as gently as if a rich curtain were swaying there. I used sometimes on these occasions to think of the Misses Bordereau and of the pity of their being shut up in apartments which in the Venetian July even Venetian vastness did not prevent from being stuffy. Their life seemed miles away from the life of the Piazza, and no doubt it was really too late to make the austere Juliana change her habits. But poor Miss Tita would have enjoyed one of Florian's ices, I was sure; sometimes I even had thoughts of carrying one home to her. Fortunately my patience bore fruit and I was not obliged to do anything so ridiculous.

One evening about the middle of July I came in earlier than usual – I forget what chance had led to this – and instead of going up to my quarters made my way into the garden. The temperature was very high; it was such a night as one would gladly have spent in the open air and I was in no hurry to go to bed. I had floated home in my gondola, listening to the slow splash of the oar in the narrow dark canals, and now the only thought that solicited me was the vague reflection that it would be pleasant to recline at one's length in the fragrant darkness on a garden bench. The odour of the canal was doubtless at the bottom of that aspiration and the breath of the garden, as I entered it, gave consistency to my purpose. It was delicious – just such an air as must have trembled with Romeo's vows when he stood among the flowers and raised his arms to his mistress's balcony. I looked at the windows of the palace to see if by chance the example of Verona (Verona being not far off) had been followed; but everything was dim, as usual, and everything was still. Juliana, on summer nights in her youth, might have murmured down from open windows at Jeffrey Aspern, but Miss Tita was not a poet's mistress any more than I was a poet. This however did not prevent my gratification from being great as I became aware on reaching the end of the garden that Miss Tita was seated in my little bower. At first I only made out an indistinct figure, not in the least counting on such an overture from one of my hostesses; it even occurred to me that some sentimental maid-servant had stolen in to keep a tryst with her sweetheart. I was going to turn away, not to frighten her, when the figure rose to its height and I recognized Miss Bordereau's niece. I must do myself the justice to say that I did not wish to frighten her either, and much as I had longed for some such accident I should have been capable of retreating. It was as if I had laid a trap for her by coming home earlier than usual and adding to that eccentricity by creeping into the garden. As she rose she spoke to me, and then I reflected that perhaps, secure in my almost inveterate absence, it was her nightly practice to take a lonely airing. There was no trap, in truth, because I had had no suspicion. At first I took for granted that the words she uttered expressed discomfiture at my arrival; but as she repeated them – I had not caught them clearly – I had the surprise of hearing her say, 'Oh, dear, I'm so very glad you've come!' She and her aunt had in common the property of unexpected speeches. She came out of the arbour almost as if she were going to throw herself into my arms.

I hasten to add that she did nothing of the kind; she did not even shake hands with me. It was a gratification to her to see me and presently she told me why – because she was nervous when she was out of doors at night alone. The plants and bushes looked so strange in the dark, and there were all sorts of queer sounds she could not tell what they were – like the noises of animals. She stood close to me, looking about her with an air of greater security but without any demonstration of interest in me as an individual. Then I guessed that nocturnal prowlings were not in the least her habit, and I was also reminded (I had been struck with the circumstance in talking with her before I took possession) that it was impossible to over-estimate her simplicity.

'You speak as if you were lost in the backwoods,' I said, laughing. 'How you manage to keep out of this charming place when you have only three steps to take to get into it, is more than I have yet been able to discover. You hide away mighty well so long as I am on the premises, I know; but I had a hope that you peeped out a little at other times. You and your poor aunt are worse off than Carmelite nuns in their cells. Should you mind telling me how you exist without air, without exercise, without any sort of human contact? I don't see how you carry on the common business of life.'

She looked at me as if I were talking some strange tongue and her answer was so little of an answer that I was considerably irritated. 'We go to bed very early – earlier than you would believe.' I was on the point of saying that this only deepened the mystery when she gave me some relief by adding, 'Before you came we were not so private. But I never have been out at night.'

'Never in these fragrant alleys, blooming here under your nose?'

'Ah,' said Miss Tita, 'they were never nice till now!' There was an unmistakable reference in this and a flattering comparison, so that it seemed to me I had gained a small advantage. As it would help me to follow it up to establish a sort of grievance I asked her why, since she thought my garden nice, she had never thanked me in any way for the flowers I had been sending up in such quantities for the previous three weeks. I had not been discouraged – there had been, as she would have observed, a daily armful; but I had been brought up in the common forms and a word of recognition now and then would have touched me in the right place.

'Why I didn't know they were for me!'

'They were for both of you. Why should I make a difference?'

Miss Tita reflected as if she might be thinking of a reason for that, but she failed to produce one. Instead of this she asked abruptly, 'Why in the world do you want to know us?'

'I ought after all to make a difference,' I replied. 'That question is your aunt's; it isn't yours. You wouldn't ask it if you hadn't been put up to it.'

'She didn't tell me to ask you,' Miss Tita replied, without confusion; she was the oddest mixture of the shrinking and the direct.

'Well, she has often wondered about it herself and expressed her wonder to you. She has insisted on it, so that she has put the idea into your head that I am unsufferably pushing. Upon my word I think I have been very discreet. And how completely your aunt must have lost every tradition of sociability, to see anything out of the way in the idea that respectable intelligent people, living as we do under the same roof, should occasionally exchange a remark! What could be more natural? We are of the same country and we have at least some of the same tastes, since, like you, I am intensely fond of Venice.'

My interlocutress appeared incapable of grasping more than one clause in any proposition, and she declared quickly, eagerly, as if she were answering my whole speech: 'I am not in the least fond of Venice. I should like to go far away!'

'Has she always kept you back so?' I went on, to show her that I could be as irrelevant as herself.

'She told me to come out tonight; she has told me very often,' said Miss Tita. 'It is I who wouldn't come. I don't like to leave her.'

'Is she too weak, is she failing?' I demanded, with more emotion, I think, than I intended to show. I judged this by the way her eyes rested upon me in the darkness. It embarrassed me a little, and to turn the matter off I continued genially: 'Do let us sit down together comfortably somewhere and you will tell me all about her.'

Miss Tita made no resistance to this. We found a bench less secluded, less confidential, as it were, than the one in the arbour; and we were still sitting there when I heard midnight ring out from those clear bells of Venice which vibrate with a solemnity of their own over the lagoon and hold the air so much more than the chimes of other places. We were together more than an hour and our interview gave, as it struck me, a great lift to my undertaking. Miss Tita accepted the situation without a protest; she had avoided me for three months, yet now she treated me almost as if these three months had made me an old friend. If I had chosen I might have inferred from this that though she had avoided me she had given a good deal of consideration to doing so. She paid no attention to the flight of time – never worried at my keeping her so long away from her aunt. She talked freely, answering questions and asking them and not even taking advantage of certain longish pauses with which they inevitably alternated to say she thought she had better go in. It was almost as if she were waiting for something – something I might say to her – and intended to give me my opportunity. I was the more struck by this as she told me that her aunt had been less well for a good many days and in a way that was rather new. She was weaker; at moments it seemed as if she had no strength at all; yet more than ever before she wished to be left alone. That was why she had told her to come out – not even to remain in her own room, which was alongside; she said her niece irritated her, made her nervous. She sat still for hours together, as if she were asleep; she had always done that, musing and dozing; but at such times formerly she gave at intervals some small sign of life, of interest, liking her companion to be near her with her work. Miss Tita confided to me that at present her aunt was so motionless that she sometimes feared she was dead; moreover she took hardly any food – one couldn't see what she lived on. The great thing was that she still on most days got up; the serious job was to dress her, to wheel her out of her bedroom. She clung to as many of her old habits as possible and she had always, little company as they had received for years, made a point of sitting in the parlour.

I scarcely knew what to think of all this – of Miss Tita's sudden conversion to sociability and of the strange circumstance that the more the old lady appeared to decline towards her end the less she should desire to be looked after. The story did not hang together, and I even asked myself whether it were not a trap laid for me, the result of a design to make me show my hand. I could not have told why my companions (as they could only by courtesy be called) should have this purpose – why they should try to trip up so lucrative a lodger. At any rate I kept on my guard, so that Miss Tita should not have occasion again to ask me if I had an *arrière-pensée*. Poor woman, before we parted for the night my mind was at rest as to *her* capacity for entertaining one.

She told me more about their affairs than I had hoped; there was no need to be prying, for it evidently drew her out simply to feel that I listened, that I cared. She ceased wondering why I cared, and at last, as she spoke of the brilliant life they had led years before, she almost chattered. It was Miss Tita who judged it brilliant; she said that when they first came to live in Venice, years and years before (I saw that her mind was essentially vague about dates and the order in which events had occurred), there was scarcely a week that they had not some visitor or did not make some delightful *passeggio* in the city. They had seen all the curiosities; they had even been to the Lido in a boat (she spoke as if I might think there was a way on foot); they had had a collation there, brought in three baskets and spread out on the grass. I asked her what people they had known and she said, Oh! very nice ones – the Cavaliere Bombicci and the Contessa Altemura,

with whom they had had a great friendship. Also English people –
the Churtons and the Goldies and Mrs Stock-Stock, whom they
had loved dearly; she was dead and gone, poor dear. That was
the case with most of their pleasant circle (this expression was
Miss Tita's own), though a few were left, which was a wonder
considering how they had neglected them. She mentioned the
names of two or three Venetian old women; of a certain doctor,
very clever, who was so kind – he came as a friend, he had really
given up practice; of the *avvocato* Pochintesta, who wrote beautiful poems and had addressed one to her aunt. These people came
to see them without fail every year, usually at the *capo d'anno*, and
of old her aunt used to make them some little present – her aunt
and she together: small things that she, Miss Tita, made herself,
like paper lamp-shades or mats for the decanters of wine at dinner
or those woollen things that in cold weather were worn on the
wrists. The last few years there had not been many presents; she
could not think what to make and her aunt had lost her interest
and never suggested. But the people came all the same; if the
Venetians liked you once they liked you for ever.

There was something affecting in the good faith of this sketch
of former social glories; the picnic at the Lido had remained vivid
through the ages and poor Miss Tita evidently was of the impression that she had had a brilliant youth. She had in fact had a
glimpse of the Venetian world in its gossiping, home-keeping,
parsimonious, professional walks; for I observed for the first time
that she had acquired by contact something of the trick of the
familiar, soft-sounding, almost infantile speech of the place. I
judged that she had imbibed this invertebrate dialect, from the
natural way the names of things and people – mostly purely local
– rose to her lips. If she knew little of what they represented she
knew still less of anything else. Her aunt had drawn in – her failing
interest in the table-mats and lamp-shades was a sign of that – and
she had not been able to mingle in society or to entertain it alone;
so that the matter of her reminiscences struck one as an old world
altogether. If she had not been so decent her references would
have seemed to carry one back to the queer rococo Venice of
Casanova. I found myself falling into the error of thinking of her

too as one of Jeffrey Aspern's contemporaries; this came from her having so little in common with my own. It was possible, I said to myself, that she had not even heard of him; it might very well be that Juliana had not cared to lift even for her the veil that covered the temple of her youth. In this case she perhaps would not know of the existence of the papers, and I welcomed that presumption – it made me feel more safe with her – until I remembered that we had believed the letter of disavowal received by Cumnor to be in the handwriting of the niece. If it had been dictated to her she had of course to know what it was about; yet after all the effect of it was to repudiate the idea of any connection with the poet. I held it probable at all events that Miss Tita had not read a word of his poetry. Moreover if, with her companion, she had always escaped the interviewer there was little occasion for her having got it into her head that people were 'after' the letters. People had not been after them, inasmuch as they had not heard of them; and Cumnor's fruitless feeler would have been a solitary accident.

When midnight sounded Miss Tita got up; but she stopped at the door of the house only after she had wandered two or three times with me round the garden. 'When shall I see you again?' I asked, before she went in; to which she replied with promptness that she should like to come out the next night. She added however that she should not come – she was so far from doing everything she liked.

'You might do a few things that *I* like,' I said with a sigh.

'Oh, you – I don't believe you!' she murmured, at this, looking at me with her simple solemnity.

'Why don't you believe me?'

'Because I don't understand you.'

'That is just the sort of occasion to have faith.' I could not say more, though I should have liked to, as I saw that I only mystified her; for I had no wish to have it on my conscience that I might pass for having made love to her. Nothing less should I have seemed to do had I continued to beg a lady to 'believe in me' in an Italian garden on a midsummer night. There was some merit in my scruples, for Miss Tita lingered and lingered: I perceived that she felt that she should not really soon come down again and wished therefore to protract the present. She insisted too on making the talk between us personal to ourselves; and altogether her behaviour was such as would have been possible only to a completely innocent woman.

'I shall like the flowers better now that I know they are also meant for me.'

'How could you have doubted it? If you will tell me the kind you like best I will send a double lot of them.'

'Oh, I like them all best!' Then she went on, familiarly: 'Shall you study – shall you read and write – when you go up to your rooms?'

'I don't do that at night, at this season. The lamplight brings in the animals.'

'You might have known that when you came.'

'I did know it!'

'And in winter do you work at night?'

'I read a good deal, but I don't often write.' She listened as if these details had a rare interest, and suddenly a temptation quite at variance with the prudence I had been teaching myself associated itself with her plain, mild face. Ah yes, she was safe and I could make her safer! It seemed to me from one moment to another that I could not wait longer – that I really must take a sounding. So I went on: 'In general before I go to sleep – very often in bed (it's a bad habit, but I confess to it), I read some great poet. In nine cases out of ten it's a volume of Jeffrey Aspern.'

I watched her well as I pronounced that name but I saw nothing wonderful. Why should I indeed – was not Jeffrey Aspern the property of the human race?

'Oh, we read him – we *have* read him,' she quietly replied.

'He is my poet of poets – I know him almost by heart.'

For an instant Miss Tita hesitated; then her sociability was too much for her.

'Oh, by heart – that's nothing!' she murmured, smiling. 'My aunt used to know him – to know him' – she paused an instant and I wondered what she was going to say – 'to know him as a visitor.'

'As a visitor?' I repeated, staring.

'He used to call on her and take her out.'

I continued to stare. 'My dear lady, he died a hundred years ago!'

'Well,' she said, mirthfully, 'my aunt is a hundred and fifty.'

'Mercy on us!' I exclaimed; 'why didn't you tell me before? I should like so to ask her about him.'

'She wouldn't care for that – she wouldn't tell you,' Miss Tita replied.

'I don't care what she cares for! She *must* tell me – it's not a chance to be lost.'

'Oh, you should have come twenty years ago: then she still talked about him.'

'And what did she say?' I asked, eagerly.

'I don't know – that he liked her immensely.'

'And she – didn't she like him?'

'She said he was a god.' Miss Tita gave me this information flatly, without expression; her tone might have made it a piece of trivial gossip. But it stirred me deeply as she dropped the words into the summer night; it seemed such a direct testimony.

'Fancy, fancy!' I murmured. And then, 'Tell me this, please – has she got a portrait of him? They are distressingly rare.'

'A portrait? I don't know,' said Miss Tita; and now there was discomfiture in her face. 'Well, good-night!' she added; and she turned into the house.

I accompanied her into the wide, dusky, stone-paved passage which on the ground floor corresponded with our grand sala. It opened at one end into the garden, at the other upon the canal, and was lighted now only by the small lamp that was always left for me to take up as I went to bed. An extinguished candle which Miss Tita apparently had brought down with her stood on the same table with it. 'Good-night, good-night!' I replied, keeping beside her as she went to get her light. 'Surely you would know, shouldn't you, if she had one?'

'If she had what?' the poor lady asked, looking at me queerly over the flame of her candle.

'A portrait of the god. I don't know what I wouldn't give to see it.'

'I don't know what she has got. She keeps her things locked up.' And Miss Tita went away, towards the staircase, with the sense evidently that she had said too much.

I let her go – I wished not to frighten her – and I contented myself with remarking that Miss Bordereau would not have locked up such a glorious possession as that – a thing a person would be proud of and hang up in a prominent place on the parlour-wall. Therefore of course she had not any portrait. Miss Tita made no direct answer to this and candle in hand, with her back to me, ascended two or three stairs. Then she stopped short and turned round looking at me across the dusky space.

'Do you write – do you write?' There was a shake in her voice – she could scarcely bring out what she wanted to ask.

'Do I write? Oh, don't speak of my writing on the same day with Aspern's!'

'Do you write about *him* – do you pry into his life?'

'Ah, that's your aunt's question; it can't be yours!' I said, in a tone of slightly wounded sensibility.

'All the more reason then that you should answer it. Do you, please?'

I thought I had allowed for the falsehoods I should have to tell; but I found that in fact when it came to the point I had not. Besides, now that I had an opening there was a kind of relief in being frank. Lastly (it was perhaps fanciful, even fatuous), I guessed that Miss Tita personally would not in the last resort be less my friend. So after a moment's hesitation I answered, 'Yes, I have written about him and I am looking for more material. In heaven's name have you got any?'

'*Santo Dio!*' she exclaimed, without heeding my question; and she hurried upstairs and out of sight. I might count upon her in the last resort, but for the present she was visibly alarmed. The proof of it was that she began to hide again, so that for a fortnight I never beheld her. I found my patience ebbing and after four or five days of this I told the gardener to stop the flowers.

6

ONE afternoon, as I came down from my quarters to go out, I found Miss Tita in the sala: it was our first encounter on that ground since I had come to the house. She put on no air of being there by accident; there was an ignorance of such arts in her angular, diffident directness. That I might be quite sure she was waiting for me she informed me of the fact and told me that Miss Bordereau wished to see me: she would take me into the room at that moment if I had time. If I had been late for a love-tryst I would have stayed for this, and I quickly signified that I should be delighted to wait upon the old lady. 'She wants to talk with you – to know you,' Miss Tita said, smiling as if she herself appreciated that idea; and she led me to the door of her aunt's apartment. I stopped her a moment before she had opened it, looking at her with some curiosity. I told her that this was a great satisfaction to me and a great honour; but all the same I should like to ask what had made Miss Bordereau change so suddenly. It was only the other day that she wouldn't suffer me near her. Miss Tita was not embarrassed by my question; she had as many little unexpected serenities as if she told fibs, but the odd part of them was that they had on the contrary their source in her truthfulness. 'Oh, my aunt changes,' she answered; 'it's so terribly dull – I suppose she's tired.'

'But you told me that she wanted more and more to be alone.'

Poor Miss Tita coloured, as if she found me over-insistent. 'Well, if you don't believe she wants to see you – I haven't invented it! I think people often are capricious when they are very old.'

'That's perfectly true. I only wanted to be clear as to whether you have repeated to her what I told you the other night.'

'What you told me?'

'About Jeffrey Aspern – that I am looking for materials.'

'If I had told her do you think she would have sent for you?'

'That's exactly what I want to know. If she wants to keep him to herself she might have sent for me to tell me so.'

'She won't speak of him,' said Miss Tita. Then as she opened the door she added in a lower tone, 'I have told her nothing.'

The old woman was sitting in the same place in which I had seen her last, in the same position, with the same mystifying bandage over her eyes. Her welcome was to turn her almost invisible face to me and show me that while she sat silent she saw me clearly. I made no motion to shake hands with her; I felt too well on this occasion that that was out of place for ever. It had been sufficiently enjoined upon me that she was too sacred for that sort of reciprocity – too venerable to touch. There was something so grim in her aspect (it was partly the accident of her green shade), as I stood there to be measured, that I ceased on the spot to feel any doubt as to her knowing my secret, though I did not in the least suspect that Miss Tita had not just spoken the truth. She had not betrayed me, but the old woman's brooding instinct had served her; she had turned me over and over in the long, still hours and she had guessed. The worst of it was that she looked terribly like an old woman who at a pinch would burn her papers. Miss Tita pushed a chair forward, saying to me, 'This will be a good place for you to sit.' As I took possession of it I asked after Miss Bordereau's health; expressed the hope that in spite of the very hot weather it was satisfactory. She replied that it was good enough – good enough; that it was a great thing to be alive.

'Oh, as to that, it depends upon what you compare it with!' I exclaimed, laughing.

'I don't compare – I don't compare. If I did that I should have given everything up long ago.'

I liked to think that this was a subtle allusion to the rapture she had known in the society of Jeffrey Aspern – though it was true that such an allusion would have accorded ill with the wish I imputed to her to keep him buried in her soul. What it accorded with was my constant conviction that no human being had ever had a more delightful social gift than his, and what it seemed to convey was that nothing in the world was worth speaking of if one pretended to speak of that. But one did not! Miss Tita sat down beside her aunt, looking as if she had reason to believe some very remarkable conversation would come off between us.

'It's about the beautiful flowers,' said the old lady; 'you sent us so many – I ought to have thanked you for them before. But I don't write letters and I receive only at long intervals.'

She had not thanked me while the flowers continued to come, but she departed from her custom so far as to send for me as soon as she began to fear that they would not come any more. I noted this; I remembered what an acquisitive propensity she had shown when it was a question of extracting gold from me, and I privately rejoiced at the happy thought I had had in suspending my tribute. She had missed it and she was willing to make a concession to bring it back. At the first sign of this concession I could only go to meet her. 'I am afraid you have not had many, of late, but they shall begin again immediately – tomorrow, tonight.'

'Oh, do send us some tonight!' Miss Tita cried, as if it were an immense circumstance.

'What else should you do with them? It isn't a manly taste to make a bower of your room,' the old woman remarked.

'I don't make a bower of my room, but I am exceedingly fond of growing flowers, of watching their ways. There is nothing un-manly in that: it has been the amusement of philosophers, of statesmen in retirement; even I think of great captains.'

'I suppose you know you can sell them – those you don't use,' Miss Bordereau went on. 'I dare say they wouldn't give you much for them; still you could make a bargain.'

'Oh, I have never made a bargain, as you ought to know. My gardener disposes of them and I ask no questions.'

'I would ask a few, I can promise you!' said Miss Bordereau; and it was the first time I had heard her laugh. I could not get used to the idea that this vision of pecuniary profit was what drew out the divine Juliana most.

'Come into the garden yourself and pick them; come as often as you like; come every day. They are all for you,' I pursued, addressing Miss Tita and carrying off this veracious statement by treating it as an innocent joke. 'I can't imagine why she doesn't come down,' I added, for Miss Bordereau's benefit.

'You must make her come; you must come up and fetch her,' said the old woman, to my stupefaction. 'That odd thing you have made in the corner would be a capital place for her to sit.'

The allusion to my arbour was irreverent; it confirmed the impression I had already received that there was a flicker of impertinence in Miss Bordereau's talk, a strange mocking lambency which must have been a part of her adventurous youth and which had outlived passions and faculties. None the less I asked, 'Wouldn't it be possible for you to come down there yourself? Wouldn't it do you good to sit there in the shade, in the sweet air?'

'Oh, sir, when I move out of this it won't be to sit in the air, and I'm afraid that any that may be stirring around me won't be particularly sweet! It will be a very dark shade indeed. But that won't be just yet,' Miss Bordereau continued, cannily, as if to correct any hopes that this courageous allusion to the last receptacle of her mortality might lead me to entertain. 'I have sat here many a day and I have had enough of arbours in my time. But I'm not afraid to wait till I'm called.'

Miss Tita had expected some interesting talk, but perhaps she found it less genial on her aunt's side (considering that I had been sent for with a civil intention) than she had hoped. As if to give the conversation a turn that would put our companion in a light more favourable she said to me, 'Didn't I tell you the other night that she had sent me out? You see that I can do what I like!'

'Do you pity her – do you teach her to pity herself?' Miss Bordereau demanded, before I had time to answer this appeal. 'She has a much easier life than I had when I was her age.'

'You must remember that it has been quite open to me to think you rather inhuman.'

'Inhuman? That's what the poets used to call the women a hundred years ago. Don't try that; you won't do as well as they!' Juliana declared. 'There is no more poetry in the world – that I know of at least. But I won't bandy words with you,' she pursued, and I well remember the old-fashioned, artificial sound she gave to the speech. 'You have made me talk, talk! It isn't good for me at all.' I got up at this and told her I would take no more of her time; but she detained me to ask, 'Do you remember, the day I saw you about the rooms, that you offered us the use of your gondola?' And when I assented, promptly, struck again with her disposition to make a 'good thing' of being there and wondering what she now had in her eye, she broke out, 'Why don't you take that girl out in it and show her the place?'

'Oh dear aunt, what do you want to do with me?' cried the 'girl', with a piteous quaver. 'I know all about the place!'

'Well then, go with him as a cicerone!' said Miss Bordereau, with an effect of something like cruelty in her implacable power of retort – an incongruous suggestion that she was a sarcastic, profane, cynical old woman. 'Haven't we heard that there have been all sorts of changes in all these years? You ought to see them and at your age (I don't mean because you're so young), you ought to take the chances that come. You're old enough, my dear, and this gentleman won't hurt you. He will show you the famous sunsets, if they still go on – *do* they go on? The sun set for me so long ago. But that's not a reason. Besides, I shall never miss you; you think you are too important. Take her to the Piazza; it used to be very pretty,' Miss Bordereau continued, addressing herself to me. 'What have they done with the funny old church? I hope it hasn't tumbled down. Let her look at the shops; she may take some money, she may buy what she likes.'

Poor Miss Tita had got up, discountenanced and helpless, and as we stood there before her aunt it would certainly have seemed to a spectator of the scene that the old woman was amusing herself at our expense. Miss Tita protested, in a confusion of exclamations and murmurs; but I lost no time in saying that if she would do me the honour to accept the hospitality of my boat I would engage that she should not be bored. Or if she did not want so much of my company the boat itself, with the gondolier, was at her service; he was a capital oar and she might have every confidence. Miss Tita, without definitely answering this speech, looked away from me, out of the window, as if she were going to cry; and I remarked that once we had Miss Bordereau's approval we could easily come to an understanding. We would take an hour, whichever she liked, one of the very next days. As I made my obeisance to the old lady I asked her if she would kindly permit me to see her again.

For a moment she said nothing; then she inquired, 'Is it very necessary to your happiness?'

'It diverts me more than I can say.'

'You are wonderfully civil. Don't you know it almost kills *me*?'

'How can I believe that when I see you more animated, more brilliant than when I came in?'

'That is very true, aunt,' said Miss Tita. 'I think it does you good.'

'Isn't it touching, the solicitude we each have that the other shall enjoy herself?' sneered Miss Bordereau. 'If you think me brilliant today you don't know what you are talking about; you have never seen an agreeable woman. Don't try to pay me a compliment; I have been spoiled,' she went on. 'My door is shut, but you may sometimes knock.'

With this she dismissed me and I left the room. The latch closed behind me, but Miss Tita, contrary to my hope, had remained within. I passed slowly across the hall and before taking my way downstairs I waited a little. My hope was answered; after a minute Miss Tita followed me. 'That's a delightful idea about the Piazza,' I said. 'When will you go – tonight, tomorrow?'

She had been disconcerted, as I have mentioned, but I had already perceived and I was to observe again that when Miss Tita was embarrassed she did not (as most women would have done) turn away from you and try to escape, but came closer, as it were, with a deprecating, clinging appeal to be spared, to be protected. Her attitude was perpetually a sort of prayer for assistance, for explanation; and yet no woman in the world could have been less of a comedian. From the moment you were kind to her she depended on you absolutely; her self-consciousness dropped from her and she took the greatest intimacy, the innocent intimacy which was the only thing she could conceive, for granted. She told me she did not know what had got into her aunt; she had changed so quickly, she had got some idea. I replied that she must find out what the idea was and then let me know; we would go and have an ice together at Florian's and she should tell me while we listened to the band.

'Oh, it will take me a long time to find out!' she said, rather ruefully; and she could promise me this satisfaction neither for that night nor for the next. I was patient now, however, for I felt that I had only to wait; and in fact at the end of the week, one lovely evening after dinner, she stepped into my gondola, to which in honour of the occasion I had attached a second oar.

We swept in the course of five minutes into the Grand Canal; whereupon she uttered a murmur of ecstasy as fresh as if she had been a tourist just arrived. She had forgotten how splendid the great water-way looked on a clear, hot summer evening, and how the sense of floating between marble palaces and reflected lights disposed the mind to sympathetic talk. We floated long and far, and though Miss Tita gave no high-pitched voice to her satisfaction I felt that she surrendered herself. She was more than pleased, she was transported; the whole thing was an immense liberation. The gondola moved with slow strokes, to give her time to enjoy it, and she listened to the plash of the oars, which grew louder and more musically liquid as we passed into narrow canals, as if it were a revelation of Venice. When I asked her how long it was since she had been in a boat she answered, 'Oh, I don't know; a long time – not since my aunt began to be ill.' This was not the only example she gave me of her extreme vagueness about the previous years and the line which marked off the period when Miss Bordereau flourished. I was not at liberty to keep her out too long, but we took a considerable *giro* before going to the Piazza. I asked her no questions, keeping the conversation on purpose away from her domestic situation and the things I wanted to know; I poured treasures of information about Venice into her ears, described Florence and Rome, discoursed to her on the charms and advantages of travel. She reclined, receptive, on the deep leather cushions, turned her eyes conscientiously to everything I pointed out to her, and never mentioned to me till some time afterwards that she might be supposed to know Florence better than I, as she had lived there for years with Miss Bordereau. At last she asked, with the shy impatience of a child, 'Are we not really going to the Piazza? That's what I want to see!' I immediately gave the order that we should go straight; and then we sat silent with the expectation of arrival. As some time still passed, however, she said suddenly, of her own movement, 'I have found out what is the matter with my aunt: she is afraid you will go!'

'What has put that into her head?'

'She has had an idea you have not been happy. That is why she is different now.'

'You mean she wants to make me happier?'

'Well, she wants you not to go; she wants you to stay.'

'I suppose you mean on account of the rent,' I remarked candidly.

Miss Tita's candour showed itself a match for my own. 'Yes, you know; so that I shall have more.'

'How much does she want you to have?' I asked, laughing. 'She ought to fix the sum, so that I may stay till it's made up.'

'Oh, that wouldn't please me,' said Miss Tita. 'It would be unheard of, your taking that trouble.'

'But suppose I should have my own reasons for staying in Venice?'

'Then it would be better for you to stay in some other house.'

'And what would your aunt say to that?'

'She wouldn't like it at all. But I should think you would do well to give up your reasons and go away altogether.'

'Dear Miss Tita,' I said, 'it's not so easy to give them up!'

She made no immediate answer to this, but after a moment she broke out: 'I think I know what your reasons are!'

'I dare say, because the other night I almost told you how I wish you would help me to make them good.'

'I can't do that without being false to my aunt.'

'What do you mean, being false to her?'

'Why, she would never consent to what you want. She has been asked, she has been written to. It made her fearfully angry.'

'Then she *has* got papers of value?' I demanded, quickly.

'Oh, she has got everything!' sighed Miss Tita, with a curious weariness, a sudden lapse into gloom.

These words caused all my pulses to throb, for I regarded them as precious evidence. For some minutes I was too agitated to speak, and in the interval the gondola approached the Piazzetta.

After we had disembarked I asked my companion whether she would rather walk round the square or go and sit at the door of the café; to which she replied that she would do whichever I liked best – I must only remember again how little time she had. I assured her there was plenty to do both, and we made the circuit of the long arcades. Her spirits revived at the sight of the bright shop-windows, and she lingered and stopped, admiring or disapproving of their contents, asking me what I thought of things, theorizing about prices. My attention wandered from her; her words of a while before, 'Oh, she has got everything!' echoed so in my consciousness. We sat down at last in the crowded circle at Florian's, finding an unoccupied table among those that were ranged in the square. It was a splendid night and all the world was out of doors; Miss Tita could not have wished the elements more auspicious for her return to society. I saw that she enjoyed it even more than she told; she was agitated with the multitude of her impressions. She had forgotten what an attractive thing the world is, and it was coming over her that somehow she had for the best years of her life been cheated of it. This did not make her angry; but as she looked all over the charming scene her face had, in spite of its smile of appreciation, the flush of a sort of wounded surprise. She became silent, as if she were thinking with a secret sadness of opportunities, for ever lost, which ought to have been easy; and this gave me a chance to say to her, 'Did you mean a while ago that your aunt has a plan of keeping me on by admitting me occasionally to her presence?'

'She thinks it will make a difference with you if you sometimes see her. She wants you so much to stay that she is willing to make that concession.'

'And what good does she consider that I think it will do me to see her?'

'I don't know; she thinks it's interesting,' said Miss Tita, simply. 'You told her you found it so.'

'So I did; but every one doesn't think so.'

'No, of course not, or more people would try.'

'Well, if she is capable of making that reflection she is capable also of making this further one,' I went on: 'that I must have a particular reason for not doing as others do, in spite of the interest she offers – for not leaving her alone.' Miss Tita looked as if she failed to grasp this rather complicated proposition; so I continued 'If you have not told her what I said to you the other night may she not at least have guessed it?'

'I don't know; she is very suspicious.'

'But she has not been made so by indiscreet curiosity, by persecution?'

'No, no; it isn't that,' said Miss Tita, turning on me a somewhat troubled face. 'I don't know how to say it: it's on account of something – ages ago, before I was born – in her life.'

'Something? What sort of thing?' I asked, as if I myself could have no idea.

'Oh, she has never told me,' Miss Tita answered; and I was sure she was speaking the truth.

Her extreme limpidity was almost provoking, and I felt for the moment that she would have been more satisfactory if she had been less ingenuous. 'Do you suppose it's something to which Jeffrey Aspern's letters and papers – I mean the things in her possession – have reference?'

'I dare say it is!' my companion exclaimed, as if this were a very happy suggestion. 'I have never looked at any of those things.'

'None of them? Then how do you know what they are?'

'I don't,' said Miss Tita, placidly. 'I have never had them in my hands. But I have seen them when she has had them out.'

'Does she have them out often?'

'Not now, but she used to. She is very fond of them.'

'In spite of their being compromising?'

'Compromising?' Miss Tita repeated, as if she was ignorant of the meaning of the word. I felt almost as one who corrupts the innocence of youth.

'I mean their containing painful memories.'

'Oh, I don't think they are painful.'

'You mean you don't think they affect her reputation?'

At this a singular look came into the face of Miss Bordereau's niece – a kind of confession of helplessness, an appeal to me to deal fairly, generously with her. I had brought her to the Piazza, placed her among charming influences, paid her an attention she appreciated, and now I seemed to let her perceive that all this had been a bribe – a bribe to make her turn in some way against her aunt. She was of a yielding nature and capable of doing almost anything to please a person who was kind to her; but the greatest kindness of all would be not to presume too much on this. It was strange enough, as I afterwards thought, that she had not the least air of resenting my want of consideration for her aunt's character, which would have been in the worst possible taste if anything less vital (from my point of view) had been at stake. I don't think she really measured it. 'Do you mean that she did something bad?' she asked in a moment.

'Heaven forbid I should say so, and it's none of my business. Besides, if she did,' I added, laughing, 'it was in other ages, in another world. But why should she not destroy her papers?'

'Oh, she loves them too much.'

'Even now, when she may be near her end?'

'Perhaps when she's sure of that she will.'

'Well, Miss Tita,' I said, 'it's just what I should like you to prevent.'

'How can I prevent it?'

'Couldn't you get them away from her?'

'And give them to you?'

This put the case very crudely, though I am sure there was no irony in her intention. 'Oh, I mean that you might let me see them and look them over. It isn't for myself; there is no personal avidity in my desire. It is simply that they would be of such immense interest to the public, such immeasurable importance as a contribution to Jeffrey Aspern's history.'

She listened to me in her usual manner, as if my speech were full of reference to things she had never heard of, and I felt particularly like the reporter of a newspaper who forces his way into a house of mourning. This was especially the case when after a moment she said, 'There was a gentleman who some time ago wrote to her in very much those words. He also wanted her papers.'

'And did she answer him?' I asked, rather ashamed of myself for not having her rectitude.

'Only when he had written two or three times. He made her very angry.'

'And what did she say?'

'She said he was a devil,' Miss Tita replied, simply.

'She used that expression in her letter?'

'Oh no; she said it to me. She made me write to him.'

'And what did you say?'

'I told him there were no papers at all.'

'Ah, poor gentleman!' I exclaimed.

'I knew there were, but I wrote what she bade me.'

'Of course you had to do that. But I hope I shall not pass for a devil.'

'It will depend upon what you ask me to do for you,' said Miss Tita, smiling.

'Oh, if there is a chance of *your* thinking so my affair is in a bad way! I sha'n't ask you to steal for me, nor even to fib – for you can't fib, unless on paper. But the principal thing is this – to prevent her from destroying the papers.'

'Why, I have no control of her,' said Miss Tita. 'It's she who controls me.'

'But she doesn't control her own arms and legs, does she? The way she would naturally destroy her letters would be to burn them. Now she can't burn them without fire, and she can't get fire unless you give it to her.'

'I have always done everything she has asked,' my companion rejoined. 'Besides, there's Olimpia.'

I was on the point of saying that Olimpia was probably corruptible, but I thought it best not to sound that note. So I simply inquired if that faithful domestic could not be managed.

'Every one can be managed by my aunt,' said Miss Tita. And then she observed that her holiday was over; she must go home.

I laid my hand on her arm, across the table, to stay her a moment. 'What I want of you is a general promise to help me.'

'Oh, how can I – how can I?' she asked, wondering and troubled. She was half surprised, half frightened at my wishing to make her play an active part.

'This is the main thing: to watch her carefully and warn me in time, before she commits that horrible sacrilege.'

'I can't watch her when she makes me go out.'

'That's very true.'

'And when you do too.'

'Mercy on us; do you think she will have done anything to-night?'

'I don't know; she is very cunning.'

'Are you trying to frighten me?' I asked.

I felt this inquiry sufficiently answered when my companion murmured in a musing, almost envious way, 'Oh, but she loves them – she loves them!'

This reflection, repeated with such emphasis, gave me great comfort; but to obtain more of that balm I said, 'If she shouldn't intend to destroy the objects we speak of before her death she will probably have made some disposition by will.'

'By will?'

'Hasn't she made a will for your benefit?'

'Why, she has so little to leave. That's why she likes money,' said Miss Tita.

'Might I ask, since we are really talking things over, what you and she live on?'

'On some money that comes from America, from a lawyer. He sends it every quarter. It isn't much!'

'And won't she have disposed of that?'

My companion hesitated – I saw she was blushing. 'I believe it's mine,' she said; and the look and tone which accompanied these words betrayed so the absence of the habit of thinking of herself that I almost thought her charming. The next instant she added, 'But she had a lawyer once, ever so long ago. And some people came and signed something.'

'They were probably witnesses. And you were not asked to sign? Well then,' I argued, rapidly and hopefully, 'it is because you are the legatee; she has left all her documents to you!'

66

'If she has it's with very strict conditions,' Miss Tita responded, rising quickly, while the movement gave the words a little character of decision. They seemed to imply that the bequest would be accompanied with a command that the articles bequeathed should remain concealed from every inquisitive eye and that I was very much mistaken if I thought she was the person to depart from an injunction so solemn.

'Oh, of course you will have to abide by the terms,' I said; and she uttered nothing to mitigate the severity of this conclusion. None the less, later, just before we disembarked at her own door, on our return, which had taken place almost in silence, she said to me abruptly, 'I will do what I can to help you.' I was grateful for this – it was very well so far as it went; but it did not keep me from remembering that night in a worried waking hour that I now had her word for it to reinforce my own impression that the old woman was very cunning.

7

THE fear of what this side of her character might have led her to do made me nervous for days afterwards. I waited for an intimation from Miss Tita; I almost figured to myself that it was her duty to keep me informed, to let me know definitely whether or no Miss Bordereau had sacrificed her treasures. But as she gave no sign I lost patience and determined to judge so far as was possible with my own senses. I sent late one afternoon to ask if I might pay the ladies a visit, and my servant came back with surprising news. Miss Bordereau could be approached without the least difficulty; she had been moved out into the sala and was sitting by the window that overlooked the garden. I descended and found this picture correct; the old lady had been wheeled forth into the world and had a certain air, which came mainly perhaps from some brighter element in her dress, of being prepared again to have converse with it. It had not yet, however, begun to flock about her; she was perfectly alone and, though the door leading to her own quarters stood open, I had at first no glimpse of Miss Tita. The window at which she sat had the afternoon shade and, one of the shutters having been pushed back, she could see the pleasant garden, where the summer sun had by this time dried up too many of the plants – she could see the yellow light and the long shadows.

'Have you come to tell me that you will take the rooms for six months more?' she asked, as I approached her, startling me by something coarse in her cupidity almost as much as if she had not already given me a specimen of it. Juliana's desire to make our acquaintance lucrative had been, as I have sufficiently indicated, a false note in my image of the woman who had inspired a great poet with immortal lines; but I may say here definitely that I recognized after all that it behoved me to make a large allowance for her. It was I who had kindled the unholy flame; it was I who had put into her head that she had the means of making money. She appeared never to have thought of that; she had been living wastefully for years, in a house five times too big for her, on a footing that I could explain only by the presumption that, excessive as it was, the space she enjoyed cost her next to nothing and that small as were her revenues they left her, for Venice, an appreciable margin. I had descended on her one day and taught her to calculate, and my almost extravagant comedy on the subject of the garden had presented me irresistibly in the light of a victim. Like all persons who achieve the miracle of changing their point of view when they are old she had been intensely converted; she had seized my hint with a desperate, tremulous clutch.

I invited myself to go and get one of the chairs that stood, at a distance, against the wall (she had given herself no concern as to whether I should sit or stand); and while I placed it near her I began, gaily, 'Oh, dear madam, what an imagination you have, what an intellectual sweep! I am a poor devil of a man of letters who lives from day to day. How can I take palaces by the year? My existence is precarious. I don't know whether six months hence I shall have bread to put in my mouth. I have treated myself for once; it has been an immense luxury. But when it comes to going on – !'

'Are your rooms too dear? if they are you can have more for

the same money,' Juliana responded. 'We can arrange, we can *combinare*, as they say here.'

'Well yes, since you ask me, they are too dear,' I said. 'Evidently you suppose me richer than I am.'

She looked at me in her barricaded way. 'If you write books don't you sell them?'

'Do you mean don't people buy them? A little – not so much as I could wish. Writing books, unless one be a great genius – and even then! – is the last road to fortune. I think there is no more money to be made by literature.'

'Perhaps you don't choose good subjects. What do you write about?' Miss Bordereau inquired.

'About the books of other people. I'm a critic, an historian, in a small way.' I wondered what she was coming to.

'And what other people, now?'

'Oh, better ones than myself: the great writers mainly – the great philosophers and poets of the past; those who are dead and gone and can't speak for themselves.'

'And what do you say about them?'

'I say they sometimes attached themselves to very clever women!' I answered, laughing. I spoke with great deliberation, but as my words fell upon the air they struck me as imprudent. However, I risked them and I was not sorry, for perhaps after all the old woman would be willing to treat. It seemed to be tolerably obvious that she knew my secret: why therefore drag the matter out? But she did not take what I had said as a confession: she only asked:

'Do you think it's right to rake up the past?'

'I don't know that I know what you mean by raking it up; but how can we get at it unless we dig a little? The present has such a rough way of treading it down.'

'Oh, I like the past, but I don't like critics,' the old woman declared, with her fine tranquillity.

'Neither do I, but I like their discoveries.'

'Aren't they mostly lies?'

'The lies are what they sometimes discover,' I said, smiling at the quiet impertinence of this. 'They often lay bare the truth.'

'The truth is God's, it isn't man's; we had better leave it alone. Who can judge of it – who can say?'

'We are terribly in the dark, I know,' I admitted; 'but if we give up trying what becomes of all the fine things? What becomes of the work I just mentioned, that of the great philosophers and poets? It is all vain words if there is nothing to measure it by.'

'You talk as if you were a tailor,' said Miss Bordereau, whimsically; and then she added quickly, in a different manner, 'This house is very fine; the proportions are magnificent. Today I wanted to look at this place again. I made them bring me out here. When your man came, just now, to learn if I would see you, I was on the point of sending for you, to ask if you didn't mean to go on. I wanted to judge what I'm letting you have. This sala is very grand,' she pursued, like an auctioneer, moving a little, as I guessed, her invisible eyes. 'I don't believe you often have lived in such a house, eh?'

'I can't often afford to!' I said.

'Well then, how much will you give for six months?'

I was on the point of exclaiming – and the air of excruciation in my face would have denoted a moral fact – 'Don't, Juliana; for *his* sake, don't!' But I controlled myself and asked less passionately: 'Why should I remain so long as that?'

'I thought you liked it,' said Miss Bordereau, with her shrivelled dignity.

'So I thought I should.'

For a moment she said nothing more, and I left my own words to suggest to her what they might. I half expected her to say, coldly enough, that if I had been disappointed we need not continue the discussion, and this in spite of the fact that I believed her now to have in her mind (however it had come there), what would have told her that my disappointment was natural. But to my extreme surprise she ended by observing: 'If you don't think we have treated you well enough perhaps we can discover some way of treating you better.' This speech was somehow so incongruous that it made me laugh again, and I excused myself by saying that she talked as if I were a sulky boy, pouting in the corner, to be 'brought round'. I had not a grain of complaint to make; and could anything have exceeded Miss Tita's graciousness in accompanying me a few nights before to the Piazza? At this the old woman went on: 'Well, you brought it on yourself!' And then in a different tone, 'She is a very nice girl.' I assented cordially to this proposition, and she expressed the hope that I did so not merely to be obliging, but that I really liked her. Meanwhile I wondered still more what Miss Bordereau was coming to. 'Except for me, today,' she said, 'she has not a relation in the world.' Did she by describing her niece as amiable and unencumbered wish to represent her as a *parti*?

It was perfectly true that I could not afford to go on with my rooms at a fancy price and that I had already devoted to my undertaking almost all the hard cash I had set apart for it. My patience and my time were by no means exhausted, but I should be able to draw upon them only on a more usual Venetian basis. I was willing to pay the venerable woman with whom my pecuniary dealings were such a discord twice as much as any other *padrona di casa* would have asked, but I was not willing to pay her twenty times as much. I told her so plainly, and my plainness appeared to have some success, for she exclaimed, 'Very good; you have done what I asked – you have made an offer!'

'Yes, but not for half a year. Only by the month.'

'Oh, I must think of that then.' She seemed disappointed that I would not tie myself to a period, and I guessed that she wished both to secure me and to discourage me; to say, severely, 'Do you dream that you can get off with less than six months? Do you dream that even by the end of that time you will be appreciably nearer your victory?' What was more in my mind was that she had a fancy to play me the trick of making me engage myself when in fact she had annihilated the papers. There was a moment when my suspense on this point was so acute that I all but broke out with the question, and what kept it back was but a kind of instinctive recoil (lest it should be a mistake), from the last violence of self-exposure. She was such a subtle old witch that one could never tell where one stood with her. You may imagine whether it cleared up the puzzle when, just after she had said she would think of my proposal and without any formal transition, she drew out of her pocket with an embarrassed hand a small object wrapped in crumpled white paper. She held it there a moment and then she asked, 'Do you know much about curiosities?'

'About curiosities?'

'About antiquities, the old gimcracks that people pay so much for today. Do you know the kind of price they bring?'

I thought I saw what was coming, but I said ingenuously, 'Do you want to buy something?'

'No, I want to sell. What would an amateur give me for that?' She unfolded the white paper and made a motion for me to take from her a small oval portrait. I possessed myself of it with a hand of which I could only hope that she did not perceive the tremor, and she added, 'I would part with it only for a good price.'

At the first glance I recognized Jeffrey Aspern, and I was well aware that I flushed with the act. As she was watching me however I had the consistency to exclaim, 'What a striking face! Do tell me who it is.'

'It's an old friend of mine, a very distinguished man in his day. He gave it to me himself, but I'm afraid to mention his name, lest you never should have heard of him, critic and historian as you are. I know the world goes fast and one generation forgets another. He was all the fashion when I was young.'

She was perhaps amazed at my assurance, but I was surprised at hers; at her having the energy, in her state of health and at her time of life, to wish to sport with me that way simply for her private entertainment – the humour to test me and practise on me. This, at least, was the interpretation that I put upon her production of the portrait, for I could not believe that she really desired to sell it or cared for any information I might give her. What she wished was to dangle it before my eyes and put a prohibitive price on it. 'The face comes back to me, it torments me,' I said, turning the object this way and that and looking at it very critically. It was a careful but not a supreme work of art, larger than the ordinary miniature and representing a young man with a remarkably handsome face, in a high-collared green coat and a buff waistcoat. I judged the picture to have a valuable quality of resemblance and to have been painted when the model was about twenty-five years old. There are, as all the world knows, three other portraits of the poet in existence, but none of them is of so early a date as this elegant production. 'I have never seen the original but I have seen other likenesses,' I went on. 'You expressed doubt of this generation having heard of the gentleman, but he strikes me for all the world as a celebrity. Now who is he? I can't put my finger on him – I can't give him a label. Wasn't he a writer? Surely he's a poet.' I was determined that it should be she, not I, who should first pronounce Jeffrey Aspern's name.

My resolution was taken in ignorance of Miss Bordereau's extremely resolute character, and her lips never formed in my hearing the syllables that meant so much for her. She neglected to answer my question but raised her hand to take back the picture, with a gesture which though ineffectual was in a high degree peremptory. 'It's only a person who should know for himself that would give me my price,' she said with a certain dryness.

'Oh, then, you have a price?' I did not restore the precious thing; not from any vindictive purpose but because I instinctively clung to it. We looked at each other hard while I retained it.

'I know the least I would take. What it occurred to me to ask you about is the most I shall be able to get.'

She made a movement, drawing herself together as if, in a spasm of dread at having lost her treasure, she were going to attempt the immense effort of rising to snatch it from me. I instantly placed it in her hand again, saying as I did so, 'I should like to have it myself, but with your ideas I could never afford it.'

She turned the small oval plate over in her lap, with its face down, and I thought I saw her catch her breath a little, as if she had had a strain or an escape. This however did not prevent her saying in a moment, 'You would buy a likeness of a person you don't know, by an artist who has no reputation?'

'The artist may have no reputation, but that thing is wonderfully well painted,' I replied, to give myself a reason.

'It's lucky you thought of saying that, because the painter was my father.'

'That makes the picture indeed precious!' I exclaimed,

laughing; and I may add that a part of my laughter came from my satisfaction in finding that I had been right in my theory of Miss Bordereau's origin. Aspern had of course met the young lady when he went to her father's studio as a sitter. I observed to Miss Bordereau that if she would entrust me with her property for twenty-four hours I should be happy to take advice upon it; but she made no answer to this save to slip it in silence into her pocket. This convinced me still more that she had no sincere intention of selling it during her lifetime, though she may have desired to satisfy herself as to the sum her niece, should she leave it to her, might expect eventually to obtain for it. 'Well, at any rate I hope you will not offer it without giving me notice,' I said, as she remained irresponsive. 'Remember that I am a possible purchaser.'

'I should want your money first!' she returned, with unexpected rudeness; and then, as if she bethought herself that I had just cause to complain of such an insinuation and wished to turn the matter off, asked abruptly what I talked about with her niece when I went out with her that way in the evening.

'You speak as if we had set up the habit,' I replied. 'Certainly I should be very glad if it were to become a habit. But in that case I should feel a still greater scruple at betraying a lady's confidence.'

'Her confidence? Has she got confidence?'

'Here she is – she can tell you herself,' I said; for Miss Tita now appeared on the threshold of the old woman's parlour. 'Have you got confidence, Miss Tita? Your aunt wants very much to know.'

'Not in her, not in her!' the younger lady declared, shaking her head with a dolefulness that was neither jocular nor affected. 'I don't know what to do with her; she has fits of horrid imprudence. She is so easily tired – and yet she has begun to roam – to drag herself about the house.' And she stood looking down at her immemorial companion with a sort of helpless wonder, as if all their years of familiarity had not made her perversities, on occasion, any more easy to follow.

'I know what I'm about. I'm not losing my mind. I dare say you would like to think so,' said Miss Bordereau, with a cynical little sigh.

'I don't suppose you came out here yourself. Miss Tita must have had to lend you a hand,' I interposed, with a pacifying intention.

'Oh, she insisted that we should push her; and when she insists!' said Miss Tita, in the same tone of apprehension; as if there were no knowing what service that she disapproved of her aunt might force her next to render.

'I have always got most things done I wanted, thank God! The people I have lived with have humoured me,' the old woman continued, speaking out of the grey ashes of her vanity.

'I suppose you mean that they have obeyed you.'

'Well, whatever it is, when they like you.'

'It's just because I like you that I want to resist,' said Miss Tita, with a nervous laugh.

'Oh, I suspect you'll bring Miss Bordereau upstairs next, to pay me a visit,' I went on; to which the old lady replied:

'Oh no; I can keep an eye on you from here!'

'You are very tired; you will certainly be ill tonight!' cried Miss Tita.

'Nonsense, my dear; I feel better at this moment than I have done for a month. Tomorrow I shall come out again. I want to be where I can see this clever gentleman.'

'Shouldn't you perhaps see me better in your sitting-room?' I inquired.

'Don't you mean shouldn't you have a better chance at me?' she returned, fixing me a moment with her green shade.

'Ah, I haven't that anywhere! I look at you but I don't see you.'

'You excite her dreadfully – and that is not good,' said Miss Tita, giving me a reproachful, appealing look.

'I want to watch you – I want to watch you!' the old lady went on.

'Well then, let us spend as much of our time together as possible – I don't care where – and that will give you every facility.'

'Oh, I've seen you enough for today. I'm satisfied. Now I'll go home.' Miss Tita laid her hands on the back of her aunt's chair and began to push, but I begged her to let me take her place. 'Oh yes, you may move me this way – you sha'n't in any other!' Miss Bordereau exclaimed, as she felt herself propelled firmly and easily over the smooth, hard floor. Before we reached the door of her own apartment she commanded me to stop, and she took a long, last look up and down the noble sala. 'Oh, it's a magnificent house!' she murmured; after which I pushed her forward. When we had entered the parlour Miss Tita told me that she should now be able to manage, and at the same moment the little red-haired *donna* came to meet her mistress. Miss Tita's idea was evidently to get her aunt immediately back to bed. I confess that in spite of this urgency I was guilty of the indiscretion of lingering; it held me there to think that I was nearer the documents I coveted – that they were probably put away somewhere in the faded, unsociable room. The place had indeed a bareness which did not suggest hidden treasures; there were no dusky nooks nor curtained corners, no massive cabinets nor chests with iron bands. More-over it was possible, it was perhaps even probable that the old lady had consigned her relics to her bedroom, to some battered box that was shoved under the bed, to the drawer of some lame dressing-table, where they would be in the range of vision by the dim night-lamp. None the less I scrutinized every article of furni-ture, every conceivable cover for a hoard, and noticed that there were half a dozen things with drawers, and in particular a tall old secretary, with brass ornaments of the style of the Empire – a receptacle somewhat rickety but still capable of keeping a great many secrets. I don't know why this article fascinated me so, inas-much as I certainly had no definite purpose of breaking into it; but I stared at it so hard that Miss Tita noticed me and changed colour. Her doing this made me think I was right and that wherever they might have been before the Aspern papers at that moment languished behind the peevish little lock of the secretary. It was hard to remove my eyes from the dull mahogany front when I reflected that a simple panel divided me from the goal of my hopes; but I remembered my prudence and with an effort took leave of Miss Bordereau. To make the effort graceful I said to her that I should certainly bring her an opinion about the little picture.

'The little picture?' Miss Tita asked, surprised.

'What do *you* know about it, my dear?' the old woman demanded. 'You needn't mind. I have fixed my price.'

'And what may that be?'

'A thousand pounds.'

'Oh Lord!' cried poor Miss Tita, irrepressibly.

'Is that what she talks to you about?' said Miss Bordereau.

'Imagine your aunt's wanting to know!' I had to separate from Miss Tita with only those words, though I should have liked immensely to add, 'For heaven's sake meet me tonight in the garden!'

8

As it turned out the precaution had not been needed, for three hours later, just as I had finished my dinner, Miss Bordereau's niece appeared, unannounced, in the open doorway of the room in which my simple repasts were served. I remember well that I felt no surprise at seeing her; which is not a proof that I did not believe in her timidity. It was immense, but in a case in which there was a particular reason for boldness it never would have prevented her from running up to my rooms. I saw that she was now quite full of a particular reason; it threw her forward – made her seize me, as I rose to meet her, by the arm.

'My aunt is very ill; I think she is dying!'

'Never in the world,' I answered, bitterly. 'Don't you be afraid!'

'Do go for a doctor – do, do! Olimpia is gone for the one we always have, but she doesn't come back; I don't know what has happened to her. I told her that if he was not at home she was to follow him where he had gone; but apparently she is following him all over Venice. I don't know what to do – she looks so as if she were sinking.'

'May I see her, may I judge?' I asked. 'Of course I shall be delighted to bring some one; but hadn't we better send my man instead, so that I may stay with you?'

Miss Tita assented to this and I despatched my servant for the best doctor in the neighbourhood. I hurried downstairs with her, and on the way she told me that an hour after I quitted them in the afternoon Miss Bordereau had had an attack of 'oppression', a terrible difficulty in breathing. This had subsided but had left her so exhausted that she did not come up: she seemed all gone. I repeated that she was not gone, that she would not go yet; whereupon Miss Tita gave me a sharper sidelong glance than she had ever directed at me and said, 'Really, what do you mean? I suppose you don't accuse her of making-believe!' I forget what reply I made to this, but I grant that in my heart I thought the old woman capable of any weird manoeuvre. Miss Tita wanted to know what I had done to her; her aunt had told her that I had made her so angry. I declared I had done nothing – I had been exceedingly careful; to which my companion rejoined that Miss Bordereau had assured her she had had a scene with me – a scene that had upset her. I answered with some resentment that it was a scene of her own making – that I couldn't think what she was angry with me for unless for not seeing my way to give a thousand pounds for the portrait of Jeffrey Aspern. 'And did she show you that? Oh gracious – oh deary me!' groaned Miss Tita, who appeared to feel that the situation was passing out of her control, and that the elements of her fate were thickening around her. I said that I would give anything to possess it, yet that I had not a thousand pounds; but I stopped when we came to the door of Miss Bordereau's room. I had an immense curiosity to pass it, but I thought it my duty to represent to Miss Tita that if I made the invalid angry she ought perhaps to be spared the sight of me. 'The sight of you? Do you think she can *see*?' my companion demanded, almost with indignation. I did think so but forbore to say it, and I softly followed my conductress.

I remember that what I said to her as I stood for a moment beside the old woman's bed was, 'Does she never show you her eyes then? Have you never seen them?' Miss Bordereau had been divested of her green shade, but (it was not my fortune to behold

Juliana in her night cap) the upper half of her face was covered by the fall of a piece of dingy lacelike muslin, a sort of extemporized hood which, wound round her head, descended to the end of her nose, leaving nothing visible but her white withered cheeks and puckered mouth, closed tightly and, as it were, consciously. Miss Tita gave me a glance of surprise, evidently not seeing a reason for my impatience. 'You mean that she always wears something? She does it to preserve them.'

'Because they are so fine?'

'Oh, today, today!' And Miss Tita shook her head, speaking very low. 'But they used to be magnificent!'

'Yes indeed, we have Aspern's word for that.' And as I looked again at the old woman's wrappings I could imagine that she had not wished to allow people a reason to say that the great poet had overdone it. But I did not waste my time in considering Miss Bordereau, in whom the appearance of respiration was so slight as to suggest that no human attention could ever help her more. I turned my eyes all over the room, rummaging with them the closets, the chests of drawers, the tables. Miss Tita met them quickly and read, I think, what was in them; but she did not answer it, turning away restlessly, anxiously, so that I felt rebuked, with reason, for a preoccupation that was almost profane in the presence of our dying companion. All the same I took another look, endeavouring to pick out mentally the place to try first, for a person who should wish to put his hand on Miss Bordereau's papers directly after her death. The room was a dire confusion; it looked like the room of an old actress. There were clothes hanging over chairs, odd-looking, shabby bundles here and there, and various pasteboard boxes piled together, battered, bulging and discoloured, which might have been fifty years old. Miss Tita after a moment noticed the direction of my eyes again and, as if she guessed how I judged the air of the place (forgetting I had no business to judge it at all), said, perhaps to defend herself from the imputation of complicity in such untidiness:

'She likes it this way; we can't move things. There are old band-boxes she has had most of her life.' Then she added, half taking pity on my real thought, 'Those things were *there*.' And she pointed to a small, low trunk which stood under a sofa where there was just room for it. It appeared to be a queer, super-annuated coffer, of painted wood, with elaborate handles and shrivelled straps and with the colour (it had last been endued with a coat of light green) much rubbed off. It evidently had travelled with Juliana in the olden time – in the days of her adventures, which it had shared. It would have made a strange figure arriving at a modern hotel.

' *Were* there – they aren't now?' I asked, startled by Miss Tita's implication.

She was going to answer, but at that moment the doctor came in – the doctor whom the little maid had been sent to fetch and whom she had at last overtaken. My servant, going on his own errand, had met her with her companion in tow, and in the soci-able Venetian spirit, retracing his steps with them, had also come up to the threshold of Miss Bordereau's room, where I saw him peeping over the doctor's shoulder. I motioned him away the more instantly that the sight of his prying face reminded me that I myself had almost as little to do there – an admonition con-firmed by the sharp way the little doctor looked at me, appearing to take me for a rival who had the field before him. He was a short, fat, brisk gentleman who wore the tall hat of his profession and seemed to look at everything but his patient. He looked par-ticularly at me, as if it struck him that I should be better for a dose, so that I bowed to him and left him with the women, going down to smoke a cigar in the garden. I was nervous; I could not go further; I could not leave the place. I don't know exactly what I thought might happen, but it seemed to me important to be there. I wandered about in the alleys – the warm night had come on – smoking cigar after cigar and looking at the light in Miss Bordereau's windows. They were open now, I could see; the situation was different. Sometimes the light moved, but not quickly; it did not suggest the hurry of a crisis. Was the old woman dying or was she already dead? Had the doctor said that there was nothing to be done at her tremendous age but to let her quietly pass away; or had he simply announced with a look a little more conventional that the end of the end had come? Were the other two women moving about to perform the offices that follow in such a case? It made me uneasy not to be nearer, as if I thought the doctor himself might carry away the papers with him. I bit my cigar hard as it came over me again that perhaps there were now no papers to carry!

I wandered about for an hour – for an hour and a half. I looked out for Miss Tita at one of the windows, having a vague idea that she might come there to give me some sign. Would she not see the red tip of my cigar moving about in the dark and feel that I wanted eminently to know what the doctor had said? I am afraid it is a proof my anxieties had made me gross that I should have taken in some degree for granted that at such an hour, in the midst of the greatest change that could take place in her life, they were uppermost also in poor Miss Tita's mind. My servant came down and spoke to me; he knew nothing save that the doctor had gone after a visit of half an hour. If he had stayed half an hour then Miss Bordereau was still alive: it could not have taken so much time as that to enunciate the contrary. I sent the man out of the house; there were moments when the sense of his curiosity annoyed me and this was one of them. *He* had been watching my cigar-tip from an upper window, if Miss Tita had not; he could not know what I was after and I could not tell him, though I was conscious he had fantastic private theories about me which he thought fine and which I, had I known them, should have thought offensive.

I went upstairs at last but I ascended no higher than the sala. The door of Miss Bordereau's apartment was open, showing from the parlour the dimness of a poor candle. I went towards it with a light tread and at the same moment Miss Tita appeared and stood looking at me as I approached. 'She's better – she's better,' she said, even before I had asked. 'The doctor has given her something; she woke up, came back to life while he was there. He says there is no immediate danger.'

'No immediate danger? Surely he thinks her condition strange!'

'Yes, because she had been excited. That affects her dreadfully.'

'It will do so again then, because she excites herself. She did so this afternoon.'

'Yes; she mustn't come out any more,' said Miss Tita, with one of her lapses into a deeper placidity.

'What is the use of making such a remark as that if you begin to rattle her about again the first time she bids you?'

'I won't – I won't do it any more.'

'You must learn to resist her,' I went on.

'Oh yes, I shall; I shall do so better if you tell me it's right.'

'You mustn't do it for me; you must do it for yourself. It all comes back to you, if you are frightened.'

'Well, I am not frightened now,' said Miss Tita, cheerfully. 'She is very quiet.'

'Is she conscious again – does she speak?'

'No, she doesn't speak, but she takes my hand. She holds it fast.'

'Yes,' I rejoined, 'I can see what force she still has by the way she grabbed that picture this afternoon. But if she holds you fast how comes it that you are here?'

Miss Tita hesitated a moment; though her face was in deep shadow (she had her back to the light in the parlour and I had put down my own candle far off, near the door of the sala), I thought I saw her smile ingenuously. 'I came on purpose – I heard your step.'

'Why, I came on tiptoe, as inaudibly as possible.'

'Well, I heard you,' said Miss Tita.

'And is your aunt alone now?'

'Oh no; Olimpia is sitting there.'

On my side I hesitated. 'Shall we then step in there?' And I nodded at the parlour; I wanted more and more to be on the spot.

'We can't talk there – she will hear us.'

I was on the point of replying that in that case we would sit silent, but I was too conscious that this would not do, as there was something I desired immensely to ask her. So I proposed that we should walk a little in the sala, keeping more at the other end, where we should not disturb the old lady. Miss Tita assented unconditionally; the doctor was coming again, she said, and she would be there to meet him at the door. We strolled through the fine superfluous hall, where on the marble floor – particularly as at first we said nothing – our footsteps were more audible than I had expected. When we reached the other end – the wide window, inveterately closed, connecting with the balcony that overhung the canal – I suggested that we should remain there, as she would see the doctor arrive still better. I opened the window and we passed out on the balcony. The air of the canal seemed even heavier, hotter than that of the sala. The place was hushed and void; the quiet neighbourhood had gone to sleep. A lamp, here and there, over the narrow black water, glimmered in double; the voice of a man going homeward singing, with his jacket on his shoulder and his hat on his ear, came to us from a distance. This did not prevent the scene from being very *comme il faut*, as Miss Bordereau had called it the first time I saw her. Presently a gondola passed along the canal with its slow rhythmical plash, and as we listened we watched it in silence. It did not stop, it did not carry the doctor; and after it had gone on I said to Miss Tita:

'And where are they now – the things that were in the trunk?'

'In the trunk?'

'That green box you pointed out to me in her room. You said her papers had been there; you seemed to imply that she had transferred them.'

'Oh yes; they are not in the trunk,' said Miss Tita.

'May I ask if you have looked?'

'Yes, I have looked – for you.'

'How for me, dear Miss Tita? Do you mean you would have given them to me if you had found them?' I asked, almost trembling.

She delayed to reply and I waited. Suddenly she broke out, 'I don't know what I would do – what I wouldn't!'

'Would you look again – somewhere else?'

She had spoken with a strange, unexpected emotion, and she went on in the same tone: 'I can't – I can't – while she lies there. It isn't decent.'

'No, it isn't decent,' I replied, gravely. 'Let the poor lady rest in peace.' And the words, on my lips, were not hypocritical, for I felt reprimanded and shamed.

Miss Tita added in a moment, as if she had guessed this and were sorry for me, but at the same time wished to explain that I did drive her on or at least did insist too much: 'I can't deceive her that way. I can't deceive her – perhaps on her death-bed.'

'Heaven forbid I should ask you, though I have been guilty myself!'

'You have been guilty?'

'I have sailed under false colours,' I felt now as if I must tell her that I had given her an invented name, on account of my fear that her aunt would have heard of me and would refuse to take me in. I explained this and also that I had really been a party to the letter written to them by John Cumnor months before.

She listened with great attention, looking at me with parted lips, and when I had made my confession she said, 'Then your real name – what is it?' She repeated it over twice when I had told her, accompanying it with the exclamation 'Gracious, gracious!' Then she added, 'I like your own best.'

'So do I,' I said, laughing. 'Ouf! it's a relief to get rid of the other.'

'So it was a regular plot – a kind of conspiracy?'

'Oh, a conspiracy – we were only two,' I replied, leaving out Mrs Prest of course.

She hesitated; I thought she was perhaps going to say that we had been very base. But she remarked after a moment, in a candid, wondering way, 'How much you must want them!'

'Oh, I do, passionately!' I conceded, smiling. And this chance made me go on, forgetting my compunction of a moment before. 'How can she possibly have changed their place herself? How can she walk? How can she arrive at that sort of muscular exertion? How can she lift and carry things?'

'Oh, when one wants and when one has so much will!' said Miss Tita, as if she had thought over my question already herself and had simply had no choice but that answer – the idea that in the dead of night, or at some moment when the coast was clear, the old woman had been capable of a miraculous effort.

'Have you questioned Olimpia? Hasn't she helped her – hasn't she done it for her?' I asked; to which Miss Tita replied promptly and positively that their servant had had nothing to do with the matter, though without admitting definitely that she had spoken to her. It was as if she were a little shy, a little ashamed now of letting me see how much she had entered into my uneasiness and had me on her mind. Suddenly she said to me, without any immediate relevance:

'I feel as if you were a new person, now that you have got a new name.'

'It isn't a new one; it is a very good old one, thank heaven!'

She looked at me a moment. 'I do like it better.'

'Oh, if you didn't I would almost go on with the other!'

'Would you really?'

I laughed again, but for all answer to this inquiry I said, 'Of course if she can rummage about that way she can perfectly have burnt them.'

'You must wait – you must wait,' Miss Tita moralized mournfully; and her tone ministered little to my patience, for it seemed after all to accept that wretched possibility. I would teach myself to wait, I declared nevertheless; because in the first place I could not do otherwise and in the second I had her promise, given me the other night, that she would help me.

'Of course if the papers are gone that's no use,' she said; not as if she wished to recede, but only to be conscientious.

'Naturally. But if you could only find out!' I groaned, quivering again.

'I thought you said you would wait.'

'Oh, you mean wait even for that?'

'For what then?'

'Oh, nothing,' I replied, rather foolishly, being ashamed to tell her what had been implied in my submission to delay – the idea that she would do more than merely find out. I know not whether she guessed this; at all events she appeared to become aware of the necessity for being a little more rigid.

'I didn't promise to deceive, did I? I don't think I did.'

'It doesn't much matter whether you did or not, for you couldn't!'

I don't think Miss Tita would have contested this even had she not been diverted by our seeing the doctor's gondola shoot into the little canal and approach the house. I noted that he came as fast as if he believed that Miss Bordereau was still in danger. We looked down at him while he disembarked and then went back into the sala to meet him. When he came up however I naturally left Miss Tita to go off with him alone, only asking her leave to come back later for news.

I went out of the house and took a long walk, as far as the Piazza, where my restlessness declined to quit me. I was unable to sit down (it was very late now but there were people still at the little tables in front of the cafés); I could only walk round and round, and I did so half a dozen times. I was uncomfortable, but it gave me a certain pleasure to have told Miss Tita who I really was. At last I took my way home again, slowly getting all but inextricably lost, as I did whenever I went out in Venice: so that it was considerably past midnight when I reached my door. The sala, upstairs, was as dark as usual and my lamp as I crossed it found nothing satisfactory to show me. I was disappointed, for I had notified Miss Tita that I would come back for a report, and I thought she might have left a light there as a sign. The door of the ladies' apartment was closed; which seemed an intimation that my faltering friend had gone to bed, tired of waiting for me. I stood in the middle of the place, considering, hoping she would hear me and perhaps peep out, saying to myself too that she would never go to bed with her aunt in a state so critical; she would sit up and watch – she would be in a chair, in her dressing-gown. I went nearer the door; I stopped there and listened. I heard nothing at all and at last I tapped gently. No answer came and after another minute I turned the handle. There was no light in the room; this ought to have prevented me from going in, but it had no such effect. If I have candidly narrated the importunities, the indelicacies, of which my desire to possess myself of Jeffrey Aspern's papers had rendered me capable I need not shrink from confessing this last indiscretion. I think it was the worst thing I did; yet there were extenuating circumstances. I was deeply though doubtless not disinterestedly anxious for more news of the old lady, and Miss Tita had accepted from me, as it were, a rendezvous which it might have been a point of honour with me to keep. It may be said that her leaving the place dark was a positive sign that she released me, and to this I can only reply that I desired not to be released.

The door of Miss Bordereau's room was open and I could see beyond it the faintness of a taper. There was no sound – my foot-step caused no one to stir. I came further into the room; I lingered there with my lamp in my hand. I wanted to give Miss Tita a chance to come to me if she were with her aunt, as she must be. I made no noise to call her; I only waited to see if she would not notice my light. She did not, and I explained this (I found after-wards I was right) by the idea that she had fallen asleep. If she had fallen asleep her aunt was not on her mind, and my explanation ought to have led me to go out as I had come. I must repeat again that it did not, for I found myself at the same moment thinking of something else. I had no definite purpose, no bad intention, but I felt myself held to the spot by an acute, though absurd, sense of opportunity. For what I could not have said, inasmuch as it was not in my mind that I might commit a theft. Even if it had been I was confronted with the evident fact that Miss Bordereau did not leave her secretary, her cupboard and the drawers of her tables gaping. I had no keys, no tools and no ambition to smash her furniture. None the less it came to me that I was now, perhaps alone, unmolested, at the hour of temptation and secrecy, nearer to the tormenting treasure than I had ever been. I held up my lamp, let the light play on the different objects as if it could tell me something. Still there came no movement from the other room. If Miss Tita was sleeping she was sleeping sound. Was she doing so – generous creature – on purpose to leave me the field? Did she know I was there and was she just keeping quiet to see what I would do – what I *could* do? But what could I do, when it came to that? She herself knew even better than I how little.

I stopped in front of the secretary, looking at it very idiotically;

for what had it to say to me after all? In the first place it was locked, and in the second it almost surely contained nothing in which I was interested. Ten to one the papers had been destroyed; and even if they had not been destroyed the old woman would not have put them in such a place as that after removing them from the green trunk – would not have transferred them, if she had the idea of their safety on her brain, from the better hiding-place to the worse. The secretary was more conspicuous, more accessible in a room in which she could no longer mount guard. It opened with a key, but there was a little brass handle, like a button, as well; I saw this as I played my lamp over it. I did something more than this at that moment: I caught a glimpse of the possibility that Miss Tita wished me really to understand. If she did not wish me to understand, if she wished me to keep away, why had she not locked the door of communication between the sitting-room and the sala? That would have been a definite sign that I was to leave them alone. If I did not leave them alone she meant me to come for a purpose – a purpose now indicated by the quick, fantastic idea that to oblige me she had unlocked the secretary. She had not left the key, but the lid would probably move if I touched the button. This theory fascinated me, and I bent over very close to judge. I did not propose to do anything, not even – not in the least – to let down the lid; I only wanted to test my theory, to see if the cover *would* move. I touched the button with my hand – a mere touch would tell me; and as I did so (it is embarrassing for me to relate it), I looked over my shoulder. It was a chance, an instinct, for I had not heard anything. I almost let my luminary drop and certainly I stepped back, straightening myself up at what I saw. Miss Bordereau stood there in her night-dress, in the doorway of her room, watching me; her hands were raised, she had lifted the everlasting curtain that covered half her face, and for the first, the last, the only time I beheld her extraordinary eyes. They glared at me, they made me horribly ashamed. I never shall forget her strange little bent white tottering figure, with its lifted head, her attitude, her expression; neither shall I forget the tone in which as I turned, looking at her, she hissed out passionately, furiously:

'Ah, you publishing scoundrel!'

I know not what I stammered, to excuse myself, to explain; but I went towards her, to tell her I meant no harm. She waved me off with her old hands, retreating before me in horror; and the next thing I knew she had fallen back with a quick spasm, as if death had descended on her, into Miss Tita's arms.

9

I LEFT Venice the next morning, as soon as I learnt that the old lady had not succumbed, as I feared at the moment, to the shock I had given her – the shock I may also say she had given me. How in the world could I have supposed her capable of getting out of bed by herself? I failed to see Miss Tita before going; I only saw the *donna*, whom I entrusted with a note for her younger mistress. In this note I mentioned that I should be absent but for a few days. I went to Treviso, to Bassano, to Castelfranco; I took walks and drives and looked at musty old churches with ill-lighted pictures and spent hours seated smoking at the doors of cafés, where there were flies and yellow curtains, on the shady side of sleepy little squares. In spite of these pastimes, which were mechanical and perfunctory, I scantily enjoyed my journey: there was too strong a taste of the disagreeable in my life. It had been devilish awkward, as the young men say, to be found by Miss Bordereau in the dead of night examining the attachment of her bureau; and it had not been less so to have to believe for a good many hours afterwards that it was highly probable I had killed her. In writing to Miss Tita I attempted to minimize these irregularities; but as she gave me no word of answer I could not know what impression I made upon her. It rankled in my mind that I had been called a publishing scoundrel, for certainly I did publish and certainly I had not been very delicate. There was a moment when I stood convinced that the only way to make up for this latter fault was to take myself away altogether on the instant; to sacrifice my hopes and relieve the two poor women for ever of the oppression of my intercourse. Then I reflected that I had better try a short absence first, for I must already have had a sense (unexpressed and dim) that in disappearing completely it would not be merely my own hopes that I should condemn to extinction. It would perhaps be sufficient if I stayed away long enough to give the elder lady time to think she was rid of me. That she would wish to be rid of me after this (if I was not rid of her) was now not to be doubted: that nocturnal scene would have cured her of the disposition to put up with my company for the sake of my dollars. I said to myself that after all I could not abandon Miss Tita, and I continued to say this even while I observed that she quite failed to comply with my earnest request (I had given her two or three addresses, at little towns, *poste restante*) that she would let me know how she was getting on. I would have made my servant write to me but that he was unable to manage a pen. It struck me there was a kind of scorn in Miss Tita's silence (little disdainful as she had ever been), so that I was uncomfortable and sore. I had scruples about going back and yet I had others about not doing so, for I wanted to put myself on a better footing. The end of it was that I did return to Venice on the twelfth day; and as my gondola gently bumped against Miss Bordereau's steps a certain palpitation of suspense told me that I had done myself a violence in holding off so long.

I had faced about so abruptly that I had not telegraphed to my servant. He was therefore not at the station to meet me, but he poked out his head from an upper window when I reached the house. 'They have put her into the earth, *la vecchia*,' he said to me in the lower hall, while he shouldered my valise; and he grinned and almost winked, as if he knew I should be pleased at the news.

'She's dead!' I exclaimed, giving him a very different look.

'So it appears, since they have buried her.'

'It's all over? When was the funeral?'

'The other yesterday. But a funeral you could scarcely call it, signore; it was a dull little *passeggio* of two gondolas. Poveretta!' the man continued, referring apparently to Miss Tita. His conception of funerals was apparently that they were mainly to amuse the living.

I wanted to know about Miss Tita – how she was and where she was – but I asked him no more questions till we had got upstairs. Now that the fact had met me I took a bad view of it, especially of the idea that poor Miss Tita had had to manage by herself after the end. What did she know about arrangements, about the steps to take in such a case? Poveretta indeed! I could only hope that the doctor had given her assistance and that she had not been neglected by the old friends of whom she had told me, the little band of the faithful whose fidelity consisted in coming to the house once a year. I elicited from my servant that two old ladies and an old gentleman had in fact rallied round Miss Tita and had supported her (they had come for her in a gondola of their own) during the journey to the cemetery, the little red-walled island of tombs which lies to the north of the town, on the way to Murano. It appeared from these circumstances that the Misses Bordereau were Catholics, a discovery I had never made, as the old woman could not go to church and her niece, so far as I perceived, either did not or went only to early mass in the parish, before I was stirring. Certainly even the priests respected their seclusion; I had never caught the whisk of the curato's skirt. That evening, an hour later, I sent my servant down with five words written on a card, to ask Miss Tita if she would see me for a few moments. She was not in the house, where he had sought her, he told me when he came back, but in the garden walking about to refresh herself and gathering flowers. He had found her there and she would be very happy to see me.

I went down and passed half an hour with poor Miss Tita. She had always had a look of musty mourning (as if she were wearing out old robes of sorrow that would not come to an end), and in this respect there was no appreciable change in her appearance. But she evidently had been crying, crying a great deal – simply, satisfyingly, refreshingly, with a sort of primitive, retarded sense of loneliness and violence. But she had none of the formalism or the self-consciousness of grief, and I was almost surprised to see her standing there in the first dusk with her hands full of flowers, smiling at me with her reddened eyes. Her white face, in the frame of her mantilla, looked longer, leaner than usual. I had had an idea that she would be a good deal disgusted with me – would consider that I ought to have been on the spot to advise her, to help her; and, though I was sure there was no rancour in her composition and no great conviction of the importance of her affairs, I had prepared myself for a difference in her manner, for some little injured look, half familiar, half estranged, which should say to my conscience, 'Well, you are a nice person to have professed things!' But historic truth compels me to declare that Tita Bordereau's countenance expressed unqualified pleasure in seeing her late aunt's lodger. That touched him extremely and he thought it simplified his situation until he found it did not. I was as kind to her that evening as I knew how to be, and I walked about the garden with her for half an hour. There was no explanation of any sort between us; I did not ask her why she had not answered my letter. Still less did I repeat what I had said to her in that communication; if she chose to let me suppose that she had forgotten the position in which Miss Bordereau surprised me that night and the effect of the discovery on the old woman I was quite willing to take it that way: I was grateful to her for not treating me as if I had killed her aunt.

We strolled and strolled and really not much passed between us save the recognition of her bereavement, conveyed in my manner and in a visible air that she had of depending on me now, since I let her see that I took an interest in her. Miss Tita had none of the pride that makes a person wish to preserve the look of independence; she did not in the least pretend that she knew at present what would become of her. I forbore to touch particularly on that however, for I certainly was not prepared to say that I would take charge of her. I was cautious; not ignobly, I think, for I felt that her knowledge of life was so small that in her unsophisticated vision there would be no reason why – since I seemed to pity her – I should not look after her. She told me how her aunt had died, very peacefully at the last, and how everything had been done afterwards by the care of her good friends (fortunately, thanks to me, she said, smiling, there was money in the house; and she repeated that when once the Italians like you they are your friends for life); and when we had gone into this she asked me about my *giro*, my impressions, the places I had seen. I told her what I could, making it up partly, I am afraid, as in my depression I had not seen much; and after she had heard me she exclaimed, quite as if she had forgotten her aunt and her sorrow, 'Dear, dear, how much I should like to do such things – to take a little journey!' It came over me for the moment that I ought to propose some tour, say I would take her anywhere she liked; and I remarked at any rate that some excursion – to give her a change – might be managed: we would think of it, talk it over. I said never a word to her about the Aspern documents; asked no questions as to what she had ascertained or what had otherwise happened with regard to them before Miss Bordereau's death. It was not that I was not on pins and needles to know, but that I thought it more decent not to betray my anxiety so soon after the catastrophe. I hoped she herself would say something, but she never glanced that way, and I thought this natural at the time. Later, however, that night, it occurred to me that her silence was somewhat strange; for if she had talked of my movements, of anything so detached as the Giorgione at Castelfranco, she might have alluded to what she could easily remember was in my mind. It was not to be supposed that the emotion produced by her aunt's death had blotted out the recollection that I was interested in that lady's relics, and I fidgeted afterwards as it came to me that her reticence might very possibly mean simply that nothing had been found. We separated in the garden (it was she who said she must go in); now that she was alone in the rooms I felt that (judged, at any rate, by Venetian ideas) I was on rather a different footing in regard to visiting her there. As I shook hands with her for good night I asked her if she had any general plan – had thought over what she had better do. 'Oh yes, oh yes, but I haven't settled anything yet,' she replied, quite cheerfully. Was her cheerfulness explained by the impression that I would settle for her?

I was glad the next morning that we had neglected practical questions, for this gave me a pretext for seeing her again immediately. There was a very practical question to be touched upon. I owed it to her to let her know formally that of course I did not expect her to keep me on as a lodger, and also to show some interest in her own tenure, what she might have on her hands in the way of a lease. But I was not destined, as it happened, to converse with her for more than an instant on either of these points. I sent her no message; I simply went down to the sala and walked to and fro there. I knew she would come out; she would very soon discover I was there. Somehow I preferred not to be shut up with her; gardens and big halls seemed better places to talk. It was a splendid morning, with something in the air that told of the waning of the long Venetian summer; a freshness from the sea which stirred the flowers in the garden and made a pleasant draught in the house, less shuttered and darkened now than when the old woman was alive. It was the beginning of autumn, of the end of the golden months. With this it was the end of my experiment – or would be in the course of half an hour, when I should really have learned that the papers had been reduced to ashes. After that there would be nothing left for me but to go to the station; for seriously (and as it struck me in the morning light) I could not linger there to act as guardian to a piece of middle-aged female helplessness. If she had not saved the papers wherein should I be indebted to her? I think I winced a little as I asked myself how much, if she *had* saved them, I should have to recognize and, as it were, to reward such a courtesy. Might not that circumstance after all saddle me with a guardianship? If this idea did not make me more uncomfortable as I walked up and down it was because I was convinced I had nothing to look to. If the old woman had not destroyed everything before she pounced upon me in the parlour she had done so afterwards.

It took Miss Tita rather longer than I had expected to guess that I was there; but when at last she came out she looked at me without surprise. I said to her that I had been waiting for her and she asked why I had not let her know. I was glad the next day that I had checked myself before remarking that I had wished to see if a friendly intuition would not tell her: it became a satisfaction to me that I had not indulged in that rather tender joke. What I did say was virtually the truth – that I was too nervous, since I expected her now to settle my fate.

'Your fate?' said Miss Tita, giving me a queer look; and as she spoke I noticed a rare change in her. She was different from what she had been the evening before – less natural, less quiet. She had been crying the day before and she was not crying now, and yet she struck me as less confident. It was as if something had happened to her during the night, or at least as if she had thought of something that troubled her – something in particular that affected her relations with me, made them more embarrassing and complicated. Had she simply perceived that her aunt's not being there now altered my position?

'I mean about our papers. *Are* there any? You must know now.'

'Yes, there are a great many; more than I supposed.' I was struck with the way her voice trembled as she told me this.

'Do you mean that you have got them in there – and that I may see them?'

'I don't think you can see them,' said Miss Tita, with an extra-ordinary expression of entreaty in her eyes, as if the dearest hope she had in the world now was that I would not take them from her. But how could she expect me to make such a sacrifice as that after all that had passed between us? What had I come back to Venice for but to see them, to take them? My delight at learning they were still in existence was such that if the poor woman had gone down on her knees to beseech me never to mention them again I would have treated the proceeding as a bad joke. 'I have got them but I can't show them,' she added.

'Not even to me? Ah, Miss Tita!' I groaned, with a voice of infinite remonstrance and reproach.

She coloured and the tears came back to her eyes; I saw that it cost her a kind of anguish to take such a stand but that a dreadful sense of duty had descended upon her. It made me quite sick to find myself confronted with that particular obstacle; all the more that it appeared to me I had been extremely encouraged to leave it out of account. I almost considered that Miss Tita had assured me that if she had no greater hindrance than that –! 'You don't mean to say you made her a deathbed promise? It was precisely against your doing anything of that sort that I thought I was safe. Oh, I would rather she had burned the papers outright than that!'

'No, it isn't a promise,' said Miss Tita.

'Pray what is it then?'

She hesitated and then she said, 'She tried to burn them, but I prevented it. She had hid them in her bed.'

'In her bed?'

'Between the mattresses. That's where she put them when she took them out of the trunk. I can't understand how she did it, because Olimpia didn't help her. She tells me so and I believe her. My aunt only told her afterwards, so that she shouldn't touch the bed – anything but the sheets. So it was badly made,' added Miss Tita, simply.

'I should think so! And how did she try to burn them?'

'She didn't try much; she was too weak, those last days. But she told me – she charged me. Oh, it was terrible! She couldn't speak after that night; she could only make signs.'

'And what did you do?'

'I took them away. I locked them up.'

'In the secretary?'

'Yes, in the secretary,' said Miss Tita, reddening again.

'Did you tell her you would burn them?'

'No, I didn't – on purpose.'

'On purpose to gratify me?'

'Yes, only for that.'

'And what good will you have done me if after all you won't show them?'

'Oh, none; I know that – I know that.'

'And did she believe you had destroyed them?'

'I don't know what she believed at the last. I couldn't tell – she was too far gone.'

'Then if there was no promise and no assurance I can't see what ties you.'

'Oh, she hated it so – she hated it so! She was so jealous. But here's the portrait – you may have that,' Miss Tita announced, taking the little picture, wrapped up in the same manner in which her aunt had wrapped it, out of her pocket.

'I may have it – do you mean you give it to me?' I questioned, staring, as it passed into my hand.

'Oh yes.'

'But it's worth money – a large sum.'

'Well!' said Miss Tita, still with her strange look.

I did not know what to make of it, for it could scarcely mean that she wanted to bargain like her aunt. She spoke as if she wished to make me a present. 'I can't take it from you as a gift,' I said, 'and yet I can't afford to pay you for it according to the ideas Miss Bordereau had of its value. She rated it at a thousand pounds.'

'Couldn't we sell it?' asked Miss Tita.

'God forbid! I prefer the picture to the money.'

'Well then keep it.'

'You are very generous.'

'So are you.'

'I don't know why you should think so,' I replied, and this was a truthful speech, for the singular creature appeared to have some very fine reference in her mind, which I did not in the least seize.

'Well, you have made a great difference for me,' said Miss Tita.

I looked at Jeffrey Aspern's face in the little picture, partly in order not to look at that of my interlocutress, which had begun to trouble me, even to frighten me a little – it was so self-conscious, so unnatural. I made no answer to this last declaration; I only privately consulted Jeffrey Aspern's delightful eyes with my own (they were so young and brilliant, and yet so wise, so full of vision); I asked him what on earth was the matter with Miss Tita. He seemed to smile at me with friendly mockery, as if he were amused at my case. I had got into a pickle for him – as if he needed it! He was unsatisfactory, for the only moment since I had known him. Nevertheless, now that I held the little picture in my hand I felt that it would be a precious possession. 'Is this a bribe to make me give up the papers?' I demanded in a moment, per- versely. 'Much as I value it, if I were to be obliged to choose, the papers are what I should prefer. Ah, but ever so much!'

'How can you choose – how can you choose?' Miss Tita asked, slowly, lamentably.

'I see! Of course there is nothing to be said, if you regard the interdiction that rests upon you as quite insurmountable. In this case it must seem to you that to part with them would be an impiety of the worst kind, a simple sacrilege!'

Miss Tita shook her head, full of her dolefulness. 'You would understand if you had known her. I'm afraid,' she quavered suddenly – 'I'm afraid! She was terrible when she was angry.'

'Yes, I saw something of that, that night. She was terrible. Then I saw her eyes. Lord, they were fine!'

'I see them – they stare at me in the dark!' said Miss Tita.

'You are nervous, with all you have been through.'

'Oh yes, very – very!'

'You mustn't mind; that will pass away,' I said, kindly. Then I added, resignedly, for it really seemed to me that I must accept the situation, 'Well, so it is, and it can't be helped. I must renounce.' Miss Tita, at this, looking at me, gave a low, soft moan, and I went on: 'I only wish to heaven she had destroyed them; then there would be nothing more to say. And I can't understand why, with her ideas, she didn't.'

'Oh, she lived on them!' said Miss Tita.

'You can imagine whether that makes me want less to see them,' I answered, smiling. 'But don't let me stand here as if I had it in my soul to tempt you to do anything base. Naturally you will understand I give up my rooms. I leave Venice immediately.' And I took up my hat, which I had placed on a chair. We were still there rather awkwardly, on our feet, in the middle of the sala. She had left the door of the apartments open behind her but she had not led me that way.

A kind of spasm came into her face as she saw me take my hat. 'Immediately – do you mean today?' The tone of the words was tragical – they were a cry of desolation.

'Oh no; not so long as I can be of the least service to you.'

'Well, just a day or two more – just two or three days,' she panted. Then controlling herself she added in another manner, 'She wanted to say something to me – the last day – something very particular, but she couldn't.'

'Something very particular?'

'Something more about the papers.'

'And did you guess – have you any idea?'

'No, I have thought – but I don't know. I have thought all kinds of things.'

'And for instance?'

'Well, that if you were a relation it would be different.'

'If I were a relation?'

'If you were not a stranger. Then it would be the same for you as for me. Anything that is mine – would be yours, and you could do what you like. I couldn't prevent you   and you would have no responsibility.'

She brought out this droll explanation with a little nervous rush, as if she were speaking words she had got by heart. They gave me an impression of subtlety and at first I failed to follow. But after a moment her face helped me to see further, and then a light came into my mind. It was embarrassing, and I bent my head over Jeffrey Aspern's portrait. What an odd expression was in his face! 'Get out of it as you can, my dear fellow!' I put the picture into the pocket of my coat and said to Miss Tita, 'Yes, I'll sell it for you. I sha'n't get a thousand pounds by any means, but I shall get something good.'

She looked at me with tears in her eyes, but she seemed to try to smile as she remarked, 'We can divide the money.'

'No, no, it shall be all yours.' Then I went on, 'I think I know what your poor aunt wanted to say. She wanted to give directions that her papers should be buried with her.'

Miss Tita appeared to consider this suggestion for a moment; after which she declared, with striking decision, 'Oh no, she wouldn't have thought that safe!'

'It seems to me nothing could be safer.'

'She had an idea that when people want to publish they are capable –' And she paused, blushing.

'Of violating a tomb? Mercy on us, what must she have thought of me!'

'She was not just, she was not generous!' Miss Tita cried with sudden passion.

The light that had come into my mind a moment before increased. 'Ah, don't say that, for we *are* a dreadful race.' Then I pursued, 'If she left a will, that may give you some idea.'

'I have found nothing of the sort – she destroyed it. She was very fond of me,' Miss Tita added, incongruously. 'She wanted me to be happy. And if any person should be kind to me – she wanted to speak of that.'

I was almost awestricken at the astuteness with which the good lady found herself inspired, transparent astuteness as it was and sewn, as the phrase is, with white thread. 'Depend upon it she didn't want to make any provision that would be agreeable to me.'

'No, not to you but to me. She knew I should like it if you could carry out your idea. Not because she cared for you but because she did think of me,' Miss Tita went on, with her unexpected, persuasive volubility. 'You could see them – you could use them.' She stopped, seeing that I perceived the sense of that conditional – stopped long enough for me to give some sign which I did not give. She must have been conscious however that though my face showed the greatest embarrassment that was ever painted on a human countenance it was not set as a stone, it was also full of compassion. It was a comfort to me a long time afterwards to consider that she could not have seen in me the smallest symptom of disrespect. 'I don't know what to do; I'm too tormented, I'm too ashamed!' she continued, with vehemence. Then turning away from me and burying her face in her hands she burst into a flood of tears. If she did not know what to do it may be imagined whether I did any better. I stood there dumb, watching her while her sobs resounded in the great empty hall. In a moment she was facing me again, with her streaming eyes. 'I would give you everything – and she would understand, where she is – she would forgive me!'

'Ah, Miss Tita – ah, Miss Tita,' I stammered, for all reply. I did not know what to do, as I say, but at a venture I made a wild, vague movement, in consequence of which I found myself at the door. I remember standing there and saying, 'It wouldn't do – it wouldn't do!' pensively, awkwardly, grotesquely, while I looked away to the opposite end of the sala as if there were a beautiful view there. The next thing I remember is that I was downstairs and out of the house. My gondola was there and my gondolier, reclining on the cushions, sprang up as soon as he saw me. I jumped in and to his usual ' *Dove commanda ?*' I replied, in a tone that made him stare, 'Anywhere, anywhere; out into the lagoon!'

He rowed me away and I sat there prostrate, groaning softly to myself, with my hat pulled over my face. What in the name of the preposterous did she mean if she did not mean to offer me her hand? That was the price – that was the price! And did she think I wanted it, poor deluded, infatuated, extravagant lady? My gondolier, behind me, must have seen my ears red as I wondered, sitting there under the fluttering *tenda*, with my hidden face, noticing nothing as we passed – wondered whether her delusion, her infatuation had been my own reckless work. Did she think I had made love to her, even to get the papers? I had not, I had not; I repeated that over to myself for an hour, for two hours, till I was wearied if not convinced. I don't know where my gondolier took me; we floated aimlessly about on the lagoon, with slow, rare strokes. At last I became conscious that we were near the Lido, far up, on the right hand, as you turn your back to Venice, and I made him put me ashore. I wanted to walk, to move, to shed some of my bewilderment. I crossed the narrow strip and got to the sea-beach – I took my way towards Malamocco. But presently I flung myself down again on the warm sand, in the breeze, on the coarse dry grass. It took it out of me to think I had been so much at fault, that I had unwittingly but none the less deplorably trifled. But I had not given her cause – distinctly I had not. I had said to Mrs Prest that I would make love to her; but it had been a joke without consequences and I had never said it to Tita Bordereau. I had been as kind as possible, because I really liked her; but since when had that become a crime where a woman of such an age and such an appearance was concerned? I am far from remembering clearly the succession of events and feelings during this long day of confusion, which I spent entirely in wandering about, without going home, until late at night; it only comes back to me that there were moments when I pacified my conscience and others when I lashed it into pain. I did not laugh all day – that I do recollect; the case, however it might have struck others, seemed to me so little amusing. It would have been better perhaps for me to feel the comic side of it. At any rate, whether I had given cause or not it went without saying that I could not pay the price. I could not accept. I could not, for a bundle of tattered papers, marry a ridiculous, pathetic, provincial old woman. It was a proof that she did not think the idea would come to me, her having determined to suggest it herself in that practical, argumentative, heroic way, in which the timidity however had been so much more striking than the boldness that her reasons appeared to come first and her feelings afterwards.

As the day went on I grew to wish that I had never heard of Aspern's relics, and I cursed the extravagant curiosity that had put John Cumnor on the scent of them. We had more than enough material without them and my predicament was the just punishment of that most fatal of human follies, our not having known when to stop. It was very well to say it was no predicament, that the way out was simple, that I had only to leave Venice by the first train in the morning, after writing a note to Miss Tita, to be placed in her hand as soon as I got clear of the house; for it was a strong sign that I was embarrassed that when I tried to make up the note in my mind in advance (I would put it on paper as soon as I got home, before going to bed), I could not think of anything but 'How can I thank you for the rare confidence you have placed in me?' That would never do; it sounded exactly as if an acceptance were to follow. Of course I might go away without writing a word, but that would be brutal and my idea was still to exclude brutal solutions. As my confusion cooled I was lost in wonder at the importance I had attached to Miss Bordereau's crumpled scraps; the thought of them became odious to me and I was as vexed with the old witch for the superstition that had prevented her from destroying them as I was with myself for having already spent more money than I could afford in attempting to control their fate. I forget what I did, where I went after leaving the Lido and at what hour or with what recovery of composure I made my way back to my boat. I only know that in the afternoon, when the air was aglow with the sunset, I was standing before the church of Saints John and Paul and looking up at the small square-jawed face of Bartolommeo Colleoni, the terrible *condot-*

tiere who sits so sturdily astride of his huge bronze horse, on the high pedestal on which Venetian gratitude maintains him. The statue is incomparable, the finest of all mounted figures, unless that of Marcus Aurelius, who rides benignant before the Roman Capitol, be finer: but I was not thinking of that; I only found myself staring at the triumphant captain as if he had an oracle on his lips. The western light shines into all his grimness at that hour and makes it wonderfully personal. But he continued to look far over my head, at the red immersion of another day – he had seen so many go down into the lagoon through the centuries – and if he were thinking of battles and stratagems they were of a different quality from any I had to tell him of. He could not direct me what to do, gaze up at him as I might. Was it before this or after that I wandered about for an hour in the small canals, to the continued stupefaction of my gondolier, who had never seen me so restless and yet so void of a purpose and could extract from me no order but 'Go anywhere – everywhere – all over the place'? He reminded me that I had not lunched and expressed therefore respectfully the hope that I would dine earlier. He had had long periods of leisure during the day, when I had left the boat and rambled, so that I was not obliged to consider him, and I told him that that day, for a change, I would touch no meat. It was an effect of poor Miss Tita's proposal, not altogether auspicious, that I had quite lost my appetite. I don't know why it happened that on this occasion I was more than ever struck with that queer air of sociability, of cousinship and family life, which makes up half the expression of Venice. Without streets and vehicles, the uproar of wheels, the brutality of horses, and with its little winding ways where people crowd together, where voices sound as in the corridors of a house, where the human step circulates as if it skirted the angles of furniture and shoes never wear out, the place has the character of an immense collective apartment, in which Piazza San Marco is the most ornamented corner and palaces and churches, for the rest, play the part of great divans of repose, tables of entertainment, expanses of decoration. And somehow the splendid common domicile, familiar, domestic and resonant, also resembles a theatre, with actors clicking over bridges and, in straggling processions, tripping along fondamentas. As you sit in your gondola the footways that in certain parts edge the canals assume to the eye the importance of a stage, meeting it at the same angle, and the Venetian figures, moving to and fro against the battered scenery of their little houses of comedy, strike you as members of an endless dramatic troupe.

I went to bed that night very tired, without being able to compose a letter to Miss Tita. Was this failure the reason why I became conscious the next morning as soon as I awoke of a determination to see the poor lady again the first moment she would receive me? That had something to do with it, but what had still more was the fact that during my sleep a very odd revulsion had taken place in my spirit. I found myself aware of this almost as soon as I opened my eyes; it made me jump out of my bed with the movement of a man who remembers that he has left the house-door ajar or a candle burning under a shelf. Was I still in time to save my goods? That question was in my heart; for what had now come to pass was that in the unconscious cerebration of sleep I had swung back to a passionate appreciation of Miss Bordereau's papers. They were now more precious than ever and a kind of ferocity had come into my desire to possess them. The condition Miss Tita had attached to the possession of them no longer appeared an obstacle worth thinking of, and for an hour, that morning, my repentant imagination brushed it aside. It was absurd that I should be able to invent nothing; absurd to renounce so easily and turn away helpless from the idea that the only way to get hold of the papers was to unite myself to her for life. I would not unite myself and yet I would have them. I must add that by the time I sent down to ask if she would see me I had invented no alternative, though to do so I had had all the time that I was dressing. This failure was humiliating, yet what could the alternative be? Miss Tita sent back word that I might come; and as I descended the stairs and crossed the sala to her door – this time she received me in her aunt's forlorn parlour – I hoped she would not think my errand was to tell her I accepted her hand. She certainly would have made the day before the reflection that I declined it.

As soon as I came into the room I saw that she had drawn this inference, but I also saw something which had not been in my forecast. Poor Miss Tita's sense of her failure had produced an extraordinary alteration in her, but I had been too full of my literary concupiscence to think of that. Now I perceived it; I can scarcely tell how it startled me. She stood in the middle of the room with a face of mildness bent upon me, and her look of forgiveness, of absolution made her angelic. It beautified her; she was younger; she was not a ridiculous old woman. This optical trick gave her a sort of phantasmagoric brightness, and while I was still the victim of it I heard a whisper somewhere in the depths of my conscience: 'Why not, after all – why not?' It seemed to me I was ready to pay the price. Still more distinctly however than the whisper I heard Miss Tita's own voice. I was so struck with the different effect she made upon me that at first I was not clearly aware of what she was saying; then I perceived she had bade me good-bye – she said something about hoping I should be very happy.

'Good-bye – good-bye?' I repeated, with an inflection interrogative and probably foolish.

I saw she did not feel the interrogation, she only heard the words; she had strung herself up to accepting our separation and they fell upon her ear as a proof. 'Are you going today?' she asked. 'But it doesn't matter, for whenever you go I shall not see you again. I don't want to.' And she smiled strangely, with an infinite gentleness. She had never doubted that I had left her the day before in horror. How could she, since I had not come back before night to contradict, even as a simple form, such an idea? And now she had the force of soul – Miss Tita with force of soul was a new conception – to smile at me in her humiliation.

'What shall you do – where shall you go?' I asked.

'Oh, I don't know. I have done the great thing. I have destroyed the papers.'

'Destroyed them?' I faltered.

'Yes; what was I to keep them for? I burnt them last night, one by one, in the kitchen.'

'One by one?' I repeated, mechanically.

'It took a long time – there were so many.' The room seemed to go round me as she said this and a real darkness for a moment descended upon my eyes. When it passed Miss Tita was there still, but the transfiguration was over and she had changed back to a plain, dingy, elderly person. It was in this character she spoke as she said, 'I can't stay with you longer, I can't;' and it was in this character that she turned her back upon me, as I had turned mine upon her twenty-four hours before, and moved to the door of her room. Here she did what I had not done when I quitted her – she paused long enough to give me one look. I have never forgotten it and I sometimes still suffer from it, though it was not resentful. No, there was no resentment, nothing hard or vindictive in poor Miss Tita; for when, later, I sent her in exchange for the portrait of Jeffrey Aspern a larger sum of money than I had hoped to be able to gather for her, writing to her that I had sold the picture, she kept it with thanks; she never sent it back. I wrote to her that I had sold the picture, but I admitted to Mrs Prest, at the time (I met her in London, in the autumn), that it hangs above my writing table. When I look at it my chagrin at the loss of the letters becomes almost intolerable.

THE REAL THING

1

WHEN the porter's wife (she used to answer the house-bell) announced 'A gentleman with a lady, sir,' I had, as I often had in those days, for the wish was father to the thought, an immediate vision of sitters. Sitters my visitors in this case proved to be; but not in the sense I should have preferred. However, there was nothing at first to indicate that they might not have come for a portrait. The gentleman, a man of fifty, very high and very straight, with a moustache slightly grizzled and a dark grey walking-coat admirably fitted, both of which I noted professionally – I don't mean as a barber or yet as a tailor – would have struck me as a celebrity if celebrities often were striking. It was a truth of which I had for some time been conscious that a figure with a good deal of frontage was, as one might say, almost never a public institution. A glance at the lady helped to remind me of this paradoxical law: she also looked too distinguished to be a 'personality'. Moreover one would scarcely come across two variations together.

Neither of the pair spoke immediately – they only prolonged the preliminary gaze which suggested that each wished to give the other a chance. They were visibly shy; they stood there letting me take them in – which, as I afterwards perceived, was the most practical thing they could have done. In this way their embarrassment served their cause. I had seen people painfully reluctant to mention that they desired anything so gross as to be represented on canvas; but the scruples of my new friends appeared almost insurmountable. Yet the gentleman might have said 'I should like a portrait of my wife,' and the lady might have said 'I should like a portrait of my husband.' Perhaps they were not husband and wife – this naturally would make the matter more delicate. Perhaps they wished to be done together – in which case they ought to have brought a third person to break the news.

'We come from Mr Rivet,' the lady said at last, with a dim smile which had the effect of a moist sponge passed over a 'sunk' piece of painting, as well as of a vague allusion to vanished beauty. She was as tall and straight, in her degree, as her companion, and with ten years less to carry. She looked as sad as a woman could look whose face was not charged with expression; that is her tinted oval mask showed friction as an exposed surface shows it. The hand of time had played over her freely, but only to simplify. She was slim and stiff, and so well-dressed, in dark blue cloth, with lappets and pockets and buttons, that it was clear she employed the same tailor as her husband. The couple had an indefinable air of prosperous thrift – they evidently got a good deal of luxury for their money. If I was to be one of their luxuries it would behove me to consider my terms.

'Ah, Claude Rivet recommended me?' I inquired; and I added that it was very kind of him, though I could reflect that, as he only painted landscape, this was not a sacrifice.

The lady looked very hard at the gentleman, and the gentleman looked round the room. Then staring at the floor a moment and stroking his moustache, he rested his pleasant eyes on me with the remark: 'He said you were the right one.'

'I try to be, when people want to sit.'

'Yes, we should like to,' said the lady anxiously.

'Do you mean together?'

My visitors exchanged a glance. 'If you could do anything with *me*, I suppose it would be double,' the gentleman stammered.

'Oh yes, there's naturally a higher charge for two figures than for one.'

'We should like to make it pay,' the husband confessed.

'That's very good of you,' I returned, appreciating so unwonted a sympathy – for I supposed he meant pay the artist.

A sense of strangeness seemed to dawn on the lady. 'We mean for the illustrations – Mr Rivet said you might put one in.'

'Put one in – an illustration?' I was equally confused.

'Sketch her off, you know,' said the gentleman, colouring.

It was only then that I understood the service Claude Rivet had rendered me; he had told them that I worked in black and white, for magazines, for story-books, for sketches of contemporary life, and consequently had frequent employment for models. These things were true, but it was not less true (I may confess it now – whether because the aspiration was to lead to everything or to nothing I leave the reader to guess), that I couldn't get the honours, to say nothing of the emoluments, of a great painter of portraits out of my head. My 'illustrations' were my pot-boilers; I looked to a different branch of art (far and away the most interesting it had always seemed to me), to perpetuate my fame. There was no shame in looking to it also to make my fortune; but that fortune was by so much further from being made from the moment my visitors wished to be 'done' for nothing. I was disappointed; for in the pictorial sense I had immediately *seen* them. I had seized their type – I had already settled what I would do with it. Something that wouldn't absolutely have pleased them, I afterwards reflected.

'Ah, you're – you're – a – ?' I began, as soon as I had mastered my surprise. I couldn't bring out the dingy word 'models'; it seemed to fit the case so little.

'We haven't had much practice,' said the lady.

'We've got to *do* something, and we've thought that an artist in your line might perhaps make something of us,' her husband threw off. He further mentioned that they didn't know many artists and that they had gone first, on the off-chance (he painted views of course, but sometimes put in figures – perhaps I remembered), to Mr Rivet, whom they had met a few years before at a place in Norfolk where he was sketching.

'We used to sketch a little ourselves,' the lady hinted.

'It's very awkward, but we absolutely *must* do something,' her husband went on.

'Of course, we're not so *very* young,' she admitted, with a wan smile.

With the remark that I might as well know something more about them, the husband had handed me a card extracted from a neat new pocket-book (their appurtenances were all of the freshest) and inscribed with the words 'Major Monarch'. Impressive as these words were they didn't carry my knowledge much further; but my visitor presently added: 'I've left the army, and we've had the misfortune to lose our money. In fact our means are dreadfully small.'

'It's an awful bore,' said Mrs Monarch.

They evidently wished to be discreet – to take care not to swagger because they were gentlefolks. I perceived they would have been willing to recognize this as something of a drawback, at the same time that I guessed at an underlying sense – their consolation in adversity – that they *had* their points. They certainly had; but these advantages struck me as preponderantly social; such for instance as would help to make a drawing-room look well. However, a drawing-room was always, or ought to be, a picture.

In consequence of his wife's allusion to their age Major Monarch observed: 'Naturally, it's more for the figure that we thought of going in. We can still hold ourselves up.' On the instant I saw that the figure was indeed their strong point. His 'naturally' didn't sound vain, but it lighted up the question. '*She* has got the best,' he continued, nodding at his wife, with a pleasant after-dinner absence of circumlocution. I could only reply, as if we were in fact sitting over our wine, that this didn't prevent his own from being very good; which led him in turn to rejoin: 'We thought that if you ever have to do people like us, we might be something like it. *She*, particularly – for a lady in a book, you know.'

I was so amused by them that, to get more of it, I did my best to take their point of view; and though it was an embarrassment to find myself appraising physically, as if they were animals on hire or useful blacks, a pair whom I should have expected to meet only in one of the relations in which criticism is tacit, I looked at Mrs Monarch judicially enough to be able to exclaim, after a moment, with conviction: 'Oh yes, a lady in a book!' She was singularly like a bad illustration.

'We'll stand up, if you like,' said the Major; and he raised himself before me with a really grand air.

I could take his measure at a glance – he was six feet two and a perfect gentleman. It would have paid any club in process of formation and in want of a stamp to engage him at a salary to stand in the principal window. What struck me immediately was that in coming to me they had rather missed their vocation; they could surely have been turned to better account for advertising purposes. I couldn't of course see the thing in detail, but I could see them make someone's fortune – I don't mean their own. There was something in them for a waistcoat-maker, an hotel-keeper or a soap-vendor. I could imagine 'We always use it' pinned on their bosoms with the greatest effect; I had a vision of the promptitude with which they would launch a table d'hôte.

Mrs Monarch sat still, not from pride but from shyness, and presently her husband said to her: 'Get up my dear and show how smart you are.' She obeyed, but she had no need to get up to show it. She walked to the end of the studio, and then she came back blushing, with her fluttered eyes on her husband. I was reminded of an incident I had accidentally had a glimpse of in Paris – being with a friend there, a dramatist about to produce a play – when an actress came to him to ask to be intrusted with a part. She went through her paces before him, walked up and down as Mrs Monarch was doing. Mrs Monarch did it quite as well, but I abstained from applauding. It was very odd to see such people apply for such poor pay. She looked as if she had ten thousand a year. Her husband had used the word that described her: she was, in the London current jargon, essentially and typically 'smart'. Her figure was, in the same order of ideas, conspicuously and irreproachably 'good'. For a woman of her age her waist was surprisingly small; her elbow moreover had the orthodox crook. She held her head at the conventional angle; but why did she come to *me*? She ought to have tried on jackets at a big shop. I feared my visitors were not only destitute, but 'artistic' – which would be a great complication. When she sat down again I thanked her, observing that what a draughtsman most valued in his model was the faculty of keeping quiet.

'Oh, *she* can keep quiet,' said Major Monarch. Then he added, jocosely: 'I've always kept her quiet.'

'I'm not a nasty fidget, am I?' Mrs Monarch appealed to her husband.

He addressed his answer to me. 'Perhaps it isn't out of place to mention – because we ought to be quite businesslike, oughtn't we? – that when I married her she was known as the Beautiful Statue.'

'Oh dear!' said Mrs Monarch, ruefully.

'Of course I should want a certain amount of expression,' I rejoined.

'Of *course*!' they both exclaimed.

'And then I suppose you know that you'll get awfully tired.'

'Oh, we *never* get tired!' they eagerly cried.

'Have you had any kind of practice?'

They hesitated – they looked at each other. 'We've been photographed, *immensely*,' said Mrs Monarch.

'She means the fellows have asked us,' added the Major.

'I see – because you're so good-looking.'

'I don't know what they thought, but they were always after us.'

'We always got our photographs for nothing,' smiled Mrs Monarch.

'We might have brought some, my dear,' her husband remarked.

'I'm not sure we have any left. We've given quantities away,' she explained to me.

'With our autographs and that sort of thing,' said the Major.

'Are they to be got in the shops?' I inquired, as a harmless pleasantry.

'Oh, yes; *hers* – they used to be.'

'Not now,' said Mrs Monarch, with her eyes on the floor.

2

I COULD fancy the 'sort of thing' they put on the presentation-copies of their photographs, and I was sure they wrote a beautiful hand. It was odd how quickly I was sure of everything that concerned them. If they were now so poor as to have to earn shillings and pence, they never had had much of a margin. Their good looks had been their capital, and they had good-humouredly made the most of the career that this resource marked out for them. It was in their faces, the blankness, the deep intellectual repose of the twenty years of country-house visiting which had given them pleasant intonations. I could see the sunny drawing-rooms, sprinkled with periodicals she didn't read, in which Mrs Monarch had continuously sat; I could see the wet shrubberies in which she had walked, equipped to admiration for either exercise. I could see the rich coverts the Major had helped to shoot and the wonderful garments in which, late at night, he repaired to the smoking-room to talk about them. I could imagine their leggings and waterproofs, their knowing tweeds and rugs, their rolls of sticks and cases of tackle and neat umbrellas; and I could evoke the exact appearance of their servants and the compact variety of their luggage on the platforms of country stations.

They gave small tips, but they were liked; they didn't do any-thing themselves, but they were welcome. They looked so well everywhere; they gratified the general relish for stature, com-plexion and 'form'. They knew it without fatuity or vulgarity, and they respected themselves in consequence. They were not super-ficial; they were thorough and kept themselves up – it had been their line. People with such a taste for activity had to have some line. I could feel how, even in a dull house, they could have been counted upon for cheerfulness. At present something had hap-pened – it didn't matter what, their little income had grown less, it had grown least – and they had to do something for pocket-money. Their friends liked them, but didn't like to support them. There was something about them that represented credit – their clothes, their manners, their type; but if credit is a large empty pocket in which an occasional chink reverberates, the chink at least must be audible. What they wanted of me was to help to make it so. Fortunately they had no children – I soon divined that. They would also perhaps wish our relations to be kept secret: this was why it was 'for the figure' – the reproduction of the face would betray them.

I liked them – they were so simple; and I had no objection to them if they would suit. But, somehow, with all their perfections I didn't easily believe in them. After all they were amateurs, and the ruling passion of my life was the detestation of the amateur. Combined with this was another perversity – an innate preference for the represented subject over the real one: the defect of the real one was so apt to be a lack of representation. I liked things that appeared; then one was sure. Whether they *were* or not was a subordinate and almost always a profitless question. There were other considerations, the first of which was that I already had two or three people in use, notably a young person with big feet, in alpaca, from Kilburn, who for a couple of years had come to me regularly for my illustrations and with whom I was still – perhaps ignobly – satisfied. I frankly explained to my visitors how the case stood; but they had taken more precautions than I supposed. They had reasoned out their opportunity, for Claude Rivet had told them of the projected *édition de luxe* of one of the writers of our day – the rarest of the novelists – who, long neglected by the multitudinous vulgar and dearly prized by the attentive (need I mention Philip Vincent?) had had the happy fortune of seeing, late in life, the dawn and then the full light of a higher criticism – an estimate in which, on the part of the public, there was something really of expiation. The edition in question, planned by a publisher of taste, was practically an act of high reparation; the woodcuts with which it was to be enriched were the homage of English art to one of the most independent representatives of English letters. Major and Mrs Monarch confessed to me that they had hoped I might be able to work *them* into my share of the enterprise. They knew I was to do the first of the books, 'Rutland Ramsay', but I had to make clear to them that my participation in the rest of the affair – this first book was to be a test – was to depend on the satisfaction I should give. If this should be limited my employers would drop me without a scruple. It was therefore a crisis for me, and naturally I was making special preparations, looking about for new people, if they should be necessary, and securing the best types. I admitted however that I should like to settle down to two or three good models who would do for everything.

'Should we have often to – a – put on special clothes?' Mrs Monarch timidly demanded.

'Dear, yes – that's half the business.'

'And should we be expected to supply our own costumes?'

'Oh, no; I've got a lot of things. A painter's models put on – or put off – anything he likes.'

'And do you mean – a – the same?'

'The same?'

Mrs Monarch looked at her husband again.

'Oh, she was just wondering,' he explained, 'if the costumes are in *general* use.' I had to confess that they were, and I mentioned further that some of them (I had a lot of genuine, greasy last-century things), had served their time, a hundred years ago, on living, world-stained men and women. 'We'll put on anything that *fits*,' said the Major.

'Oh, I arrange that – they fit in the pictures.'

'I'm afraid I should do better for the modern books. I would come as you like,' said Mrs Monarch.

'She has got a lot of clothes at home: they might do for contemporary life,' her husband continued.

'Oh, I can fancy scenes in which you'd be quite natural.' And indeed I could see the slipshod rearrangements of stale properties – the stories I tried to produce pictures for without the exasperation of reading them – whose sandy tracts the good lady might help to people. But I had to return to the fact that for this sort of work – the daily mechanical grind – I was already equipped; the people I was working with were fully adequate.

'We only thought we might be more like *some* characters,' said Mrs Monarch mildly, getting up.

Her husband also rose; he stood looking at me with a dim wistfulness that was touching in so fine a man. 'Wouldn't it be rather a pull sometimes to have – a – to have – ?' He hung fire; he wanted me to help him by phrasing what he meant. But I couldn't – I didn't know. So he brought it out, awkwardly: 'The *real* thing; a gentleman, you know, or a lady.' I was quite ready to give a general assent – I admitted that there was a great deal in that. This encouraged Major Monarch to say, following up his appeal with an unacted gulp: 'It's awfully hard – we've tried everything.' The gulp was communicative; it proved too much for his wife. Before I knew it Mrs Monarch had dropped again upon a divan and burst into tears. Her husband sat down beside her, holding one of her hands; whereupon she quickly dried her eyes with the other, while I felt embarrassed as she looked up at me. 'There isn't a confounded job I haven't applied for – waited for – prayed for. You can fancy we'd be pretty bad first. Secretaryships and that sort of thing? You might as well ask for a peerage. I'd be *anything* – I'm strong; a messenger or a coalheaver. I'd put on a gold-laced cap and open carriage-doors in front of the haberdasher's; I'd hang about a station, to carry portmanteaus; I'd be a postman. But they won't *look* at you; there are thousands, as good as yourself, already on the ground. *Gentlemen*, poor beggars, who have drunk their wine, who have kept their hunters!'

I was as reassuring as I knew how to be, and my visitors were presently on their feet again while, for the experiment, we agreed on an hour. We were discussing it when the door opened and Miss Churm came in with a wet umbrella. Miss Churm had to take the omnibus to Maida Vale and then walk half-a-mile. She looked a trifle blowsy and slightly splashed. I scarcely ever saw her come in without thinking afresh how odd it was that, being so little in herself, she should yet be so much in others. She was a meagre little Miss Churm, but she was an ample heroine of romance. She was only a freckled cockney, but she could represent everything, from a fine lady to a shepherdess; she had the faculty, as she might have had a fine voice or long hair. She couldn't spell, and she loved beer, but she had two or three 'points', and practice, and a knack, and mother-wit, and a kind of whimsical sensibility, and a love of the theatre, and seven sisters, and not an ounce of respect, especially for the *h*. The first thing my visitors saw was that her umbrella was wet, and in their spotless perfection they visibly winced at it. The rain had come on since their arrival.

'I'm all in a soak; there *was* a mess of people in the 'bus. I wish you lived near a stytion,' said Miss Churm. I requested her to get ready as quickly as possible, and she passed into the room in which she always changed her dress. But before going out she asked me what she was to get into this time.

'It's the Russian princess, don't you know?' I answered; 'the one with the "golden eyes", in black velvet, for the long thing in the *Cheapside*.'

'Golden eyes? I *say*!' cried Miss Churm, while my companions watched her with intensity as she withdrew. She always arranged herself, when she was late, before I could turn round; and I kept my visitors a little, on purpose, so that they might get an idea, from seeing her, what would be expected of themselves. I mentioned that she was quite my notion of an excellent model – she was really very clever.

'Do you think she looks like a Russian princess?' Major Monarch asked, with lurking alarm.

'When I make her, yes.'

'Oh, if you have to *make* her –!' he reasoned, acutely.

'That's the most you can ask. There are so many that are not makeable.'

'Well now, *here's* a lady' – and with a persuasive smile he passed his arm into his wife's – 'who's already made!'

'Oh, I'm not a Russian princess,' Mrs Monarch protested, a little coldly. I could see that she had known some and didn't like them. There, immediately, was a complication of a kind that I never had to fear with Miss Churm.

This young lady came back in black velvet – the gown was rather rusty and very low on her lean shoulders – and with a Japanese fan in her red hands. I reminded her that in the scene I was doing she had to look over someone's head. 'I forget whose it is; but it doesn't matter. Just look over a head.'

'I'd rather look over a stove,' said Miss Churm; and she took her station near the fire. She fell into position, settled herself into a tall attitude, gave a certain backward inclination to her head and a certain forward droop to her fan, and looked, at least to my prejudiced sense, distinguished and charming, foreign and dangerous. We left her looking so, while I went downstairs with Major and Mrs Monarch.

'I think I could come about as near it as that,' said Mrs Monarch.

'Oh, you think she's shabby, but you must allow for the alchemy of art.'

However, they went off with an evident increase of comfort, founded on their demonstrable advantage in being the real thing. I could fancy them shuddering over Miss Churm. She was very droll about them when I went back, for I told her what they wanted.

'Well, if *she* can sit I'll tyke to book-keeping,' said my model.

'She's very lady-like,' I replied, as an innocent form of aggravation.

'So much the worse for *you*. That means she can't turn round.'

'She'll do for the fashionable novels.'

'Oh yes, she'll *do* for them!' my model humorously declared. 'Ain't they bad enough without her?' I had often sociably denounced them to Miss Churm.

3

IT was for the elucidation of a mystery in one of these works that I first tried Mrs Monarch. Her husband came with her, to be useful if necessary – it was sufficiently clear that as a general thing he would prefer to come with her. At first I wondered if this were for 'propriety's' sake – if he were going to be jealous and meddling. The idea was too tiresome, and if it had been confirmed it would speedily have brought our acquaintance to a close. But I soon saw there was nothing in it and that if he accompanied Mrs Monarch it was (in addition to the chance of being wanted), simply because he had nothing else to do. When she was away from him his occupation was gone – she never *had* been away from him. I judged, rightly, that in their awkward situation their close union was their main comfort and that this union had no weak spot. It was a real marriage, an encouragement to the hesitating, a nut for pessimists to crack. Their address was humble (I remember afterwards thinking it had been the only thing about them that was really professional), and I could fancy the lamentable lodgings in which the Major would have been left alone. He could bear them with his wife – he couldn't bear them without her.

He had too much tact to try and make himself agreeable when

he couldn't be useful; so he simply sat and waited, when I was too absorbed in my work to talk. But I liked to make him talk – it made my work, when it didn't interrupt it, less sordid, less special. To listen to him was to combine the excitement of going out with the economy of staying at home. There was only one hindrance: that I seemed not to know any of the people he and his wife had known. I think he wondered extremely, during the term of our intercourse, whom the deuce I *did* know. He hadn't a stray six-pence of an idea to fumble for; so we didn't spin it very fine – we confined ourselves to questions of leather and even of liquor (saddlers and breeches-makers and how to get good claret cheap), and matters like 'good trains' and the habits of small game. His lore on these last subjects was astonishing, he managed to inter-weave the stationmaster with the ornithologist. When he couldn't talk about greater things he could talk cheerfully about smaller, and since I couldn't accompany him into reminiscences of the fashionable world he could lower the conversation without a visible effort to my level.

So earnest a desire to please was touching in a man who could so easily have knocked one down. He looked after the fire and had an opinion on the draught of the stove, without my asking him, and I could see that he thought many of my arrangements not half clever enough. I remember telling him that if I were only rich I would offer him a salary to come and teach me how to live. Some-times he gave a random sigh, of which the essence was: 'Give me even such a bare old barrack as *this*, and I'd do something with it!' When I wanted to use him he came alone; which was an illustration of the superior courage of women. His wife could bear her solitary second floor, and she was in general more discreet; showing by various small reserves that she was alive to the pro-priety of keeping our relations markedly professional – not letting them slide into sociability. She wished it to remain clear that she and the Major were employed, not cultivated, and if she approved of me as a superior, who could be kept in his place, she never thought me quite good enough for an equal.

She sat with great intensity, giving the whole of her mind to it, and was capable of remaining for an hour almost as motionless as if she were before a photographer's lens. I could see she had been photographed often, but somehow the very habit that made her good for that purpose unfitted her for mine. At first I was extremely pleased with her lady-like air, and it was a satisfaction, on coming to follow her lines, to see how good they were and how far they could lead the pencil. But after a few times I began to find her too insurmountably stiff; do what I would with it my drawing looked like a photograph or a copy of a photograph. Her figure had no variety of expression – she herself had no sense of variety. You may say that this was my business, was only a question of placing her. I placed her in every conceivable position, but she managed to obliterate their differences. She was always a lady certainly, and into the bargain was always the same lady. She was the real thing, but always the same thing. There were moments when I was oppressed by the serenity of her confidence that she *was* the real thing. All her dealings with me and all her husband's were an implication that this was lucky for *me*. Meanwhile I found myself trying to invent types that approached her own, instead of making her own transform itself – in the clever way that was not impossible, for instance, to poor Miss Churm. Arrange as I would and take the precautions I would, she always, in my pictures, came out too tall – landing me in the dilemma of having represented a fascinating woman as seven feet high, which, out of respect perhaps to my own very much scantier inches, was far from my idea of such a personage.

The case was worse with the Major – nothing I could do would keep *him* down, so that he became useful only for the representation of brawny giants. I adored variety and range, I cherished human accidents, the illustrative note; I wanted to characterize closely, and the thing in the world I most hated was the danger of being ridden by a type. I had quarrelled with some of my friends about it – I had parted company with them for maintaining that one *had* to be, and that if the type was beautiful (witness Raphael and Leonardo), the servitude was only a gain. I was neither Leonardo nor Raphael; I might only be a presumptuous young modern searcher, but I held that everything was to be sacrificed sooner than character. When they averred that the haunting type in question could easily *be* character, I retorted, perhaps superficially: 'Whose?' It couldn't be everybody's – it might end in being nobody's.

After I had drawn Mrs Monarch a dozen times I perceived more clearly than before that the value of such a model as Miss Churm resided precisely in the fact that she had no positive stamp, combined of course with the other fact that what she did have was a curious and inexplicable talent for imitation. Her usual appearance was like a curtain which she could draw up at request for a capital performance. This performance was simply suggestive; but it was a word to the wise – it was vivid and pretty. Sometimes, even, I thought it, though she was plain herself, too insipidly pretty; I made it a reproach to her that the figures drawn from her were monotonously (*bêtement*, as we used to say) graceful. Nothing made her more angry; it was so much her pride to feel that she could sit for characters that had nothing in common with each other. She would accuse me at such moments of taking away her 'reputytion'.

It suffered a certain shrinkage, this queer quantity, from the repeated visits of my new friends. Miss Churm was greatly in demand, never in want of employment, so I had no scruple in putting her off occasionally, to try them more at my ease. It was certainly amusing at first to do the real thing – it was amusing to do Major Monarch's trousers. They *were* the real thing, even if he did come out colossal. It was amusing to do his wife's back hair (it was so mathematically neat), and the particular 'smart' tension of her tight stays. She lent herself especially to positions in which the face was somewhat averted or blurred; she abounded in lady-like back views and *profils perdus*. When she stood erect she took naturally one of the attitudes in which court-painters represent queens and princesses; so that I found myself wondering whether, to draw out this accomplishment, I couldn't get the editor of the *Cheapside* to publish a really royal romance, 'A Tale of Buckingham Palace'. Sometimes, however, the real thing and the make-believe came into contact; by which I mean that Miss Churm, keeping an appointment or coming to make one on days when I had much work in hand, encountered her invidious rivals. The encounter was not on their part, for they noticed her no more than if she had been the housemaid; not from intentional loftiness, but simply because, as yet, professionally, they didn't know how to fraternize, as I could guess that they would have liked – or at least that the Major would. They couldn't talk about the omnibus – they always walked; and they didn't know what else to try – she wasn't interested in good trains or cheap claret. Besides, they must have felt – in the air – that she was amused at them, secretly derisive of their ever knowing how. She was not a person to conceal her scepticism if she had had a chance to show it. On the other hand Mrs Monarch didn't think her tidy; for why else did she take pains to say to me (it was going out of the way, for Mrs Monarch), that she didn't like dirty women?

One day when my young lady happened to be present with my other sitters (she even dropped in, when it was convenient, for a chat), I asked her to be so good as to lend a hand in getting tea – a service with which she was familiar and which was one of a class that, living as I did in a small way, with slender domestic resources, I often appealed to my models to render. They liked to lay hands on my property, to break the sitting, and sometimes the china – I made them feel Bohemian. The next time I saw Miss Churm after this incident she surprised me greatly by making a scene about it – she accused me of having wished to humiliate her. She had not resented the outrage at the time, but had seemed obliging and amused, enjoying the comedy of asking Mrs Monarch, who sat vague and silent, whether she would have cream and sugar, and putting an exaggerated simper into the question. She had tried intonations – as if she too wished to pass for the real thing; till I was afraid my other visitors would take offence.

Oh, *they* were determined not to do this; and their touching patience was the measure of their great need. They would sit by the hour, uncomplaining, till I was ready to use them; they would come back on the chance of being wanted and would walk away cheerfully if they were not. I used to go to the door with them to see in what magnificent order they retreated. I tried to find other employment for them – I introduced them to several artists. But they didn't 'take', for reasons I could appreciate, and I became conscious, rather anxiously, that after such disappointments they fell back upon me with a heavier weight. They did me the honour to think that it was I who was most *their* form. They were not picturesque enough for the painters, and in those days there were not so many serious workers in black and white. Besides, they had an eye to the great job I had mentioned to them – they had secretly set their hearts on supplying the right essence for my pictorial vindication of our fine novelist. They knew that for this undertaking I should want no costume-effects, none of the frippery of past ages – that it was a case in which everything would be contemporary and satirical and, presumably, genteel. If I could work them into it their future would be assured, for the labour would of course be long and the occupation steady.

One day Mrs Monarch came without her husband – she explained his absence by his having had to go to the City. While she sat there in her usual anxious stiffness there came, at the door, a knock which I immediately recognized as the subdued appeal of a model out of work. It was followed by the entrance of a young man whom I easily perceived to be a foreigner and who proved in fact an Italian acquainted with no English word but my name, which he uttered in a way that made it seem to include all others. I had not then visited his country, nor was I proficient in his tongue; but as he was not so meanly constituted – what Italian is? – as to depend only on that member for expression he conveyed to me, in familiar but graceful mimicry, that he was in search of exactly the employment in which the lady before me was engaged. I was not struck with him at first, and while I continued to draw I emitted rough sounds of discouragement and dismissal. He stood his ground, however, not importunately, but with a dumb, dog-like fidelity in his eyes which amounted to innocent impudence – the manner of a devoted servant (he might have been in the house for years), unjustly suspected. Suddenly I saw that this very attitude and expression made a picture, whereupon I told him to sit down and wait till I should be free. There was another picture in the way he obeyed me, and I observed as I worked that there were others still in the way he looked wonderingly, with his head thrown back, about the high studio. He might have been crossing himself in St Peter's. Before I finished I said to myself: 'The fellow's a bankrupt orange-monger, but he's a treasure.'

When Mrs Monarch withdrew he passed across the room like a flash to open the door for her, standing there with the rapt, pure gaze of the young Dante spellbound by the young Beatrice. As I never insisted, in such situations, on the blankness of the British domestic, I reflected that he had the making of a servant (and I needed one, but couldn't pay him to be only that), as well as of a model; in short I made up my mind to adopt my bright adventurer if he would agree to officiate in the double capacity. He jumped at my offer, and in the event my rashness (for I had known nothing about him), was not brought home to me. He proved a sympathetic though a desultory ministrant, and had in a wonderful degree the *sentiment de la pose*. It was uncultivated, instinctive; a part of the happy instinct which had guided him to my door and helped him to spell out my name on the card nailed to it. He had had no other introduction to me than a guess, from the shape of my high north window, seen outside, that my place was a studio, and that as a studio it would contain an artist. He had wandered to England in search of a fortune, like other itinerants, and had embarked, with a partner and a small green handcart, on the sale of penny ices. The ices had melted away and the partner had dissolved in their train. My young man wore tight yellow trousers with reddish stripes and his name was Oronte. He was sallow but fair, and when I put him into some old clothes of my own he looked like an Englishman. He was as good as Miss Churm, who could look, when required, like an Italian.

4

I THOUGHT Mrs Monarch's face slightly convulsed when, on her coming back with her husband, she found Oronte installed. It was strange to have to recognize in a scrap of a lazzarone a competitor to her magnificent Major. It was she who scented danger first, for the Major was anecdotically unconscious. But Oronte gave us tea, with a hundred eager confusions (he had never seen such a queer process), and I think she thought better of me for having at last an 'establishment'. They saw a couple of drawings that I had made of the establishment, and Mrs Monarch hinted that it never would have struck her that he had sat for them. 'Now the drawings you make from *us*, they look exactly like us,' she reminded me, smiling in triumph; and I recognized that this was indeed just their defect. When I drew the Monarchs I couldn't, somehow, get away from them – get into the character I wanted to represent; and I had not the least desire my model should be discoverable in my picture. Miss Churm never was, and Mrs Monarch thought I hid her, very properly, because she was vulgar; whereas if she was lost it was only as the dead who go to heaven are lost – in the gain of an angel the more.

By this time I had got a certain start with 'Rutland Ramsay', the first novel in the great projected series; that is I had produced a dozen drawings, several with the help of the Major and his wife, and I had sent them in for approval. My understanding with the publishers, as I have already hinted, had been that I was to be left to do my work, in this particular case, as I liked, with the whole book committed to me; but my connection with the rest of the series was only contingent. There were moments when, frankly, it *was* a comfort to have the real thing under one's hand; for there were characters in 'Rutland Ramsay' that were very much like it. There were people presumably as straight as the Major and women of as good a fashion as Mrs Monarch. There was a great deal of country-house life – treated, it is true, in a fine, fanciful, ironical, generalized way – and there was a considerable impli-cation of knickerbockers and kilts. There were certain things I had to settle at the outset; such things for instance as the exact appearance of the hero, the particular bloom of the heroine. The author of course gave me a lead, but there was a margin for interpretation. I took the Monarchs into my confidence, I told them frankly what I was about, I mentioned my embarrassments and alternatives. 'Oh, take *him*!' Mrs Monarch murmured sweetly looking at her husband; and 'What could you want better than my wife?' the Major inquired, with the comfortable candour that now prevailed between us.

I was not obliged to answer these remarks – I was only obliged to place my sitters. I was not easy in mind, and I postponed, a little timidly perhaps, the solution of the question. The book was a large canvas, the other figures were numerous, and I worked off at first some of the episodes in which the hero and the heroine were not concerned. When once I had set *them* up I should have to stick to them – I couldn't make my young man seven feet high in one place and five feet nine in another. I inclined on the whole to the latter measurement, though the Major more than once reminded me that *he* looked about as young as anyone. It was indeed quite possible to arrange him, for the figure, so that it would have been difficult to detect his age. After the spontaneous Oronte had been with me a month, and after I had given him to understand several different times that this native exuberance would presently constitute an insurmountable barrier to our further intercourse, I waked to a sense of his heroic capacity. He was only five feet seven, but the remaining inches were latent. I tried him almost secretly at first, for I was really rather afraid of the judgement my other models would pass on such a choice. If they regarded Miss Churm as little better than a snare, what would they think of the representation by a person so little the real thing as an Italian street-vendor of a protagonist formed by a public school?

If I went a little in fear of them it was not because they bullied me, because they had got an oppressive foothold, but because in their really pathetic decorum and mysteriously permanent newness they counted on me so intensely. I was therefore very glad when Jack Hawley came home: he was always of such good counsel. He painted badly himself, but there was no one like him for putting his finger on the place. He had been absent from England for a year; he had been somewhere – I don't remember where – to get a fresh eye. I was in a good deal of dread of any such organ, but we were old friends; he had been away for months and a sense of emptiness was creeping into my life. I hadn't dodged a missile for a year.

He came back with a fresh eye, but with the same old black velvet blouse, and the first evening he spent in my studio we smoked cigarettes till the small hours. He had done no work himself, he had only got the eye; so the field was clear for the production of my little things. He wanted to see what I had done for the *Cheapside*, but he was disappointed in the exhibition. That at least seemed the meaning of two or three comprehensive groans which, as he lounged on my big divan, on a folded leg, looking at my latest drawings, issued from his lips with the smoke of the cigarette.

'What's the matter with you?' I asked.

'What's the matter with *you*?'

'Nothing save that I'm mystified.'

'You are indeed. You're quite off the hinge. What's the meaning of this new fad?' And he tossed me, with visible irreverence, a drawing in which I happened to have depicted both my majestic models. I asked if he didn't think it good, and he replied that it struck him as execrable, given the sort of thing I had always represented myself to him as wishing to arrive at; but I let that pass, I was so anxious to see exactly what he meant. The two figures in the picture looked colossal, but I supposed this was *not* what he meant, inasmuch as, for aught he knew to the contrary, I might have been trying for that. I maintained that I was working exactly in the same way as when he last had done me the honour to commend me. 'Well, there's a big hole somewhere,' he answered; 'wait a bit and I'll discover it.' I depended upon him to do so: where else was the fresh eye? But he produced at last nothing more luminous than 'I don't know – I don't like your types.' This was lame, for a critic who had never consented to discuss with me anything but the question of execution, the direction of strokes and the mystery of values.

'In the drawings you've been looking at I think my types are very handsome.'

'Oh, they won't do!'

'I've had a couple of new models.'

'I see you have. *They* won't do.'

'Are you very sure of that?'

'Absolutely – they're stupid.'

'You mean *I* am – for I ought to get round that.'

'You *can't* – with such people. Who are they?'

I told him, as far as was necessary, and he declared, heartlessly: '*Ce sont des gens qu'il faut mettre à la porte.*'

'You've never seen them; they're awfully good,' I compassionately objected.

'Not seen them? Why, all this recent work of yours drops to pieces with them. It's all I want to see of them.'

'No one else has said anything against it – the *Cheapside* people are pleased.'

'Everyone else is an ass, and the *Cheapside* people the biggest asses of all. Come, don't pretend, at this time of day, to have pretty illusions about the public, especially about publishers and editors. It's not for *such* animals you work – it's for those who know, *coloro che sanno*; so keep straight for *me* if you can't keep straight for yourself. There's a certain sort of thing you tried for from the first – and a very good thing it is. But this twaddle isn't *in* it.' When I talked with Hawley later about 'Rutland Ramsay' and its possible successors he declared that I must get back into my boat again or I would go to the bottom. His voice in short was the voice of warning.

I noted the warning, but I didn't turn my friends out of doors. They bored me a good deal; but the very fact that they bored me admonished me not to sacrifice them – if there was anything to be done with them – simply to irritation. As I look back at this phase they seem to me to have pervaded my life not a little. I have a vision of them as most of the time in my studio, seated, against the wall, on an old velvet bench to be out of the way, and looking like a pair of patient courtiers in a royal ante-chamber. I am convinced that during the coldest weeks of the winter they held their ground because it saved them fire. Their newness was losing its gloss, and it was impossible not to feel that they were objects of charity. Whenever Miss Churm arrived they went away, and after I was fairly launched in 'Rutland Ramsay' Miss Churm arrived pretty often. They managed to express to me tacitly that they supposed I wanted her for the low life of the book, and I let them suppose it, since they had attempted to study the work – it was lying about the studio – without discovering that it dealt only

with the highest circles. They had dipped into the most brilliant
of our novelists without deciphering many passages. I still took
an hour from them, now and again, in spite of Jack Hawley's
warning: it would be time enough to dismiss them, if dismissal
should be necessary, when the rigour of the season was over.
Hawley had made their acquaintance – he had met them at my
fireside – and thought them a ridiculous pair. Learning that he
was a painter they tried to approach him, to show him too that
they were the real thing; but he looked at them, across the big
room, as if they were miles away: they were a compendium of
everything that he most objected to in the social system of his
country. Such people as that, all convention and patent-leather,
with ejaculations that stopped conversation, had no business in
a studio. A studio was a place to learn to see, and how could you
see through a pair of feather beds?

The main inconvenience I suffered at their hands was that, at
first, I was shy of letting them discover how my artful little servant
had begun to sit to me for 'Rutland Ramsay'. They knew that I
had been odd enough (they were prepared by this time to allow
oddity to artists), to pick a foreign vagabond out of the streets,
when I might have had a person with whiskers and credentials;
but it was some time before they learned how high I rated his
accomplishments. They found him in an attitude more than once,
but they never doubted I was doing him as an organ-grinder.
There were several things they never guessed, and one of them
was that for a striking scene in the novel, in which a footman
briefly figured, it occurred to me to make use of Major Monarch
as the menial. I kept putting this off, I didn't like to ask him to
don the livery – besides the difficulty of finding a livery to fit him.
At last, one day late in the winter, when I was at work on the
despised Oronte (he caught one's idea in an instant), and was in
the glow of feeling that I was going very straight, they came in,
the Major and his wife, with their society laugh about nothing
(there was less and less to laugh at), like country-callers – they
always reminded me of that – who have walked across the park
after church and are presently persuaded to stay to luncheon.
Luncheon was over, but they could stay to tea – I knew they

wanted it. The fit was on me, however, and I couldn't let my ardour cool and my work wait, with the fading daylight, while my model prepared it. So I asked Mrs Monarch if she would mind laying it out – a request which, for an instant, brought all the blood to her face. Her eyes were on her husband's for a second, and some mute telegraphy passed between them. Their folly was over the next instant; his cheerful shrewdness put an end to it. So far from pitying their wounded pride, I must add, I was moved to give it as complete a lesson as I could. They bustled about together and got out the cups and saucers and made the kettle boil. I know they felt as if they were waiting on my servant, and when the tea was prepared I said: 'He'll have a cup, please – he's tired.' Mrs Monarch brought him one where he stood, and he took it from her as if he had been a gentleman at a party, squeezing a crush-hat with an elbow.

Then it came over me that she had made a great effort for me – made it with a kind of nobleness – and that I owed her a compensation. Each time I saw her after this I wondered what the compensation could be. I couldn't go on doing the wrong thing to oblige them. Oh, it *was* the wrong thing, the stamp of the work for which they sat – Hawley was not the only person to say it now. I sent in a large number of the drawings I had made for 'Rutland Ramsay', and I received a warning that was more to the point than Hawley's. The artistic adviser of the house for which I was working was of opinion that many of my illustrations were not what had been looked for. Most of these illustrations were the subjects in which the Monarchs had figured. Without going into the question of what *had* been looked for, I saw at this rate I shouldn't get the other books to do. I hurled myself in despair upon Miss Churm, I put her through all her paces. I not only adopted Oronte publicly as my hero, but one morning when the Major looked in to see if I didn't require him to finish a figure for the *Cheapside*, for which he had begun to sit the week before, I told him that I had changed my mind – I would do the drawing from my man. At this my visitor turned pale and stood looking at me. 'Is *he* your idea of an English gentleman?' he asked.

I was disappointed, I was nervous, I wanted to get on with my work; so I replied with irritation: 'Oh, my dear Major – I can't be ruined for *you*!'

He stood another moment; then, without a word, he quitted the studio. I drew a long breath when he was gone, for I said to myself that I shouldn't see him again. I had not told him definitely that I was in danger of having my work rejected, but I was vexed at his not having felt the catastrophe in the air, read with me the moral of our fruitless collaboration, the lesson that, in the deceptive atmosphere of art, even the highest respectability may fail of being plastic.

I didn't owe my friends money, but I did see them again. They reappeared together, three days later, and under the circumstances there was something tragic in the fact. It was a proof to me that they could find nothing else in life to do. They had threshed the matter out in a dismal conference – they had digested the bad news that they were not in for the series. If they were not useful to me even for the *Cheapside* their function seemed difficult to determine, and I could only judge at first that they had come, forgivingly, decorously, to take a last leave. This made me rejoice in secret that I had little leisure for a scene; for I had placed both my other models in position together and I was pegging away at a drawing from which I hoped to derive glory. It had been suggested by the passage in which Rutland Ramsay, drawing up a chair to Artemisia's piano-stool, says extraordinary things to her while she ostensibly fingers out a difficult piece of music. I had done Miss Churm at the piano before – it was an attitude in which she knew how to take on an absolutely poetic grace. I wished the two figures to 'compose' together, intensely, and my little Italian had entered perfectly into my conception. The pair were vividly before me, the piano had been pulled out; it was a charming picture of blended youth and murmured love, which I had only to catch and keep. My visitors stood and looked at it, and I was friendly to them over my shoulder.

They made no response, but I was used to silent company and went on with my work, only a little disconcerted (even though exhilarated by the sense that *this* was at least the ideal thing), at not having got rid of them after all. Presently I heard Mrs Monarch's sweet voice beside, or rather above me: 'I wish her hair was a little better done.' I looked up and she was staring with a strange fixedness at Miss Churm, whose back was turned to her. 'Do you mind my just touching it?' she went on – a question which made me spring up for an instant, as with the instinctive fear that she might do the young lady a harm. But she quieted me with a glance I shall never forget – I confess I should like to have been able to paint *that* – and went for a moment to my model. She spoke to her softly, laying a hand upon her shoulder and bending over her; and as the girl, understanding, gratefully assented, she disposed her rough curls, with a few quick passes, in such a way as to make Miss Churm's head twice as charming. It was one of the most heroic personal services I have ever seen rendered. Then Mrs Monarch turned away with a low sigh and, looking about her as if for something to do, stooped to the floor with a noble humility and picked up a dirty rag that had dropped out of my paint-box.

The Major meanwhile had also been looking for something to do and, wandering to the other end of the studio, saw before him my breakfast things, neglected, unremoved. 'I say, can't I be useful *here*?' he called out to me with an irrepressible quaver. I assented with a laugh that I fear was awkward and for the next ten minutes, while I worked, I heard the light clatter of china and the tinkle of spoons and glass. Mrs Monarch assisted her husband – they washed up my crockery, they put it away. They wandered off into my little scullery, and I afterwards found that they had cleaned my knives and that my slender stock of plate had an unprecedented surface. When it came over me, the latent eloquence of what they were doing, I confess that my drawing was blurred for a moment – the picture swam. They had accepted their failure, but they couldn't accept their fate. They had bowed their heads in bewilderment to the perverse and cruel law in virtue of which the real thing could be so much less precious than the unreal; but they didn't want to starve. If my servants were my models, my models might be my servants. They would reverse the parts – the others would sit for the ladies and gentlemen, and *they* would do the work. They would still be in the studio – it was an intense dumb appeal to me not to turn them out. 'Take us on,' they wanted to say – 'we'll do *anything*.'

When all this hung before me the *afflatus* vanished – my pencil dropped from my hand. My sitting was spoiled and I got rid of my sitters, who were also evidently rather mystified and awe-struck. Then, alone with the Major and his wife, I had a most un-comfortable moment. He put their prayer into a single sentence: 'I say, you know – just let *us* do for you, can't you?' I couldn't – it was dreadful to see them emptying my slops; but I pretended I could, to oblige them, for about a week. Then I gave them a sum of money to go away; and I never saw them again. I obtained the remaining books, but my friend Hawley repeats that Major and Mrs Monarch did me a permanent harm, got me into a second-rate trick. If it be true I am content to have paid the price – for the memory.

THE PAPERS

1

THERE was a longish period – the dense duration of a London winter, cheered, if cheered it could be called, with lurid electric, with fierce 'incandescent' flares and glares – when they repeatedly met, at feeding-time, in a small and not quite savoury pothouse a stone's-throw from the Strand. They talked always of pothouses, of feeding-time – by which they meant any hour between one and four of the afternoon; they talked of most things, even of some of the greatest, in a manner that gave, or that they desired to show as giving, in respect to the conditions of their life, the measure of their detachment, their contempt, their general irony. Their general irony, which they tried at the same time to keep gay and to make amusing at least to each other, was their refuge from the want of savour, the want of napkins, the want, too often, of shillings, and of many things besides that they would have liked to have. Almost all they had with any security was their youth, complete, admirable, very nearly invulnerable, or as yet inattackable; for they didn't count their talent, which they had originally taken for granted and had since then lacked freedom of mind, as well indeed as any offensive reason, to reappraise. They were taken up with other questions and other estimates – the remarkable limits, for instance, of their luck, the remarkable smallness of the talent of their friends. They were above all in that phase of youth and in that state of aspiration in which 'luck' is the subject of most frequent reference, as definite as the colour red, and in which it is the elegant name for money when people are as refined as they are poor. She was only a suburban young woman in a sailor hat, and he a young man destitute, in strictness, of occasion for a 'topper'; but they felt that they had in a peculiar way the freedom of the town, and the town, if it did nothing else, gave a range to the spirit. They sometimes went, on excursions that they groaned at as professional, far afield from the Strand, but the curiosity with which they came back was mostly greater than any other, the Strand being for them, with its ampler alternative Fleet Street, overwhelmingly the Papers, and the Papers being, at a rough guess, all the furniture of their consciousness.

The Daily Press played for them the part played by the embowered nest on the swaying bough for the parent birds that scour the air. It was, as they mainly saw it, a receptacle, owing its form to the instinct more remarkable, as they held the journalistic, than that even of the most highly organized animal, into which, regularly, breathlessly, contributions had to be dropped – odds and ends, all grist to the mill, all somehow digestible and convertible, all conveyed with the promptest possible beak and the flutter, often, of dreadfully fatigued little wings. If there had been no Papers there would have been no young friends for us of the figure we hint at, no chance mates, innocent and weary, yet acute even to penetration, who were apt to push off their plates and rest their elbows on the table in the interval between the turn-over of the pint-pot and the call for the awful glibness of their score. Maud Blandy drank beer – and welcome, as one may say; and she smoked cigarettes when privacy permitted, though she drew the line at this in the right place, just as she flattered herself she knew how to draw it, journalistically, where other delicacies were concerned. She was fairly a product of the day – so fairly that she might have been born afresh each morning, to serve, after the fashion of certain agitated ephemeral insects, only till the morrow. It was as if a past had been wasted on her and a future were not to be fitted; she was really herself, so far at least as her great preoccupation went, an edition, an 'extra special', coming out at the loud hours and living its life, amid the roar of vehicles, the hustle of pavements, the shriek of newsboys, according to the quantity of shock to be proclaimed and distributed, the quantity to be administered, thanks to the varying temper of Fleet Street, to the nerves of the nation. Maud was a shocker, in short, in petticoats, and alike for the thoroughfare, the club, the suburban train and the humble home; though it must honestly be added that petticoats were not of her essence. This was one of the reasons, in an age of 'emancipations', of her intense actuality, as well as, positively, of a good fortune to which, however impersonal she might have appeared, she was not herself in a position to do full justice; the felicity of her having about her naturally so much of the young bachelor that she was saved the disfigurement of any marked straddling or elbowing. It was literally true of her that she would have pleased less, or at least have offended more, had she been obliged, or been prompted, to assert – all too vainly, as it would have been sure to be – her superiority to sex. Nature, constitution, accident, whatever we happen to call it, had relieved her of this care; the struggle for life, the competition with men, the taste of the day, the fashion of the hour had *made* her superior, or had at any rate made her indifferent, and she had no difficulty in remaining so. The thing was therefore, with the aid of an extreme general flatness of person, directness of step and simplicity of motive, quietly enough done, without a grace, a weak inconsequence, a stray reminder to interfere with the success; and it is not too much to say that the success – by which I mean the plainness of the type – would probably never have struck you as so great as at the moments of our young lady's chance comradeship with Howard Bight. For the young man, though his personal signs had not, like his friend's, especially the effect of one of the stages of an evolution, might have been noted as not so fiercely or so freshly a male as to distance Maud in the show.

She presented him in truth, while they sat together, as comparatively girlish. She fell naturally into gestures, tones, expressions, resemblances, that he either suppressed, from sensibility to her personal predominance, or that were merely latent in him through much taking for granted. Mild, sensitive, none too solidly nourished, and condemned, perhaps by a deep delusion as to the final issue of it, to perpetual coming and going, he was so resigned to many things, and so disgusted even with many others, that the least of his cares was the cultivation of a bold front. What mainly concerned him was its being bold enough to get him his dinner, and it was never more void of aggression than when he solicited in person those scraps of information, snatched at those floating particles of news, on which his dinner depended. Had he had time a little more to try his case, he would have made out that if he liked Maud Blandy, it was partly by the impression of what she could do for him: what she could do for herself had never entered into his head. The positive quantity, moreover, was vague to his mind; it existed, that is, for the present, but as the proof of how, in spite of the want of encouragement, a fellow could keep going. She struck him in fact as the only encouragement he had, and this altogether by example, since precept, frankly, was deterrent on her lips, as speech was free, judgement prompt, and accent not absolutely pure. The point was that, as the easiest thing to be with her, he was so passive that it almost made him graceful and so attentive that it almost made him distinguished. She was herself neither of these things, and they were not of course what a man had most to be; whereby she contributed to their common view the impatiences required by a proper reaction, forming this for him a kind of protective hedge behind which he could wait. Much waiting, for either, was, I hasten to add, always in order, inasmuch as their novitiate seemed to them interminable and the steps of their ladder fearfully far apart. It rested – the ladder – against the great stony wall of the public attention – a sustaining mass which apparently wore somewhere, in the upper air, a big, thankless, expressionless face, a countenance equipped with eyes, ears, an uplifted nose and a gaping mouth – all convenient if they could only be reached. The ladder groaned meanwhile, swayed and shook with the weight of the close-pressed climbers, tier upon tier, occupying the upper, the middle, the nethermost rounds and quite preventing, for young persons placed as our young friends were placed, any view of the summit. It was meanwhile moreover only Howard Bight's perverse view – he was confessedly perverse – that Miss Blandy had arrived at a perch superior to his own.

She had hitherto recognized in herself indeed but a tighter clutch and a grimmer purpose; she had recognized, she believed, in keen moments, a vocation; she had recognized that there had been eleven of them at home, with herself as youngest, and distinctions by that time so blurred in her that she might as easily have been christened John. She had recognized truly, most of all, that if they came to talk they both were nowhere; yet this was compatible with her insisting that Howard had as yet comparatively had the luck. When he wrote to people they consented, or at least they answered; almost always, for that matter, they answered with greed, so that he was not without something of some sort to hawk about to buyers. Specimens indeed of human greed – *the* greed, the great one, the eagerness to figure, the snap at the bait of publicity, he had collected in such store as to stock, as to launch, a museum. In this museum the prize object, the high rare specimen, had been for some time established; a celebrity of the day enjoying, uncontested, a glass case all to himself, more conspicuous than any other, before which the arrested visitor might rebound from surprised recognition. Sir A. B. C. Beadel-Muffet K.C.B., M.P., stood forth there as large as life, owing indeed his particular place to the shade of direct acquaintance with him that Howard Bight could boast, yet with his eminent presence in such a collection but too generally and notoriously justified. He was universal and ubiquitous, commemorated, under some rank rubric, on every page of every public print every day in every year, and as inveterate a feature of each issue of any self-respecting sheet as the name, the date, the tariffed advertisements. He had always done something, or was about to do something, round which the honours of announcement clustered, and indeed, as he had inevitably thus become a subject of fallacious report, one half of his chronicle appeared to consist of official contradiction of the other half. His activity – if it had not better been called his passivity – was beyond any other that figured in the public eye, for no other assuredly knew so few or such brief intermittences. Yet, as there was the inside as well as the outside view of his current history, the quantity of it was easy to analyse for the possessor of the proper crucible. Howard Bight, with his arms on the table, took it apart and put it together again most days in the year, so that an amused comparison of notes on the subject often added a mild spice to his colloquies with Maud Blandy. They knew, the young pair, as they considered, many secrets, but they liked to think that they knew none quite so scandalous as the way that, to put it roughly, this distinguished person maintained his distinction.

It was known certainly to all who had to do with the Papers, a brotherhood, a sisterhood of course interested – for what was it, in the last resort, but the interest of their bread and butter? – in shrouding the approaches to the oracle, in not telling tales out of school. They all lived alike on the solemnity, the sanctity of the oracle, and the comings and goings, the doings and undoings, the intentions and retractations of Sir A. B. C. Beadel-Muffet K.C.B., M.P., were in their degree a part of that solemnity. The Papers, taken together the glory of the age, were, though superficially multifold, fundamentally one, so that any revelation of their being procured or procurable to float an object not intrinsically buoyant would very logically convey discredit from the circumference – where the revelation would be likely to be made – to the centre. Of so much as this our grim neophytes, in common with a thousand others, were perfectly aware; but something in the nature of their wit, such as it was, or in the condition of their nerves, such as it easily might become, sharpened almost to acerbity their relish of so artful an imitation of the voice of fame. The fame was *all* voice, as they could guarantee who had an ear always glued to the speaking-tube; the items that made the sum were individually of the last vulgarity, but the accumulation was a triumph – one of the greatest the age could show – of industry and vigilance. It was after all not true that a man had done nothing who for ten years had so fed, so dyked and directed and distributed the fitful sources of publicity. He had laboured, in his way, like a navvy with a spade; he might be said to have earned by each night's work the reward, each morning, of his small spurt of glory. Even for such a matter as its not being true that Sir A. B. C. Beadel-Muffet K.C.B., M.P., was to start on his visit to the Sultan of Samarcand on the 23rd, *but* being true that he was to start on the 29th, the personal attention required was no small affair, taking the legend with the fact, the myth with the meaning, the original artless error with the subsequent earnest truth – allowing in fine for the statement still to come that the visit would have to be relinquished in consequence of the visitor's other pressing engagements, and bearing in mind the countless channels to be successively watered. Our young man, one December afternoon, pushed an evening paper across to his companion, keeping his thumb on a paragraph at which she glanced without eagerness.

She might, from her manner, have known by instinct what it would be, and her exclamation had the note of satiety. 'Oh, he's working *them* now?'

'If he has begun he'll work them hard. By the time that has gone round the world there'll be something else to say. "We are authorized to state that the marriage of Miss Miranda Beadel-Muffet to Captain Guy Deveraux, of the Fiftieth Rifles, will not take place." Authorized to state – rather! when every wire in the machine has been pulled over and over. They're authorized to state something every day in the year, and the authorization is not difficult to get. Only his daughters, now that they're coming on, poor things – and I believe there are many – will have to be chucked into the pot and produced on occasions when other matter fails. How pleasant for them to find themselves hurtling through the air, clubbed by the paternal hand, like golf-balls in a suburb! Not that I suppose they don't like it – why should one suppose anything of the sort?' Howard Bight's impression of the general appetite appeared today to be especially vivid, and he and his companion were alike prompted to one of those slightly violent returns on themselves and the work they were doing which none but the vulgar-minded altogether avoid. 'People – as I see them – would almost rather be jabbered about unpleasantly than not be jabbered about at all: whenever you try them – whenever, at least, I do – I'm confirmed in that conviction. It isn't only that if one holds out the mere tip of the perch they jump at it like starving fish; it is that they leap straight out of the water themselves, leap in their thousands and come flopping, open-mouthed and goggle-eyed, to one's very door. What is the sense of the French expression about a person's making *des yeux de carpe*? It suggests the eyes that a young newspaper-man seems to see all round him, and I declare I sometimes feel that, if one has the courage not to blink at the show, the gilt is a good deal rubbed off the gingerbread of one's early illusions. They all do it, as the song is at the music-halls, and it's some of one's surprises that tell one most. You've thought there were some high souls that didn't do it – that wouldn't, I mean, to work the oracle, lift a little finger of their own. But, Lord bless you, give them a chance – you'll find some of the greatest the greediest. I give you my word for it, I haven't a scrap of faith left in a single human creature. Except, of course,' the young man added, 'the grand creature that *you* are, and the cold, calm, comprehensive one whom you thus admit to your familiarity. *We* face the music. We see, we understand; we know we've got to live, and how we do it. But at least, like this, alone together, we take our intellectual revenge, we escape the indignity of being fools dealing with fools. I don't say we shouldn't enjoy it more if we *were*. But it can't be helped; we haven't the gift – the gift, I mean, of not seeing. We do the worst we can for the money.'

' *You* certainly do the worst you can,' Maud Blandy soon replied, 'when you sit there, with your wanton wiles, and take the spirit out of me. I require a working faith, you know. If one isn't a fool, in our world, where *is* one?'

'Oh, I say!' her companion groaned without alarm. 'Don't you fail *me*, mind you.'

They looked at each other across their clean platters, and, little as the light of romance seemed superficially to shine in them or about them, the sense was visibly enough in each of being involved in the other. He would have been sharply alone, the softly sardonic young man, if the somewhat dry young woman hadn't affected him, in a way he was even too nervous to put to the test, as saving herself up for him; and the consciousness of absent resources that was on her own side quite compatible with this economy grew a shade or two less dismal with the imagination of his somehow being at costs for her. It wasn't an expense of shillings – there was not much question of that; what it came to was perhaps nothing more than that, being as he declared himself, 'in the know', he kept pulling her in too, as if there had been room for them both. He told her everything, all his secrets. He talked and talked, often making her think of herself as a lean, stiff person, destitute of skill or art, but with ear enough to be performed to, sometimes strangely touched, at moments completely ravished, by a fine violinist. He was her fiddler and genius; she was sure neither of her taste nor of his tunes, but if she could do nothing else for him she could hold the case while he handled the instrument. It had never passed between them that they could draw nearer, for they seemed near, near verily for pleasure, when each, in a decent young life, was so much nearer to the other than to anything else. There was no pleasure known to either that wasn't further off. What held them together was in short that they were in the same boat, a cockle-shell in a great rough sea, and that the movements required for keeping it afloat not only were what the situation safely permitted, but also made for reciprocity and intimacy. These talks over greasy white slabs, repeatedly mopped with moist grey cloths by young women in black uniforms, with inexorable braided 'buns' in the nape of weak necks, these sessions, sometimes prolonged, in halls of oilcloth, among penal-looking tariffs and pyramids of scones, enabled them to rest on their oars; the more that they were on terms with the whole families, chartered companies, of food-stations, each a race of innumerable and indistinguishable members, and had mastered those hours of comparative elegance, the earlier and the later, when the little weary ministrants were limply sitting down and the occupants of the red benches bleakly interspaced. So it was, that, at times, they renewed their understanding, and by signs, mannerless and meagre, that would have escaped the notice of witnesses. Maud Blandy had no need to kiss her hand across to him to show she felt what he meant; she had moreover never in her life kissed her hand to anyone, and her companion couldn't have imagined it of her. His romance was so grey that it wasn't romance at all; it was a reality arrived at without stages, shades, forms. If he had been ill or stricken she would have taken him – other resources failing – into her lap; but would that, which would scarce even have been motherly, have been romantic? She nevertheless at this moment put in her plea for the general element. 'I can't help it, about Beadel-Muffet; it's too magnificent – it appeals to me. And then I've a particular feeling about him – I'm waiting to see what will happen. It *is* genius, you know, to get yourself so celebrated for nothing – to carry out your idea in the face of everything. I mean your idea of *being* celebrated. It isn't as if he had done even one little thing. What *has* he done when you come to look?'

'Why, my dear chap, he has done everything. He has missed

nothing. He has been in everything, *of* everything, *at* everything, *over* everything, *under* everything, that has taken place for the last twenty years. He's *always* present, and, though he never makes a speech, he never fails to get alluded to in the speeches of others. That's doing it cheaper than anyone else does it, but it's thoroughly doing it – which is what we're talking about. And so far,' the young man contended, 'from its being "in the face" of anything, it's positively with the help of everything, since the Papers are everything and more. They're made for such people, though no doubt he's the person who has known best how to use them. I've gone through one of the biggest sometimes, from beginning to end – it's quite a thrilling little game – to catch him once out. It has happened to me to think I was near it when, on the last column of the last page – I count "advertisements", heaven help us, out! – I've found him as large as life and as true as the needle to the pole. But at last, in a way, it goes, it can't help going, of itself. He comes in, he breaks out, of himself; the letters, under the compositor's hand, form themselves, from the force of habit, into his name – any connection for it, any context, being as good as any other, and the wind, which he has originally "raised", but which continues to blow, setting perpetually in his favour. The thing would really be now, don't you see, for him to keep himself out. That would be, on my honour, it strikes me – his *getting* himself out – the biggest fact in his record.'

The girl's attention, as her friend developed the picture, had become more present. 'He *can't* get himself out. There he is.' She had a pause; she had been thinking. 'That's just my idea.'

'Your idea? Well, an idea's always a blessing. What do you want for it?'

She continued to turn it over as if weighing its value. 'Something perhaps *could* be done with it – only it would take imagination.'

He wondered, and she seemed to wonder that he didn't see. 'Is it a situation for a "ply"!'

'No, it's too good for a ply – yet it isn't quite good enough for a short story.'

'It would do then for a novel?'

144

'Well, I seem to see it,' Maud said – 'and with a lot *in* it to be got out. But I seem to see it as a question not of what you or I might be able to do with it, but of what the poor man himself may. That's what I meant just now,' she explained, 'by my having a creepy sense of what may happen for him. It has already more than once occurred to me. *Then*,' she wound up, 'we shall have real life, the case itself.'

'Do you know *you've* got imagination?' Her friend, rather interested, appeared by this time to have seized her thought.

'I see him having for some reason, very imperative, to seek retirement, lie low, to hide, in fact, like a man "wanted", but pursued all the while by the lurid glare that he has himself so started and kept up, and at last literally devoured ("like Frankenstein", of course!) by the monster he has created.'

'I say, you *have* got it!' – and the young man flushed, visibly, artistically, with the recognition of elements which his eyes had for a minute earnestly fixed. 'But it will take a lot of doing.'

'Oh,' said Maud, '*we* shan't have to do it. He'll do it himself.'

'I wonder.' Howard Bight really wondered. 'The fun would be for him to do it *for* us. I mean for him to want us to help him somehow to get out.'

'Oh, "us"!' the girl mournfully sighed.

'Why not, when he comes to us to get in?'

Maud Blandy stared. 'Do you mean to you personally? You surely know by this time that no one ever "comes" to me.'

'Why, I went to him in the first instance; I made up to him straight, I did him "at home", somewhere, as I've surely mentioned to you before, three years ago. He liked, I believe – for he's really a delightful old ass – the way I did it; he knows my name and has my address, and has written me three or four times since, with his own hand, a request to be so good as to make use of my (he hopes) still close connection with the daily Press to rectify the rumour that he has reconsidered his opinion on the subject of the blankets supplied to the Upper Tooting Workhouse Infirmary. He has reconsidered his opinion on no subject whatever – which he mentions, in the interest of historic truth, without further intrusion on my valuable time. And he regards that sort of thing as

145

a commodity that I can dispose of – thanks to my "close connection" – for several shillings.'

'And can you?'

'Not for several pence. They're all tariffed, but he's tariffed low – having a value, apparently, that money doesn't represent. He's always welcome, but he isn't always paid for. The beauty, however, is in his marvellous memory, his keeping us all so apart and not muddling the fellow to whom he has written that he hasn't done this, that or the other with the fellow to whom he has written that he has. He'll write to me again some day about something else – about his alleged position on the date of the next school-treat of the Chelsea Cabmen's Orphanage. I shall seek a market for the precious item, and that will keep us in touch; so that if the complication you have the sense of in your bones does come into play – the thought's too beautiful! – he may once more remember me. Fancy his coming to one with a "What can you do for me *now*?"'. Bight lost himself in the happy vision; it gratified so his cherished consciousness of the 'irony of fate' – a consciousness so cherished that he never could write ten lines without use of the words.

Maud showed however at this point a reserve which appeared to have grown as the possibility opened out. 'I believe in it – it must come. It can't not. It's the only end. He doesn't know; nobody knows – the simple-minded all: only you and I know. But it won't be nice, remember.'

'It won't be funny?'

'It will be pitiful. There'll have to be a reason.'

'For his turning round?' the young man nursed the vision. 'More or less – I see what you mean. But except for a "ply" will that so much matter? His reason will concern himself. What will concern us will be his funk and his helplessness, his having to stand there in the blaze, with nothing and nobody to put it out. We shall see him, shrieking for a bucket of water, wither up in the central flame.'

Her look had turned sombre. 'It makes one cruel. That is it makes *you*. I mean our trade does.'

'I dare say – I see too much. But I'm willing to chuck it.'

'Well,' she presently replied, 'I'm not willing to, but it seems pretty well on the cards that I shall have to. *I* don't see too much. I don't see enough. So, for all the good it does me – !'

She had pushed back her chair and was looking round for her umbrella. 'Why, what's the matter?' Howard Bight too blankly inquired.

She met his eyes while she pulled on her rusty old gloves. 'Well, I'll tell you another time.'

He kept his place, still lounging, contented where she had again become restless. 'Don't you call it seeing enough to see – to have had so luridly revealed to you – the doom of Beadel-Muffet?'

'Oh, he's not my business, he's yours. You're his man, or one of his men – he'll come back to you. Besides, he's a special case, and, as I say, I'm too sorry for him.'

'That's a proof then of what you do see.'

Her silence for a moment admitted it, though evidently she was making, for herself, a distinction, which she didn't express. 'I don't then see what I want, what I require. And *he*,' she added, 'if he does have some reason, will have to have an awfully strong one. To be strong enough it will have to be awful.'

'You mean he'll have done something?'

'Yes, that may remain undiscovered if he can only drop out of the papers, sit for a while in darkness. You'll know what it is; you'll not be able to help yourself. But I shan't want to, for anything.'

She had got up as she said it, and he sat looking at her, thanks to her odd emphasis, with an interest that, as he also rose, passed itself off as a joke. 'Ah, then, you sweet sensitive thing, I promise to keep it from you.'

2

THEY met again a few days later, and it seemed the law of their meetings that these should take place mainly within moderate eastward range of Charing Cross. An afternoon performance of a play translated from the Finnish, already several times given, on a series of Saturdays, had held Maud for an hour in a small, hot, dusty theatre where the air hung as heavy about the great 'trimmed' and plumed hats of the ladies as over the flora and fauna of a tropical forest; at the end of which she edged out of her stall in the last row, to join a small band of unattached critics and correspondents, spectators with ulterior views and pencilled shirt-cuffs, who, coming together in the lobby for an exchange of ideas, were ranging from 'Awful rot' to 'Rather jolly'. Ideas, of this calibre, rumbled and flashed, so that, lost in the discussion, our young woman failed at first to make out that a gentleman on the other side of the group, but standing a little off, had his eyes on her for some extravagant, though apparently quite respectable, purpose. He had been waiting for her to recognize him, and as soon as he had caught her attention he came round to her with an eager bow. She had by this time entirely placed him – placed him as the smoothest and most shining subject with which, in the exercise of her profession, she had yet experimented; but her recognition was accompanied with a pang that his amiable address made but the sharper. She had her reason for awkward-ness in the presence of a rosy, glossy, kindly, but discernibly troubled personage whom she had waited on 'at home' at her own suggestion – promptly welcomed – and the sympathetic element in whose 'personality'. the Chippendale, the photogra-phic, the autographic elements in whose flat in the Earls Court Road, she had commemorated in the liveliest prose of which she was capable. She had described with humour his favourite pug, she had revealed with permission his favourite make of Kodak, she had touched upon his favourite manner of spending his Sun-days and had extorted from him the shy confession that he preferred after all the novel of adventure to the novel of subtlety. Her embarrassment was therefore now the greater as, touching to behold, he so clearly had approached her with no intention of asperity, not even at first referring at all to the matter that couldn't have been gracefully explained.

She had seen him originally – had had the instinct of it in making up to him – as one of the happy of the earth, and the impression of him 'at home', on his proving so good-natured about the interview, had begotten in her a sharper envy, a hungrier sense of the invidious distinctions of fate, than any her literary conscience, which she deemed rigid, had yet had to reckon with. He must have been rich, rich by such estimates as hers; he at any rate had everything, while she had nothing – nothing but the vulgar need of offering him to brag, on his behalf, for money, if she could get it, about his luck. She hadn't in fact got money, hadn't so much as managed to work in her stuff anywhere; a practical comment sharp enough on her having represented to him – with wasted pathos, she was indeed soon to perceive – how 'important' it was to her that people should let her get at them. This dim celebrity had not needed that argument; he had not only, with his alacrity, allowed her, as she had said, to try her hand, but had tried *with* her, quite feverishly, and all to the upshot of showing her that there were even greater outsiders than herself. He could have put down money, could have published, as the phrase was – a bare two columns – at his own expense; but it was just a part of his rather irritating luxury that he had a scruple about that, wanted intensely to taste the sweet, but didn't want to owe it to any wire-pulling. He wanted the golden apple straight from the tree, where it yet seemed so unable to grow for him by any exuberance of its own. He had breathed to her his real secret – that to be inspired, to work with effect, he had to feel he was appreciated, to have it all somehow come back to him. The artist, necessarily sensitive, lived on encouragement, on knowing and being reminded that people cared for him a little, cared even just enough to flatter him a wee bit. They had talked that over, and he had really, as he called it, quite put himself in her power. He had whispered in her ear that it might be very weak and silly, but that positively to be himself, to do anything, certainly to do his best, he required the breath of sympathy. He did love notice, let alone praise – there it was. To be systematically ignored – well, blighted him at the root. He was afraid she would think he had said too much, but she left him with his leave, none the less, to repeat a part of it. They had agreed that she was to bring in prettily, somehow, that he did love praise; for just the right way he was sure he could trust to her taste.

She had promised to send him the interview in proof, but she had been able, after all, to send it but in type-copy. If *she*, after all, had had a flat adorned – as to the drawing-room alone – with eighty-three photographs, and all in plush frames; if she had lived in the Earls Court Road, had been rosy and glossy and well filled out; and if she had looked withal, as she always made a point of calling it when she wished to refer without vulgarity to the right place in the social scale, 'unmistakeably gentle' – if she had achieved these things she would have snapped her fingers at all other sweets, have sat as tight as possible and let the world wag, have spent her Sundays in silently thanking her stars, and not have cared to know one Kodak, or even one novelist's 'methods', from another. Except for his unholy itch he was in short so just the person she would have liked to be that the last consecration was given for her to his character by his speaking quite as if he had accosted her only to secure her view of the strange Finnish 'soul'. He had come each time – there had been four Saturdays; whereas Maud herself had had to wait till today, though her bread depended on it, for the roundabout charity of her publicly bad seat. It didn't matter *why* he had come – so that he might see it somewhere printed of him that he was 'a conspicuously faithful attendant' at the interesting series; it only mattered that he was letting her off so easily, and yet that there was a restless hunger, odd on the part of one of the filled-out, in his appealing eye, which she now saw not to be a bit intelligent, though that didn't matter either. Howard Bight came into view while she dealt with these impressions, whereupon she found herself edging a little away from her patron. Her other friend, who had but just arrived and was apparently waiting to speak to her, would be a pretext for a break before the poor gentleman should begin to accuse her of having failed him. She had failed herself so much more that she would have been ready to reply to him that *he* was scarce the one to complain; fortunately, however, the bell sounded the end of the interval and her tension was relaxed. They all flocked back to their places, and her *camarade* – she knew enough often so to designate him – was enabled, thanks to some shifting of other spectators, to occupy a seat beside her. He had brought with him the breath of business; hurrying from one appointment to another he might have time but for a single act. He had seen each of the others by itself, and the way he now crammed in the third, after having previously snatched the fourth, brought home again to the girl that he was leading the real life. Her own was a dull imitation of it. Yet it happened at the same time that before the curtain rose again he had, with a 'Who's your fat friend?' professed to have caught her in the act of making her own brighter.

'"Mortimer Marshal"?' he echoed after she had, a trifle dryly, satisfied him. 'Never heard of him.'

'Well, I shan't tell him that. But you *have*,' she said; 'you've only forgotten. I told you after I had been to him.'

Her friend thought – it came back to him. 'Oh yes, and showed me what you had made of it. I remember your stuff was charming.'

'I see you remember nothing,' Maud a little more dryly said. 'I didn't show you what I had made of it. I've never made anything. You've not seen my stuff, and nobody has. They won't have it.'

She spoke with a smothered vibration, but, as they were still waiting, it had made him look at her; by which she was slightly the more disconcerted. 'Who won't?'

'Everyone, everything won't. Nobody, nothing will. He's hopeless, or rather *I* am. I'm no good. And he knows it.'

'Oh – oh!' the young man kindly but vaguely protested. 'Has he been making that remark to you?'

'No – that's the worst of it. He's too dreadfully civil. He thinks I can do something.'

'Then why do you say he knows you can't?'

She was impatient; she gave it up. 'Well, I don't know what he knows – except that he does want to be loved.'

'Do you mean he has proposed to you to love him?'

'Loved by the great heart of the public – speaking through its natural organ. He wants to be – well, where Beadel-Muffet is.'

'Oh, I hope not!' said Bight with grim amusement.

His friend was struck with his tone. 'Do you mean it's coming on for Beadel-Muffet – what we talked about?' And then as he looked at her so queerly that her curiosity took a jump: 'It really and truly *is*? Has anything happened?'

'The rummest thing in the world – since I last saw you. We're wonderful, you know, you and I together – we *see*. And what we see always takes place, usually within the week. It wouldn't be believed. But it will do for *us*. At any rate it's high sport.'

'Do you mean,' she asked, 'that his scare has literally begun?'

He meant, clearly, quite as much as he said. 'He has written to me again he wants to see me, and we've an appointment for Monday.'

'Then why isn't it the old game?'

'Because it isn't. He wants to gather from me, as I *have* served him before, if something can't be done. *On a souvent besoin d'un plus petit que soi*. Keep quiet, and we shall see something.'

This was very well; only his manner visibly had for her the effect of a chill in the air. 'I hope,' she said, 'you're going at least to be decent to him.'

'Well, you'll judge. Nothing at all can be done – it's too ridiculously late. And it serves him right. I shan't deceive him, certainly, but I might as well enjoy him.'

The fiddles were still going, and Maud had a pause. 'Well, you know you've more or less lived on him. I mean it's the kind of thing you *are* living on.'

'Precisely – that's just why I loathe it.'

Again she hesitated. 'You mustn't quarrel, you know, with your bread and butter.'

He looked straight before him, as if she had been consciously, and the least bit disagreeably, sententious. 'What in the world's that but what I shall just be *not* doing? If our bread and butter is the universal push I consult our interest by not letting it trifle with us. They're not to blow hot and cold – it won't do. There he is – let him get out himself. What I call sport is to see if he can.'

'And not – poor wretch – to help him?'

But Bight was ominously lucid. 'The devil is that he can't *be* helped. His one idea of help, from the day he opened his eyes, has been to be prominently – damn the word! – mentioned: it's the only kind of help that exists in connection with him. What therefore is a fellow to do when he happens to want it to stop – wants a special sort of prominence that will work like a trap in a panto-mime and enable him to vanish when the situation requires it? Is one to mention that he wants *not* to be mentioned – never, never, please, any more? Do you see the success of that, all over the place, do you see the headlines in the American papers? No, he must die as he has lived – the Principal Public Person of his time.'

'Well,' she sighed, 'it's all horrible.' And then without a transi-tion: 'What do you suppose has happened to him?'

'The dreadfulness I wasn't to tell you?'

'I only mean if you suppose him in a really bad hole.'

The young man considered. 'It can't certainly be that he has had a change of heart – never. It may be nothing worse than that the woman he wants to marry has turned against it.'

'But I supposed him – with his children all so boomed – to *be* married.'

'Naturally; else he couldn't have got such a boom from the poor lady's illness, death and burial. Don't you remember two years ago? – "We are given to understand that Sir A. B. C. Beadel-Muffet K.C.B., M.P., particularly desires that no flowers be sent for the late Hon. Lady Beadel-Muffet's funeral." And then, the next day: "We are authorized to state that the impression, so generally prevailing, that Sir A. B. C. Beadel-Muffet has expressed an objection to flowers in connection with the late Hon. Lady Beadel-Muffet's obsequies, rests on a misapprehension of Sir A. B. C. Beadel-Muffet's markedly individual views. The floral tributes already delivered in Queen's Gate Gardens, and remark-able for number and variety, have been the source of such gratifi-cation to the bereaved gentleman as his situation permits." With a wind-up of course for the following week – the inevitable few heads of remark, on the part of the bereaved gentleman, on the general subject of Flowers at Funerals as a Fashion, vouchsafed, under pressure possibly indiscreet, to a rising young journalist always thirsting for the authentic word.'

'I guess now,' said Maud, after an instant, 'the rising young journalist. You egged him on.'

'Dear, no. I panted in his rear.'

'It makes you,' she added, 'more than cynical.'

'And what do you call "more than" cynical?'

'It makes you sardonic. Wicked,' she continued; 'devilish.'

'That's it – that *is* cynical. Enough's as good as a feast.' But he came back to the ground they had quitted. 'What were you going to say *he's* prominent for, Mortimer Marshal?'

She wouldn't, however, follow him there yet, her curiosity on the other issue not being spent. 'Do you know then as a fact, that he's marrying again, the bereaved gentleman?'

Her friend, at this, showed impatience. 'My dear fellow, do you *see* nothing? We had it all, didn't we, three months ago, and then we didn't have it, and then we had it again; and goodness knows where we are. But I throw out the possibility. I forget her bloated name, but she may be rich, and she may be decent. She may make it a condition that he keeps out – out, I mean, of the only things he has really ever been "in".'

'The Papers?'

'The dreadful, nasty, vulgar Papers. She may put it to him – I see it dimly and queerly, but I see it – that he must get out first, and then they'll talk; then she'll say yes, then he'll have the money. I see it – and much more sharply – that he *wants* the money, needs it, I mean, badly, desperately, so that this necessity may very well make the hole in which he finds himself. Therefore he must do something – what he's trying to do. It supplies the motive that our picture, the other day, rather missed.'

Maud Blandy took this in, but it seemed to fail to satisfy her. 'It must be something worse. You make it out *that*, so that your practical want of mercy, which you'll not be able to conceal from me, shall affect me as less inhuman.'

'I don't make it out anything, and I don't care what it is; the queerness, the grand "irony" of the case is itself enough for me. You, on your side, however, I think, make it out what you call "something worse", because of the romantic bias of your mind. You "see red". Yet isn't it, after all, sufficiently lurid that he shall lose his blooming bride?'

'You're sure,' Maud appealed, 'that he'll lose her?'

'Poetic justice screams for it; and my whole interest in the matter is staked on it.'

But the girl continued to brood. 'I thought you contend that nobody's half "decent". Where do you find a woman to make such a condition?'

'Not easily, I admit.' The young man thought. 'It will be *his* luck to have found her. That's his tragedy, say, that she can financially save him, but that she happens to be just the one freak, the creature whose stomach has turned. The spark – I mean of decency – has got, after all, somehow to be kept alive; and it may be lodged in this particular female form.'

'I see. But why should a female form that's so particular confess to an affinity with a male form that's so fearfully general? As he's *all* self-advertisement, why isn't it much more natural to her simply to loathe him?'

'Well, because, oddly enough, it seems that people don't.'

'*You* do,' Maud declared. 'You'll kill him.'

He just turned a flushed cheek to her, and she saw that she had touched something that lived in him. 'We *can*,' he consciously smiled, 'deal death. And the beauty is that it's in a perfectly straight way. We can lead them on. But have you ever seen Beadel-Muffet for yourself?' he continued.

'No. How often, please, need I tell you that I've seen nobody and nothing?'

'Well, if you had you'd understand.'

'You mean he's so fetching?'

'Oh, he's great. He's not "all" self-advertisement – or at least he doesn't seem to be: that's his pull. But I see, you female humbug,' Bight pursued, 'how much you'd like him yourself.'

'I want, while I'm about it, to pity him in sufficient quantity.'

'Precisely. Which means, for a woman, with extravagance and to the point of immorality.'

'I ain't a woman,' Maud Blandy sighed. 'I wish I were!'

'Well, about the pity,' he went on; 'you shall be immoral, I promise you, before you've done. Doesn't Mortimer Marshal,' he asked, 'take you for a woman?'

'You'll have to ask *him*. How,' she demanded, 'does one

know those things?' And she stuck to her Beadel-Muffet. 'If you're to see him on Monday shan't you then get to the bottom of it?'

'Oh, I don't conceal from you that I promise myself larks, but I won't tell you, positively I won't,' Bight said, 'what I see. You're morbid. If it's only bad enough – I mean his motive – you'll want to save him.'

'Well, isn't that what you're to profess to him that *you* want?'

'Ah,' the young man returned, 'I believe you'd really invent a way.'

'I would if I could.' And with that she dropped it. 'There's my fat friend,' she presently added, as the entr'acte still hung heavy and Mortimer Marshal, from a row much in advance of them, screwed himself round in his tight place apparently to keep her in his eye.

'He does then,' said her companion, 'take you for a woman. I seem to guess he's "littery".'

'That's it; so badly that he wrote that "littery" ply *Corisanda*, you must remember, with Beatrice Beaumont in the principal part, which was given at three matinées in this very place and which hadn't even the luck of being slated. Every creature connected with the production, from the man himself and Beatrice *her*self down to the mothers and grandmothers of the sixpenny young women, the young women of the programmes, was interviewed both before and after, and he promptly published the piece, pleading guilty to the "littery" charge – which is the great stand he takes and the subject of the discussion.'

Bight had wonderingly followed. 'Of what discussion?'

'Why, the one he thinks there ought to have been. There hasn't been any, of course, but he wants it, dreadfully misses it. People won't keep it up – whatever they *did* do, though I don't myself make out that they did anything. His state of mind requires something to start with, which has got somehow to be provided. There must have been a noise made, don't you see? to make him prominent; and in order to remain prominent, he has got to go for his enemies. The hostility to his ply, and all *because* it's "littery", we can do nothing without that; but it's uphill work to come across it. We sit up nights trying, but we seem to get no for'arder. The public attention would seem to abhor the whole matter even as nature abhors a vacuum. We've nothing to go upon, otherwise we might go far. But there we are.'

'I see,' Bight commented. 'You're nowhere at all.'

'No; it isn't even that, for we're just where *Corisanda*, on the stage and in the closet, put us at a stroke. Only there we stick fast – nothing seems to happen, nothing seems to come or to be capable of being made to come. We wait.'

'Oh, if he waits with *you*!' Bight amicably jibed.

'He may wait for ever?'

'No, but resignedly. You'll make him forget his wrongs.'

'Ah, I'm not of that sort, and I could only do it by making him come into his rights. And I recognize now that that's impossible. There are different cases, you see, whole different classes of them, and his is the opposite to Beadel-Muffet's.'

Howard Bight gave a grunt. 'Why the opposite if you also pity him? I'll be hanged,' he added, 'if you won't save *him* too.'

But she shook her head. She knew. 'No; but it's nearly, in its way, as lurid. Do you know,' she asked, 'what he has done?'

'Why, the difficulty appears to be that he can't have done anything. He should strike once more – hard, and in the same place. He should bring out another ply.'

'Why so? You can't be more than prominent, and he *is* prominent. You can't do more than subscribe, in your prominence, to thirty-seven "press-cutting" agencies in England and America, and, having done so, you can't do more than sit at home with your ear on the postman's knock, looking out for results. *There* comes in the tragedy – there are no results. Mortimer Marshal's postman doesn't knock; the press-cutting agencies can't find anything to cut. With thirty-seven, in the whole English-speaking world, scouring millions of papers for him in vain, and with a big slice of his private income all the while going to it, the "irony" is too cruel, and the way he looks at one, as in one's degree responsible, does make one wince. He expected, naturally, most from the Americans, but it's they who have failed him worst. Their silence is that of the tomb, and it seems to grow, if the silence of the tomb *can* grow. He won't admit that the thirty-seven look far enough or long enough, and he writes them, I infer, angry letters, wanting to know what the deuce they suppose he has paid them for. But what are they either, poor things, to do?'

'Do? They can print his angry letters. That, at least, will break the silence, and he'll like it better than nothing.'

This appeared to strike our young woman. 'Upon my word, I really believe he would.' Then she thought better of it. 'But they'd be afraid, for they do guarantee, you know, that there's something for everyone. They claim it's their strength – that there's enough to go round. They won't want to show that they break down.'

'Oh, well,' said the young man, 'if he can't manage to smash a pane of glass somewhere –!'

'That's what he thought *I* would do. And it's what *I* thought I might,' Maud added; 'otherwise I wouldn't have approached him. I did it on spec, but I'm no use. I'm a fatal influence. I'm a non-conductor.'

She said it with such plain sincerity that it quickly took her companion's attention. 'I *say*!' he covertly murmured. 'Have you a secret sorrow?'

'Of course I've a secret sorrow.' And she stared at it, stiff and a little sombre, not wanting it to be too freely handled, while the curtain at last rose to the lighted stage.

3

SHE was later on more open about it, sundry other things, not wholly alien, having meanwhile happened. One of these had been that her friend had waited with her to the end of the Finnish performance and that it had then, in the lobby, as they went out, not been possible for her not to make him acquainted with Mr Mortimer Marshal. This gentleman had clearly waylaid her and had also clearly divined that her companion was of the Papers – papery all through; which doubtless had something to do with his having handsomely proposed to them to accompany him somewhere to tea. They hadn't seen why they shouldn't, it being an adventure, all in their line, like another; and he had carried them, in a four-wheeler, to a small and refined club in a region which was as the fringe of the Piccadilly region, where even their own presence scarce availed to contradict the implication of the exclusive. The whole occasion, they were further to feel, was essentially a tribute to their professional connection, especially that side of it which flushed and quavered, which panted and pined in their host's personal nervousness. Maud Blandy now saw it vain to contend with his delusion that *she*, underfed and unprinted, who had never been so conscious as during these bribed moments of her non-conducting quality, was papery to any purpose – a delusion that exceeded, by her measure, every other form of pathos. The decoration of the tea-room was a pale, aesthetic green, the liquid in the delicate cups a copious potent amber; the bread and butter was thin and golden, the muffins a revelation to her that she was barbarously hungry. There were ladies at other tables with other gentlemen – ladies with long feather boas and hats not of the sailor pattern, and gentlemen whose straight collars were doubled up much higher than Howard Bight's and their hair parted far more at the side. The talk was so low, with pauses somehow so not of embarrassment that it could only have been earnest, and the air, an air of privilege and privacy to our young woman's sense, seemed charged with fine things taken for granted. If it hadn't been for Bight's company she would have grown almost frightened, so much seemed to be offered her for something she couldn't do. That word of Bight's about smashing a windowpane had lingered with her; it had made her afterwards wonder, while they sat in their stalls, if there weren't some brittle surface in range of her own elbow. She had to fall back on the consciousness of how her elbow, in spite of her type, lacked practical point, and that was just why the terms in which she saw her service now, as she believed, bid for, had the effect of scaring her. They came out most, for that matter, in Mr Mortimer Marshal's dumbly-insistent eyes, which seemed to be perpetually saying: 'You know what I mean when I'm too refined – like everything here, don't you see? – to say it out. You know there ought to be something about me somewhere, and that really, with the opportunities, the facilities you enjoy, it wouldn't be so much out of your way just to – well, reward this little attention.'

The fact that he was probably every day, in just the same anxious flurry and with just the same superlative delicacy, paying little attentions with an eye to little rewards, this fact by itself but scantily eased her, convinced as she was that no luck but her own was as hopeless as his. He squared the clever young wherever he could get at them, but it was the clever young, taking them generally, who fed from his hand and then forgot him. She didn't forget him; she pitied him too much, pitied herself, and was more and more, as she found, now pitying everyone; only she didn't know how to say to him that she could do, after all, nothing for him. She oughtn't to have come, in the first place, and wouldn't if it hadn't been for her companion. Her companion was increasingly sardonic – which was the way in which, at best, she now increasingly saw him; he was shameless in acceptance, since, as she knew, as she felt at his side, he had come only, at bottom, to mislead and to mystify. *He* was, as she wasn't, on the Papers and of them, and their baffled entertainer knew it without either a hint on the subject from herself or a need, on the young man's own lips, of the least vulgar allusion. Nothing was so much as named, the whole connection was sunk; they talked about clubs, muffins, afternoon performances, the effect of the Finnish soul upon the appetite, quite as if they had met in society. Nothing could have been less like society – she innocently supposed at least – than the real spirit of their meeting; yet Bight did nothing that he might do to keep the affair within bounds. When looked at by their friend so hard and so hintingly, he only looked back, just as dumbly, but just as intensely and, as might be said, portentously; ever so impenetrably, in fine, and ever so wickedly. He didn't smile – as if to cheer – the least little bit; which he might be abstaining from on purpose to make his promises solemn: so, as he tried to smile – she couldn't, it was all too dreadful – she wouldn't meet her friend's eyes, but kept looking, heartlessly, at the 'notes' of the place, the hats of the ladies, the tints of the rugs, the intenser Chippendale, here and there, of the chairs and tables, of the very

guests, of the very waitresses. It had come to her early: 'I've done
him, poor man, at home, and the obvious thing now will be to do
him at his club.' But this inspiration plumped against her fate
even as an imprisoned insect against the window-glass. She
couldn't do him at his club without decently asking leave; whereby he would know of her feeble feeler, feeble because she was so
sure of refusals. She would rather tell him, desperately, what she
thought of him than expose him to see again that she was herself
nowhere, herself nothing. Her one comfort was that, for the half-
hour – it had made the situation quite possible – he seemed fairly
hypnotized by her colleague; so that when they took leave he as
good as thanked her for what she had this time done for him. It
was one of the signs of his infatuated state that he clearly viewed
Bight as a mass of helpful cleverness, though the cruel creature,
uttering scarce a sound, had only fixed him in a manner that
might have been taken for the fascination of deference. He might
perfectly have been an idiot for all the poor gentleman knew. But
the poor gentleman saw a possible 'leg up' in every bush; and
nothing but impertinence would have convinced him that she
hadn't brought him, compunctiously as to the past, a master of
the proper art. Now, more than ever, how he would listen for the
postman!

The whole occasion had broken so, for busy Bight, into matters
to be attended to before Fleet Street warmed to its work, that the
pair were obliged, outside, to part company on the spot, and it
was only on the morrow, a Saturday, that they could taste again
of that comparison of notes which made for each the main savour,
albeit slightly acrid, of their current consciousness. The air was
full, as from afar, of the grand indifference of spring, of which the
breath could be felt so much before the face could be seen, and
they had bicycled side by side out to Richmond Park as with the
impulse to meet it on its way. They kept a Saturday, when possible, sacred to the Suburbs as distinguished from the Papers –
when possible being largely when Maud could achieve the use of
the somewhat fatigued family machine. Many sisters contended
for it, under whose flushed pressure it might have been seen spinning in many different directions. Superficially, at Richmond, our

young couple rested – found a quiet corner to lounge deep in the Park, with their machines propped by one side of a great tree and their associated backs sustained by another. But agitation, finer than the finest scorching, was in the air for them; it was made sharp, rather abruptly, by a vivid outbreak from Maud. It was very well, she observed, for her friend to be clever at the expense of the general 'greed', he saw it in the light of his own jolly luck, and what she saw, as it happened, was nothing but the general art of letting you starve, yourself, in your hole. At the end of five minutes her companion had turned quite pale with having to face the large extent of her confession. It was a confession for the reason that in the first place it evidently cost her an effort that pride had again and again successfully prevented, and because in the second she had thus the air of having lived overmuch on swagger. She could scarce have said at this moment what, for a good while, she had really lived on, and she didn't let him know now to complain either of her privation or of her disappointments. She did it to show why she couldn't go with him when he was so awfully sweeping. There were at any rate apparently, all over, two wholly different sets of people. If everyone rose to his bait no creature had ever risen to hers; and that was the grim truth of her position, which proved at the least that there were two quite different kinds of luck. They told two different stories of human vanity; they couldn't be reconciled. And the poor girl put it in a nutshell. 'There's but one person I've *ever* written to who has so much as noticed my letter.'

He wondered, painfully affected – it rather overwhelmed him; he took hold of it at the easiest point. 'One person – ?'

'The misguided man we had tea with. He alone – *he* rose.'

'Well then, you see that when they do rise they *are* misguided. In other words they're donkeys.'

'What I see is that I don't strike the right ones and that I haven't therefore your ferocity; that is my ferocity, if I have any, rests on a different ground. You'll say that I go for the wrong people; but I don't, God knows – witness Mortimer Marshal – fly too high. I picked him out, after prayer and fasting, as just the likeliest of the likely – not anybody a bit grand and yet not quite

162

a nobody; and by an extraordinary chance I was justified. Then I pick out others who seem just as good, I pray and fast, and no sound comes back. But I work through my ferocity too,' she stiffly continued, 'though at first it was great, feeling as I did that when my bread and butter was in it people had no right not to oblige me. It was their duty – what they were prominent *for* – to be interviewed, so as to keep me going; and I did as much for them any day as they would be doing for me.'

Bight heard her, but for a moment said nothing. 'Did you tell them that? I mean to say to them it was your little all?'

'Not vulgarly – I know how. There are ways of saying it's "important"; and I hint it just enough to see that the importance fetches them no more than anything else. It isn't important to *them*. And I, in their place,' Maud went on, 'wouldn't answer either; I'll be hanged if ever I would. That's what it comes to, that there *are* two distinct lots, and that my luck, being born so, is always to try the snubbers. You were born to know by instinct the others. But it makes me more tolerant.'

'More tolerant of what?' her friend asked.

'Well, of what you described to me. Of what you rail at.'

'Thank you for *me*!' Bight laughed.

'Why not? Don't you live on it?'

'Not in such luxury – you surely must see for yourself – as the distinction you make seems to imply. It isn't luxury to be nine-tenths of the time sick of everything. People moreover are worth to me but tuppence apiece; there are too many, confound them – so many that I don't see really how any can be left over for *your* superior lot. It *is* a chance,' he pursued – 'I've had refusals too – though I confess they've sometimes been of the funniest. Besides, I'm getting out of it,' the young man wound up. 'God knows I want to. My advice to you,' he added in the same breath, 'is to sit tight. There are as good fish in the sea –!'

She waited a moment. 'You're sick of everything and you're getting out of it; it's not good enough for you, in other words, but it's still good enough for me. Why am I to sit tight when you sit so loose?'

'Because what you want will come – can't help coming. Then,

in time, you'll also get out of it. But then you'll have had it, as I have, and the good of it.'

'But what, really, if it breeds nothing but disgust,' she asked, 'do you *call* the good of it?'

'Well, two things. First the bread and butter, and then the fun. I repeat it – sit tight.'

'Where's the fun,' she asked again, 'of learning to despise people?'

'You'll see when it comes. It will all be upon you, it will change for you any day. Sit tight, sit tight.'

He expressed such confidence that she might for a minute have been weighing it. 'If you get out of it, what will you do?'

'Well, imaginative work. This job has made me at least *see*. It has given me the loveliest tips.'

She had still another pause. 'It has given me – *my* experience has – a lovely tip too.'

'And what's that?'

'I've told you before – the tip of pity. I'm so much sorrier for them all – panting and gasping for it like fish out of water – than I am anything else.'

He wondered. 'But I thought that was what just isn't your experience.'

'Oh, I mean then,' she said impatiently, 'that my tip is from yours. It's only a different tip. I want to save them.'

'Well,' the young man replied, and as if the idea had had a meaning for him, 'saving them may perhaps work out as a branch. The question is can you be paid for it?'

'Beadel-Muffet would pay me,' Maud suddenly suggested.

'Why, that's just what I'm expecting,' her companion laughed, 'that he will, after tomorrow – directly or indirectly – do *me*.'

'Will you take it from him then only to get him in deeper, as that's what you perfectly know you'll do? You won't save him; you'll lose him.'

'What then would you, in the case,' Bight asked, 'do for your money?'

Well, the girl thought. 'I'd get him to see me – I should have first, I recognize, to catch my hare – and then I'd work up my

stuff. Which would be boldly, quite by a master-stroke, a statement of his fix – of the fix, I mean, of his wanting, his supplicating
to be dropped. I'd give out that it would really oblige. Then I'd
send my copy about, and the rest of the matter would take care of
itself. I don't say *you* could do it that way – you'd have a different
effect. But I should be able to trust the thing, being mine, not to be
looked at, or, if looked at, chucked straight into the basket. I
should so have, to that extent, handled the matter, and I should
so, by merely touching it, have broken the spell. That's my one
line – I stop things off by touching them. There'd never be a word
about him more.'

Her friend, with his legs out and his hands locked at the back of
his neck, had listened with indulgence. 'Then hadn't I better
arrange it for you that Beadel-Muffet shall see you?'

'Oh, not after you've damned him!'

'You want to see him first?'

'It will be the only way – to be of any use to him. You ought to
wire him in fact not to open his mouth till he has seen me.'

'Well, I will,' said Bight at last. 'But, you know, we shall lose
something very handsome – his struggle, all in vain, with his fate.
Noble sport, the sight of it all.' He turned a little, to rest on his
elbow, and, cycling suburban young man as he was, he might have
been, outstretched under his tree, melancholy Jacques looking off
into a forest glade, even as sailor-hatted Maud, in – for elegance –
a new cotton blouse and a long-limbed angular attitude, might
have prosefully suggested the mannish Rosalind. He raised his
face in appeal to her. 'Do you really ask me to sacrifice it?'

'Rather than sacrifice *him*? Of course I do.'

He said for a while nothing more; only, propped on his elbow,
lost himself again in the Park. After which he turned back to her.
'Will you have me?' he suddenly asked.

'"Have you" – ?'

'Be my bonny bride. For better, for worse. I hadn't, upon my
honour,' he explained with obvious sincerity, 'understood you
were so down.'

'Well, it isn't so bad as that,' said Maud Blandy.

'So bad as taking up with *me*?'

'It isn't as bad as having let you know – when I didn't want you to.'

He sank back again with his head dropped, putting himself more at his ease. 'You're too proud – that's what's the matter with you. And I'm too stupid.'

'No, you're not,' said Maud grimly. 'Not stupid.'

'Only cruel, cunning, treacherous, cold-blooded, vile?' He drawled the words out softly, as if they sounded fair.

'And I'm not stupid either,' Maud Blandy went on. 'We just, poor creatures – well, we just *know*.'

'Of course we do. So why do you want us to drug ourselves with rot? To go on as if we didn't know?'

She made no answer for a moment; then she said: 'There's good to be known too.'

'Of course, again. There are all sorts of things, and some much better than others. That's why,' the young man added, 'I just put that question to you.'

'Oh no, it isn't. You put it to me because you think I feel I'm no good.'

'How so, since I keep assuring you that you've only to wait? How so, since I keep assuring you that if you do wait it will all come with a rush? But say I *am* sorry for you,' Bight lucidly pursued; 'how does that prove either that my motive is base or that I do you a wrong?'

The girl waived this question, but she presently tried another. 'Is it your idea that we should live on all the people –?'

'The people we catch? Yes, old man, till we can do better.'

'My conviction is,' she soon returned, 'that if I were to marry you I should dish you. I should spoil the business. It would fall off; and, as I can do nothing myself, then where should we be?'

'Well,' said Bight, 'we mightn't be quite so high up in the scale of the morbid.'

'It's you that are morbid,' she answered. 'You've, in your way – like everyone else, for that matter, all over the place – "sport" on the brain.'

'Well,' he demanded, 'what is sport but success? What is success but sport?'

'Bring that out somewhere. If it be true,' she said, 'I'm glad I'm a failure.'

After which, for a longish space, they sat together in silence, a silence finally broken by a word from the young man. 'But about Mortimer Marshal – how do you propose to save *him*?'

It was a change of subject that might, by its so easy introduction of matter irrelevant, have seemed intended to dissipate whatever was left of his proposal of marriage. That proposal, however, had been somehow both too much in the tone of familiarity to linger and too little in that of vulgarity to drop. It had had no form, but the mild air kept perhaps thereby the better the taste of it. This was sensibly moreover in what the girl found to reply. 'I think, you know, that he'd be no such bad friend. I mean that, with his appetite, there would be something to be done. He doesn't half hate me.'

'Ah, my dear,' her friend ejaculated, 'don't, for God's sake, be low.'

But she kept it up. 'He clings to me. You saw. It's hideous, the way he's able to "do" himself.'

Bight lay quiet, then spoke as with a recall of the Chippendale Club. 'Yes, I couldn't "do" you as he could. But if you don't bring it off – ?'

'Why then does he cling? Oh, because, all the same, I'm potentially the Papers still. I'm at any rate the nearest he has got to them. And then I'm other things.'

'I see.'

'I'm so awfully attractive,' said Maud Blandy. She got up with this and, shaking out her frock, looked at her resting bicycle, looked at the distances possibly still to be gained. Her companion paused, but at last also rose, and by that time she was awaiting him, a little gaunt and still not quite cool, as an illustration of her last remark. He stood there watching her, and she followed this remark up. 'I do, you know, really pity him.'

It had almost a feminine fineness, and their eyes continued to meet. 'Oh, you'll work it!' And the young man went to his machine.

167

4

IT was not till five days later that they again came together, and during these days many things had happened. Maud Blandy had, with high elation, for her own portion, a sharp sense of this ; if it had at the time done nothing more intimate for her the Sunday of bitterness just spent with Howard Bight had started, all abruptly, a turn of the tide of her luck. This turn had not in the least been in the young man's having spoken to her of marriage – since she hadn't even, up to the late hour of their parting, so much as ans-wered him straight: she dated the sense of difference much rather from the throb of a happy thought that had come to her while she cycled home to Kilburnia in the darkness. The throb had made her for the few minutes, tired as she was, put on speed, and it had been the cause of still further proceedings for her the first thing the next morning. The active step that was the essence of these proceedings had almost got itself taken before she went to bed; which indeed was what had happened to the extent of her writing, on the spot, a meditated letter. She sat down to it by the light of the guttering candle that awaited her on the dining-room table and in the stale air of family food that only *had* been – a residuum so at the mercy of mere ventilation that she didn't so much as peep into a cupboard; after which she had been on the point of nipping over, as she would have said, to drop it into that opposite pillar-box whose vivid maw, opening out through thick London nights, had received so many of her fruitless little ventures. But she had checked herself and waited, waited to be sure, with the morning, that her fancy wouldn't fade; posting her note in the end, however, with a confident jerk, as soon as she was up. She had, later on, had business, or at least had sought it, among the haunts that she had taught herself to regard as professional; but neither on the Monday nor on either of the days that directly followed had she encountered there the friend whom it would take a difference in more matters than could as yet be dealt with to enable her to regard, with proper assurance or with proper modesty, as a lover. Whatever he was, none the less, it couldn't otherwise have come to her that it was possible to feel lonely in the Strand. That showed, after all, how thick they must constantly have been – which *was* perhaps a thing to begin to think of in a new, in a steadier light. But it showed doubtless still more that her companion was probably up to something rather awful; it made her wonder, holding her breath a little, about Beadel-Muffet, made her certain that he and his affairs would partly account for Bight's whirl of absence.

Ever conscious of empty pockets, she had yet always a penny, or at least a ha'penny, for a paper, and those she now scanned, she quickly assured herself, were edited quite as usual. Sir A. B. C. Beadel-Muffet K.C.B., M.P. had returned on Monday from Undertone, where Lord and Lady Wispers had, from the previous Friday, entertained a very select party; Sir A. B. C. Beadel-Muffet K.C.B., M.P. was to attend on Tuesday the weekly meeting of the society of the Friends of Rest; Sir A. B. C. Beadel-Muffet K.C.B., M.P. had kindly consented to preside on Wednesday, at Samaritan House, at the opening of the Sale of Work of the Middlesex Incurables. These familiar announcements, however, far from appeasing her curiosity, had an effect upon her nerves; she read into them mystic meanings that she had never read before. Her freedom of mind in this direction was indeed at the same time limited, for her own horizon was already, by the Monday night, bristling with new possibilities, and the Tuesday itself – well, what had the Tuesday itself become, with this eruption, from within, of interest amounting really to a revelation what had the Tuesday itself become but the greatest day yet of her life? Such a description of it would have appeared to apply predominantly to the morning had she not, under the influence, precisely, of the morning's thrill, gone, towards evening, with her design, into the Charing Cross Station. There, at the bookstall, she bought them all, every rag that was hawked; and there, as she unfolded one at a venture, in the crowd and under the lamps, she felt her consciousness further, felt it for the moment quite impressively, enriched 'Personal Peeps – Number Ninety-Three: a Chat with the New Dramatist' needed neither the 'H.B.' as a terminal signature nor a text spangled, to the exclusion of almost everything else, with

Mortimer Marshals that looked as tall as if lettered on posters, to help to account for her young man's use of his time. And yet, as she soon made out, it had been used with an economy that caused her both to wonder and to wince; the 'peep' commemorated being none other than their tea with the artless creature the previous Saturday, and the meagre incidents and pale impressions of that occasion furnishing forth the picture.

Bight had solicited no new interview; he hadn't been such a fool – for she saw, soon enough, with all her intelligence, that this was what he would have been, and that a repetition of contact would have dished him. What he *had* done, she found herself perceiving – and perceiving with an emotion that caused her face to glow – was journalism of the intensest essence; a column concocted of nothing, an omelette made, as it were, without even the breakage of the egg or two that might have been expected to be the price. The poor gentleman's whereabouts at five o'clock was the only egg broken, and this light and delicate crash was the sound in the world that would be sweetest to him. What stuff it had to be, since the writer really knew nothing about him, yet how its being just such stuff made it perfectly serve its purpose! She might have marvelled afresh, with more leisure, at such purposes, but she was lost in the wonder of seeing how, without matter, without thought, without an excuse, without a fact and yet at the same time sufficiently without a fiction, he had managed to be as resonant as if he had beaten a drum on the platform of a booth. And he had not been too personal, not made anything awkward for *her*, had given nothing and nobody away, had tossed the Chippendale Club into the air with such a turn that it had fluttered down again, like a blown feather, miles from its site. The thirty-seven agencies would already be posting to their subscriber thirty-seven copies, and their subscriber, on his side, would be posting, to his acquaintance, many times thirty-seven, and thus at least getting something for his money; but this didn't tell her why her friend had taken the trouble – if it had *been* a trouble; why at all events he had taken the time, pressed as he apparently was for that commodity. These things she was indeed presently to learn, but they were meanwhile part of a suspense composed of more

elements than any she had yet tasted. And the suspense was prolonged, though other affairs too, that were not part of it, almost
equally crowded upon her; the week having almost waned when
relief arrived in the form of a cryptic post-card. The post-card
bore the H.B., like the precious 'Peep', which had already had a
wondrous sequel, and it appointed, for the tea-hour, a place of
meeting familiar to Maud, with the simple addition of the signifi-
cant word 'Larks!'

When the time he had indicated came she waited for him, at
their small table, swabbed like the deck of a steam-packet, nose to
nose with a mustard-pot and a price-list, in the consciousness of
perhaps after all having as much to tell him as to hear from him.
It appeared indeed at first that this might well be the case, for the
questions that came up between them when he had taken his place
were overwhelmingly those he himself insisted on putting. 'What
has he done, what *has* he, and what will he?' – that inquiry, not
loud but deep, had met him as he sat down; without however
producing the least recognition. Then she as soon felt that his
silence and his manner were enough for her, or that, if they
hadn't been, his wonderful look, the straightest she had ever had
from him, would instantly have made them so. He looked at her
hard, hard, as if he had meant 'I say, mind your eyes!' and it
amounted really to a glimpse, rather fearful, of the subject. It was
no joke, the subject, clearly, and her friend had fairly gained age,
as he had certainly lost weight, in his recent dealings with it. It
struck her even, with everything else, that this was positively the
way she would have liked him to show if their union had taken the
form they hadn't reached the point of discussing; wearily coming
back to her from the thick of things, wanting to put on his slippers
and have his tea, all prepared by her and in their place, and
beautifully to be trusted to regale her in his turn. He was excited,
disavowedly, and it took more disavowal still after she had opened
her budget – which she did, in truth, by saying to him as her first
alternative: 'What did you do him *for*, poor Mortimer Marshal?
It isn't that he's not in the seventh heaven –!'

'He *is* in the seventh heaven!' Bight quickly broke in. 'He
doesn't want my blood?'

171

'Did you do him,' she asked, 'that he should want it? It's splendid how you could – simply on that show.'

'That show? Why,' said Howard Bight, 'that show was an immensity. That show was volumes, stacks, abysses.'

He said it in such a tone that she was a little at a loss. 'Oh, you don't want abysses.'

'Not much, to knock off such twaddle. There isn't a breath in it of what I saw. What I saw is my own affair. I've got the abysses for myself. They're in my head – it's always something. But the monster,' he demanded, 'has written you?'

'How couldn't he – that night? I got it the next morning, telling me how much he wanted to thank me and asking me where he might see me. So I went,' said Maud, 'to see him.'

'At his own place again?'

'At his own place again. What do I yearn for but to be received at people's own places?'

'Yes, for the stuff. But when you've had – as you had had from him – the stuff?'

'Well, sometimes, you see, I get more. He gives me all I can take.' It was in her head to ask if by chance Bight were jealous, but she gave it another turn. 'We had a big palaver, partly about you. He appreciates.'

'Me?'

'Me – first of all, I think. All the more that I've had – fancy! – a proof of my stuff, the despised and rejected, as originally concocted, and that he has now seen it. I tried it on again with *Brains*, the night of your thing – sent it off with your thing enclosed as a rouser. They took it, by return, like a shot – you'll see on Wednesday. And if the dear man lives till then, for impatience, I'm to lunch with him that day.'

'I see,' said Bight. 'Well, that was what I did it for. It shows how right I was.'

They faced each other, across their thick crockery, with eyes that said more than their words, and that, above all, said, and asked, other things. So she went on in a moment: 'I don't know what he doesn't expect. And he thinks I can keep it up.'

'Lunch with him *every* Wednesday?'

'Oh, he'd give me my lunch, and more. It was last Sunday that you were right – about my sitting close,' she pursued. 'I'd have been a pretty fool to jump. Suddenly, I see, the music begins. I'm awfully obliged to you.'

'You feel,' he presently asked, 'quite differently – so differently that I've missed my chance? I don't care for *that* serpent, but there's something else that you don't tell me.' The young man, detached and a little spent, with his shoulder against the wall and a hand vaguely playing over the knives, forks and spoons, dropped his succession of sentences without an apparent direction. 'Something else has come up, and you're as pleased as Punch. Or, rather, you're not quite entirely so, because you can't goad me to fury. You can't worry me as much as you'd like. Marry me first, old man, and *then* see if I mind. Why shouldn't you keep it up? – I mean lunching with him?' His questions came as in play that was a little pointless, without his waiting more than a moment for answers; though it was not indeed that she might not have answered even in the moment, had not the pointless play been more what she wanted. 'Was it at the place,' he went on, 'that he took us to?'

'Dear no – at his flat, where I've been before. You'll see, in *Brains*, on Wednesday. I don't think I've muffed it – it's really rather there. But he showed me everything this time – the bathroom, the refrigerator, and the machines for stretching his trousers. He has nine, and in constant use.'

'Nine?' said Bight gravely.

'Nine.'

'Nine trousers?'

'Nine machines. I don't know how many trousers.'

'Ah, my dear,' he said, 'that's a grave omission; the want of the information will be felt and resented. But does it all, at any rate,' he asked, 'sufficiently fetch you?' After which, as she didn't speak he lapsed into helpless sincerity. 'Is it really, you think, his dream to secure you?'

She replied, on this, as if his tone made it too amusing. 'Quite. There's no mistaking it. He sees me as, most days in the year, pulling the wires and beating the drum somewhere; that is he sees

173

me of course not exactly as writing about "our home" – once I've
got one – myself, but as procuring others to do it through my
being (as *you've* made him believe) in with the Organs of Public
Opinion. He doesn't see, if I'm half decent, why there shouldn't
be something about him every day in the week. He's all right, and
he's all ready. And who, after all, *can* do him so well as the partner
of his flat? It's like making, in one of those big domestic siphons,
the luxury of the poor, your own soda-water. It comes cheaper,
and it's always on the sideboard. "*Vichy chez soi.*" The interviewer at home.'

Her companion took it in. 'Your place is on *my* sideboard –
you're really a first-class fizz! He steps then, at any rate, into
Beadel-Muffet's place.'

'That,' Maud assented, 'is what he would like to do.' And she
knew more than ever there was something to wait for.

'It's a lovely opening,' Bight returned. But he still said, for the
moment, nothing else; as if, charged to the brim though he had
originally been, she had rather led his thought away.

'What have you done with poor Beadel?' she consequently
asked. 'What is it, in the name of goodness, you're doing *to* him?
It's worse than ever.'

'Of course it's worse than ever.'

'He capers,' said Maud, 'on every housetop – he jumps out of
every bush.' With which her anxiety really broke out. '*Is* it you
that are doing it?'

'If you mean am I seeing him, I certainly am. I'm seeing nobody
else. I assure you he's spread thick.'

'But you're acting for him?'

Bight waited. 'Five hundred people are acting for him; but the
difficulty is that what he calls the "terrific forces of publicity" –
by which he means ten thousand *other* persons – are acting against
him. We've all in fact been turned on – to turn everything off, and
that's exactly the job that makes the biggest noise. It appears
everywhere, in every kind of connection and every kind of type,
that Sir A. B. C. Beadel-Muffet K.C.B., M.P. desires to cease to
appear *anywhere*; and then it appears that his desiring to cease to
appear is observed to conduce directly to his more tremendously

174

appearing, or certainly, and in the most striking manner, to his not in the least *dis*appearing. The workshop of silence roars like the Zoo at dinner-time. He *can't* disappear; he hasn't weight enough to sink; the splash the diver makes, you know, tells where he is. If you ask me what I'm doing,' Bight wound up, 'I'm holding him under water. But we're in the middle of the pond, the banks are thronged with spectators, and I'm expecting from day to day to see stands erected and gate-money taken. There,' he wearily smiled, 'you have it. Besides,' he then added with an odd change of tone, 'I rather think you'll see tomorrow.'

He had made her at last horribly nervous. 'What shall I see?'

'It will all be out.'

'Then why shouldn't you tell me?'

'Well,' the young man said, 'he *has* disappeared. There you are. I mean personally. He's not to be found. But nothing could make more, you see, for ubiquity. The country will ring with it. He vanished on Tuesday night – was then last seen at his club. Since then he has given no sign. How can a man disappear who does *that* sort of thing? It is, as you say, to caper on the housetops. But it will only be known tonight.'

'Since when, then,' Maud asked, 'have you known it?'

'Since three o'clock today. But I've kept it. I *am* – a while longer – keeping it.'

She wondered; she was full of fears. 'What do you expect to get for it?'

'Nothing – if you spoil my market. I seem to make out that you want to.'

She gave this no heed; she had her thought. 'Why then did you three days ago wire me a mystic word?'

'Mystic –?'

'What do you call "Larks"?'

'Oh, I remember. Well, it was because I saw larks coming; because I saw, I mean, what has happened. I was sure it would have to happen.'

'And what the mischief *is* it?'

Bight smiled. 'Why, what I tell you. That he has gone.'

'Gone where?'

'Simply bolted to parts unknown. "Where" is what nobody who belongs to him is able in the least to say, or seems likely to be able.'

'Any more than why?'

'Any more than why.'

'Only *you* are able to say that?'

'Well,' said Bight, 'I can say what has so lately stared me in the face, what he has been thrusting at me in all its grotesqueness: his desire for a greater privacy worked through the Papers themselves. He came to me with it,' the young man presently added. 'I didn't go to *him*.'

'And he trusted you,' Maud replied.

'Well, you see what I have given him – the very flower of my genius. What more do you want? I'm spent, seedy, sore. I'm sick,' Bight declared, 'of his beastly funk.'

Maud's eyes, in spite of it, were still a little hard. 'Is he thoroughly sincere?'

'Good God, no! How *can* he be? Only trying it – as a cat, for a jump, tries too smooth a wall. He drops straight back.'

'Then isn't his funk real?'

'As real as he himself is.'

Maud wondered. 'Isn't his flight –?'

'That's what we shall see!'

'Isn't,' she continued, 'his reason?'

'Ah,' he laughed out, 'there you are again!'

But she had another thought and was not discouraged. 'Mayn't he be, honestly, mad?'

'Mad – oh yes. But not, I think, honestly. He's not honestly anything in the world but the Beadel-Muffet of our delight.'

'Your delight,' Maud observed after a moment, 'revolts me.' And then she said: 'When did you last see him?'

'On Tuesday at six, love. I was one of the last.'

'Decidedly, too, then, I judge, one of the worst.' She gave him her idea. 'You hounded him on.'

'I reported,' said Bight, 'success. Told him how it was going.'

'Oh, I can see you! So that if he's dead –'

176

'Well?' asked Bight blandly.

'His blood is on your hands.'

He eyed his hands a moment. 'They *are* dirty for him! But now, darling,' he went on, 'be so good as to show me yours.'

'Tell me first,' she objected, 'what you believe. *Is* it suicide?'

'I think that's the thing for us to make it. Till somebody,' he smiled, 'makes it something else.' And he showed how he warmed to the view. 'There are weeks of it, dearest, yet.'

He leaned more towards her, with his elbows on the table, and in this position, moved by her extreme gravity, he lightly flicked her chin with his finger. She threw herself, still grave, back from his touch, but they remained thus a while closely confronted. 'Well,' she at last remarked, 'I shan't pity you.'

'You make it, then, everyone except me?'

'I mean,' she continued, 'if you do have to loathe yourself.'

'Oh, I shan't miss it.' And then as if to show how little, 'I did mean it, you know, at Richmond,' he declared.

'I won't have you if you've killed him,' she presently returned.

'You'll decide in that case for the *nine*?' And as the allusion, with its funny emphasis, left her blank: 'You want to wear *all* the trousers?'

'You deserve,' she said, when light came, 'that I should take him.' And she kept it up. 'It's a lovely flat.'

Well, he could do as much. 'Nine, I suppose, appeals to you as the number of the muses?'

This short passage, remarkably, for all its irony, brought them together again, to the extent at least of leaving Maud's elbows on the table and of keeping her friend, now a little back in his chair, firm while he listened to her. So the girl came out. 'I've seen Mrs Chorner three times. I wrote that night, after our talk at Richmond, asking her to oblige. And I put on cheek as I had never, never put it. I said the public would be so glad to hear from her "on the occasion of her engagement".'

'Do you call that cheek?' Bight looked amused. 'She at any rate rose straight.'

'No, she rose crooked; but she rose. What you had told me there in the Park – well, immediately happened. She did consent to see me, and so far you had been right in keeping me up to it. But what do you think it was for?'

'To show you *her* flat, *her* tub, *her* petticoats?'

'She doesn't live in a flat; she lives in a house of her own, and a jolly good one, in Green Street, Park Lane; though I did, as happened, see her tub, which is a dream – all marble and silver, like a kind of a swagger sarcophagus, a thing for the Wallace Collection; and though her petticoats, as she first shows, seem all that, if you wear petticoats yourself, you can look at. There's no doubt of her money – given her place and her things, and given her appearance too, poor dear, which would take some doing.'

'She squints?' Bight sympathetically asked.

'She's so ugly that she *has* to be rich – she couldn't afford it on less than five thousand a year. As it is, I could well see, she can afford anything – even such a nose. But she's funny and decent; sharp, but a really good sort. And they're *not* engaged.'

'She told you so? Then there you are!'

'It all depends,' Maud went on; 'and you don't know where I am at all. *I* know what it depends on.'

'Then there you are again! It's a mine of gold.'

'Possibly, but not in your sense. She wouldn't give me the first word of an interview – it wasn't for that she received me. It was for something much better.'

Well, Bight easily guessed. 'For *my* job?'

'To see what can be done. She loathes his publicity.'

The young man's face lighted. 'She told you so?'

'She received me on purpose to tell me.'

'Then why do you question my "larks"? What do you want more?'

'I want nothing – with what I have: nothing, I mean, but to help her. We made friends – I like her. And she likes *me*,' said Maud Blandy.

'Like Mortimer Marshal, precisely.'

'No, precisely not like Mortimer Marshal. I caught, on the spot, her idea – *that* was what took her. Her idea is that I can help her – help her to keep them quiet about Beadel: for which purpose

178

I seem to have struck her as falling from the skies, just at the right moment, into her lap.'

Howard Bight followed, yet lingered by the way. 'To keep *whom* quiet – ?'

'Why, the beastly Papers – what we've been talking about. She wants him straight out of them – *straight*.'

'She too ?' Bight wondered. 'Then *she's* in terror ?'

'No, not in terror – or it wasn't that when I last saw her. But in mortal disgust. She feels it has gone too far – which is what she wanted me, as an honest, decent, likely young woman, up to my neck in it, as she supposed, to understand from her. My relation with her is now that I do understand and that if an improvement takes place I shan't have been the worse for it. Therefore you see,' Maud went on, 'you simply cut my throat when you prevent improvement.'

'Well, my dear,' her friend returned, 'I won't let you bleed to death.' And he showed, with this, as confessedly struck. 'She doesn't then, you think, *know* – ?'

'Know what ?'

'Why, what, about him, there may *be* to be known. Doesn't know of his flight.'

'She didn't – certainly.'

'Nor of anything to make it likely ?'

'What you call his queer reason ? No – she named it to me no more than you have; though she does mention, distinctly, that he himself hates, or pretends to hate, the exhibition daily made of him.'

'She speaks of it,' Bight asked, 'as pretending – ?'

Maud straightened it out. 'She feels him – *that* she practically told me – as rather ridiculous. She honestly has her feeling; and, upon my word, it's what I like her for. Her stomach has turned and she has made it her condition. "Muzzle your Press," she says; "*then* we'll talk." She gives him three months – she'll give him even six. And this, meanwhile – when he comes to *you* – is how you forward the muzzling.'

'The Press, my child,' Bight said, 'is the watchdog of civilization, and the watchdog happens to be – it can't be helped – in a

179

chronic state of *rabies*. Muzzling is easy talk; one can but keep the animal on the run. Mrs Chorner, however,' he added, 'seems a figure of fable.'

'It's what I told you she would have to be when, some time back, you threw out, as a pure hypothesis, to supply the man with a motive, your exact vision of her. Your motive has come true,' Maud went on – 'with the difference only, if I understand you, that this doesn't appear the whole of it. That doesn't matter' – she frankly paid him a tribute. 'Your forecast was inspiration.'

'A stroke of genius' – he had been the first to feel it. But there were matters less clear. 'When did you see her last?'

'Four days ago. It was the third time.'

'And even then she didn't imagine the truth about him?'

'I don't know, you see,' said Maud, 'what you *call* the truth.'

'Well, that he – quite by that time – didn't know where the deuce to turn. That's truth enough.'

Maud made sure. 'I don't see how she can have known it and not have been upset. She wasn't,' said the girl, 'upset. She *isn't* upset. But she's original.'

'Well, poor thing,' Bight remarked, 'she'll have to be.'

'Original?'

'Upset. Yes, and original too, if she doesn't give up the job.' It had held him an instant – but there were many things. 'She sees the wild ass he is, and yet she's willing –?'

'"Willing" is just what I asked *you* three months ago,' Maud returned, 'how she *could* be.'

He had lost it – he tried to remember. 'What then did I say?'

'Well, practically, that women are idiots. Also, I believe, that he's a dazzling beauty.'

'Ah yes, he *is*, poor wretch, though beauty today in distress.'

'Then there you are,' said Maud. They had got up, as at the end of their story, but they stood a moment while he waited for change. 'If it comes out,' the girl dropped, '*that* will save him. If he's dishonoured – as I see her – she'll have him, because then he won't be ridiculous. And I can understand it.'

Bight looked at her in such appreciation that he forgot, as he pocketed it, to glance at his change. 'Oh, you creatures –!'

'Idiots, aren't we?'

Bight let the question pass, but still with his eyes on her, 'You ought to want him to *be* dishonoured.'

'I can't want him, then – if he's to get the good of it – to be dead.'

Still for a little he looked at her. 'And if *you're* to get the good?' But she had turned away, and he went with her to the door, before which, when they had passed out, they had in the side-street, a backwater to the flood of the Strand, a further sharp colloquy. They were alone, the small street for a moment empty, and they felt at first that they had adjourned to a greater privacy, of which, for that matter, he took prompt advantage. 'You're to lunch again with the man of the flat?'

'Wednesday, as I say; 1.45.'

'Then oblige me by stopping away.'

'You don't like it?' Maud asked.

'Oblige me, oblige me,' he repeated.

'And disoblige *him*?'

'Chuck him. We've started him. It's enough.'

Well, the girl but wanted to be fair. 'It's *you* who started him; so I admit you're quits.'

'That then started *you* – made *Brains* repent; so you see what you both owe me. I let the creature off, but I hold you to your debt. There's only one way for you to meet it.' And then as she but looked into the roaring Strand: 'With worship.' It made her, after a minute, meet his eyes, but something just then occurred that stayed any word on the lips of either. A sound reached their ears, as yet unheeded, the sound of newsboys in the great thoroughfare shouting 'extra-specials' and mingling with the shout a catch that startled them. The expression in their eyes quickened as they heard, borne on the air, 'Mysterious Disappearance –!' and then lost it in the hubbub. It was easy to complete the cry, and Bight himself gasped. 'Beadel-Muffet? Confound them!'

'Already?' Maud had turned positively pale.

'They've got it first – be hanged to them!'

Bight gave a laugh – a tribute to their push – but her hand was on his arm for a sign to listen again. It was there, in the raucous throats; it was there, for a penny, under the lamps and in the thick of the stream that stared and passed and left it. They caught the whole thing – 'Prominent Public Man!' And there was something brutal and sinister in the way it was given to the flaring night, to the other competing sounds, to the general hardness of hearing and sight which was yet, on London pavements, compatible with an interest sufficient for cynicism. He had been, poor Beadel, public and prominent, but he had never affected Maud Blandy at least as so marked with this character as while thus loudly committed to extinction. It was horrid – it was tragic; yet her lament for him was dry. 'If he's gone I'm dished.'

'Oh, he's gone – now,' said Bight.

'I mean if he's dead.'

'Well, perhaps he isn't. I see,' Bight added, 'what you do mean. If he's dead you can't kill him.'

'Oh, she wants him alive,' said Maud.

'Otherwise she can't chuck him?'

To which the girl, however, anxious and wondering, made no direct reply. 'Good-bye to Mrs Chorner. And I owe it to *you*.'

'Ah, my love!' he vaguely appealed.

'Yes, it's you who have destroyed him, and it makes up for what you've done *for* me.'

'I've done it, you mean, against you? I didn't know,' he said, 'you'd take it so hard.'

Again, as he spoke, the cries sounded out: 'Mysterious Disappearance of Prominent Public Man!' It seemed to swell as they listened; Maud started with impatience. 'I hate it too much,' she said, and quitted him to join the crowd.

He was quickly at her side, however, and before she reached the Strand he had brought her again to a pause. 'Do you mean you hate it so much you won't have me?'

It had pulled her up short, and her answer was proportionately straight. 'I won't have you if he's dead.'

'Then will you if he's not?'

At this she looked at him hard. 'Do you *know*, first?'

'No – blessed if I do.'

'On your honour?'

'On my honour.'

'Well,' she said after a hesitation, 'if *she* doesn't drop me –'

'It's an understood thing?' he pressed.

But again she hung fire. 'Well, produce him first.'

They stood there striking their bargain, and it was made, by the long look they exchanged, a question of good faith. 'I'll produce him,' said Howard Bight.

5

IF it had not been a disaster, Beadel-Muffet's plunge into the obscure, it would have been a huge success; so large a space did the prominent public man occupy, for the next few days, in the Papers, so near did he come, nearer certainly than ever before, to supplanting other topics. The question of his whereabouts, of his antecedents, of his habits, of his possible motives, of his probable, or improbable, embarrassments, fairly raged, from day to day and from hour to hour, making the Strand, for our two young friends, quite fiercely, quite cruelly vociferous. They met again promptly, in the thick of the uproar, and no other eyes could have scanned the current rumours and remarks so eagerly as Maud's unless it had been those of Maud's companion. The rumours and remarks were mostly very wonderful, and all of a nature to sharpen the excitement produced in the comrades by their being already, as they felt, 'in the know'. Even for the girl this sense existed, so that she could smile at wild surmises; she struck herself as knowing much more than she did, especially as, with the alarm once given, she abstained, delicately enough, from worrying, from catechizing Bight. She only looked at him as to say 'See, while the suspense lasts, how generously I spare you,' and her attitude was not affected by the interested promise he had made her. She believed he knew more than he said, though he had sworn as to what he didn't; she saw him in short as holding some threads but having lost others, and his state of mind, so far as she could read it, represented in equal measure assurances unsupported and anxieties unconfessed. He would have liked to pass for having, on cynical grounds, and for the mere ironic beauty of it, believed that the hero of the hour was only, as he had always been, 'up to' something from which he would emerge more than ever glorious, or at least conspicuous; but, knowing the gentleman was more than anything, more than all else, asinine, he was not deprived of ground in which fear could abundantly grow. If Beadel, in other words, was ass enough, as was conceivable, to be working the occasion, he was by the same token ass enough to have lost control of it, to have committed some folly from which even fools don't rebound. That was the spark of suspicion lurking in the young man's ease, and that, Maud knew, explained something else.

The family and friends had but too promptly been approached, been besieged; yet Bight, in all the promptness, had markedly withdrawn from the game – had had, one could easily judge, already too much to do with it. Who but he, otherwise, would have been so naturally let loose upon the forsaken home, the bewildered circle, the agitated club, the friend who had last conversed with the eminent absentee, the waiter, in exclusive halls, who had served him with five-o'clock tea, the porter, in august Pall Mall, who had called his last cab, the cabman, supremely privileged, who had driven him – where? 'The Last Cab' would, as our young woman reflected, have been a heading so after her friend's own heart, and so consonant with his genius, that it took all her discretion not to ask him how he had resisted it. She didn't ask, she but herself noted the title for future use – she would have at least got that, 'The Last Cab', out of the business; and, as the days went by and the extra-specials swarmed, the situation between them swelled with all the unspoken. Matters that were grave depended on it for each – and nothing so much, for instance, as her seeing Mrs Chorner again. To see that lady as things *had* been had meant that the poor woman might have been helped to believe in her. Believing in her she would have paid her, and Maud, disposed as she was, really had felt capable of earning the pay. Whatever, as the case stood, was caused to hang in the air, nothing dangled more free than the profit derivable from muzzling the Press. With the watchdog to whom Bight had compared it barking for dear life, the moment was scarcely adapted for calling afresh upon a person who had offered a reward for silence. The only silence, as we say, was in the girl's not mentioning to her friend how these embarrassments affected her. Mrs Chorner was a person she liked – a connection more to her taste than any she had professionally made, and the thought of her now on the rack, tormented with suspense, might well have brought to her lips a 'See *there* what you've done!'

There was, for that matter, in Bight's face he couldn't keep it out – precisely the look of seeing it; which was one of her reasons too for not insisting on her wrong. If he couldn't conceal it this was a part of the rest of the unspoken; he didn't allude to the lady lest it might be too sharply said to him that it was on *her* account he should most blush. Last of all he was hushed by the sense of what he had himself said when the news first fell on their ears. His promise to 'produce' the fugitive was still in the air, but with every day that passed the prospect turned less to redemption. Therefore if her own promise, on a different head, depended on it, he was naturally not in a hurry to bring the question to a test. So it was accordingly that they but read the Papers and looked at each other. Maud felt in truth that these organs had never been so worth it, nor either she or her friend – whatever the size of old obligations – so much beholden to them. They helped them to wait, and the better, really, the longer the mystery lasted. It grew of course daily richer, adding to its mass as it went and multiplying its features, looming especially larger through the cloud of correspondence, communication, suggestion, supposition, speculation, with which it was presently suffused. Theories and explanations sprouted at night and bloomed in the morning, to be overtopped at noon by a still thicker crop and to achieve by evening the density of a tropical forest. These, again, were the green glades in which our young friends wandered.

Under the impression of the first night's shock Maud had written to Mortimer Marshal to excuse herself from her engagement to luncheon – a step of which she had promptly advised Bight as a sign of her playing fair. He took it, she could see, for what it was worth, but she could see also how little he now cared. He was thinking of the man with whose strange agitation he had so cleverly and recklessly played, and, in the face of the catastrophe of which they were still so likely to have news, the vanities of smaller fools, the conveniences of first-class flats, the memory of Chippendale teas, ceased to be actual or ceased at any rate to be importunate. Her old interview, furbished into freshness, had appeared, on its Wednesday, in *Brains*, but she had not received in person the renewed homage of its author – she had only, once more, had the vision of his inordinate purchase and diffusion of the precious number. It was a vision, however, at which neither Bight nor she smiled; it was funny on so poor a scale compared with their other show. But it befell that when this latter had, for ten days, kept being funny to the tune that so lengthened their faces, the poor gentleman glorified in *Brains* succeeded in making it clear that he was not easily to be dropped. He wanted now, evidently, as the girl said to herself, to live at concert pitch, and she gathered, from three or four notes, to which, at short intervals, he treated her, that he was watching in anxiety for reverberations not as yet perceptible. His expectation of results from what our young couple had done for him would, as always, have been a thing for pity with a young couple less imbued with the comic sense; though indeed it would also have been a comic thing for a young couple less attentive to a different drama. Disappointed of the girl's company at home the author of *Corisanda* had proposed fresh appointments, which she had desired at the moment, and indeed more each time, not to take up; to the extent even that, catching sight of him, unperceived, on one of these occasions, in her inveterate Strand, she checked on the spot a first impulse to make herself apparent. He was before her, in the crowd, and going the same way. He had stopped a little to look at a shop, and it was then that she swerved in time not to pass close to him. She turned and reversed, conscious and convinced that he was, as she mentally put it, on the prowl for her.

She herself, poor creature – as she also mentally put it – she herself was shamelessly on the prowl, but it wasn't, for her self-respect, to get herself puffed, it wasn't to pick up a personal advantage. It was to pick up news of Beadel-Muffet, to be near the extra-specials, and it was, also – as to this she was never blind

– to cultivate that nearness by chances of Howard Bight. The blessing of blindness, in truth, at this time, she scantily enjoyed – being perfectly aware of the place occupied, in her present attitude to that young man, by the simple impossibility of not seeing him. She had done with him, certainly, if he *had* killed Beadel, and nothing was now growing so fast as the presumption in favour of some catastrophe, yet shockingly to be revealed, enacted somewhere in desperate darkness – though probably 'on lines', as the Papers said, anticipated by none of the theorists in their own columns, any more than by clever people at the clubs, where the betting was so heavy. She had done with him, indubitably, but she had not – it was equally unmistakable – done with letting him see how thoroughly she *would* have done; or, to feel about it otherwise, she was laying up treasure in time – as against the privations of the future. She was affected moreover – perhaps but half-consciously – by another consideration; her attitude to Mortimer Marshal had turned a little to fright; she wondered, uneasily, at impressions she might have given him; and she had it, finally, on her mind that, whether or no the vain man believed in them, there must be a limit to the belief she had communicated to her friend. He *was* her friend, after all – whatever should happen; and there were things that, even in that hampered character, she couldn't allow him to suppose. It was a queer business now, in fact, for her to ask herself if she, Maud Blandy, had produced in any sane human sense an effect of flirtation.

She saw herself in this possibility as in some grotesque reflector, a full-length looking-glass of the inferior quality that deforms and discolours. It made her, as a flirt, a figure for frank derision, and she entertained, honest girl, none of the self-pity that would have spared her a shade of this sharpened consciousness, have taken an inch from facial proportion where it would have been missed with advantage, or added one in such other quarters as would have welcomed the gift. She might have counted the hairs of her head, for any wish she could have achieved to remain vague about them, just as she might have rehearsed, disheartened, postures of grace, for any dream she could compass of having ever accidentally struck one. Void, in short, of a personal illusion, exempt with an exemption which left her not less helplessly aware of where her hats and skirts and shoes failed, than of where her nose and mouth and complexion, and, above all, where her poor figure, without a scrap of drawing, did, she blushed to bethink herself that she might have affected her young man as really bragging of a conquest. Her *other* young man's pursuit of her, what was it but rank greed – not in the least for her person, but for the connection of which he had formed so preposterous a view? She was ready now to say to herself that she had swaggered to Bight for the joke – odd indeed though the wish to undeceive him at the moment when he would have been more welcome than ever to think what he liked. The only thing she wished him not to think, as she believed, was that she thought Mortimer Marshal thought her – or anyone on earth thought her – intrinsically charming. She didn't want to put to him 'Do you suppose I suppose that if it came to the point –?' her reasons for such avoidance being easily conceivable. He was not to suppose that, in any such quarter, she struck herself as either casting a spell or submitting to one; only, while their crisis lasted, rectifications were scarce in order. She couldn't remind him even, without a mistake, that she had but wished to worry him; because in the first place that suggested again a pretension in her (so at variance with the image in the mirror) to put forth arts – suggested possibly even that she used similar ones when she lunched, in bristling flats, with the pushing; and because in the second it would have seemed a sort of challenge to him to renew his appeal.

Then, further and most of all, she had a doubt which by itself would have made her wary, as it distinctly, in her present suspended state, made her uncomfortable; she was haunted by the after-sense of having perhaps been fatuous. A spice of conviction, in respect to what was open to her, an element of elation, in her talk to Bight about Marshal, had there not, after all, been? Hadn't she a little liked to think the wretched man *could* cling to her? and hadn't she also a little, for herself, filled out the future, in fancy, with the picture of the droll relation? She had seen it as droll, evidently; but had she seen it as impossible, unthinkable? It had become unthinkable now, and she was not wholly unconscious of how the change had worked. Such workings were queer – but there they were; the foolish man had become odious to her precisely *because* she was hardening her face for Bight. The latter was no foolish man, but this it was that made it the more a pity he should have placed the impassable between them. That was what, as the days went on, she felt herself take in. It was there, the impassable – she couldn't lucidly have said why, couldn't have explained the thing on the real scale of the wrong her comrade had done. It was a wrong, it was a wrong – she couldn't somehow get out of that; which was a proof, no doubt, that she confusedly tried. The author of *Corisanda* was sacrificed in the effort – for ourselves it may come to that. Great to poor Maud Blandy as well, for that matter, great, yet also attaching, were the obscurity and ambiguity in which some impulses lived and moved – the rich gloom of their combinations, contradictions, inconsistencies, surprises. It rested her verily a little from her straightness – the line of a character, she felt, markedly like the line of the Edgware Road and of Maida Vale – that she *could* be queerly inconsistent, and inconsistent in the hustling Strand, where, if anywhere, you had, under pain of hoofs and wheels, to decide whether or no you would cross. She had moments, before shop-windows, into which she looked without seeing, when all the unuttered came over her. She had once told her friend that she pitied everyone, and at these moments, in sharp unrest, she pitied Bight for their tension, in which nothing was relaxed.

It was all too mixed and too strange – each of them in a different corner with a different impossibility. There was her own, in far Kilburnia; and there was her friend's, everywhere – for where didn't he go? and there was Mrs Chorner's, on the very edge of Park 'Line', in spite of all petticoats and marble baths; and there was Beadel-Muffet's, the wretched man, God only knew where – which was what made the whole show supremely incoherent: he ready to give his head, if, as seemed so unlikely, he still *had* a head, to steal into cover and keep under, out of the glare; he having scoured Europe, it might so well be guessed, for some hole in which the Papers wouldn't find him out, and then having – what else was there by this time to presume? – died, in the hole, as the only way not to see, to hear, to know, let alone *be* known, heard, seen. Finally, while he lay there relieved by the only relief, here was poor Mortimer Marshal, undeterred, undismayed, unperceiving, so hungry to be paragraphed in something like the same fashion and published on something like the same scale, that, for the very blindness of it, he couldn't read the lesson that was in the air, and scrambled, to his utmost, towards the boat itself that ferried the warning ghost. Just *that*, beyond everything, was the incoherence that made for rather dismal farce, and on which Bight had put his finger in naming the author of *Corisanda* as a candidate, in turn, for the comic, the tragic vacancy. It was a wonderful moment for such an ideal, and the sight was not really to pass from her till she had seen the whole of the wonder. A fortnight had elapsed since the night of Beadel's disappearance, and the conditions attending the afternoon performances of the Finnish drama had in some degree reproduced themselves – to the extent, that is, of the place, the time and several of the actors involved; the audience, for reasons traceable, being differently composed. A lady of 'high social position', desirous still further to elevate that character by the obvious aid of the theatre, had engaged a playhouse for a series of occasions on which she was to affront in person whatever volume of attention she might succeed in collecting. Her success had not immediately been great, and by the third or the fourth day the public consciousness was so markedly astray that the means taken to recover it penetrated, in the shape of a complimentary ticket, even to our young woman. Maud had communicated with Bight, who could be sure of a ticket, proposing to him that they should go together and offering to await him in the porch of the theatre. He joined her there, but with so queer a face – for her subtlety – that she paused before him, previous to their going in, with a straight 'You *know* something!'

'About that rank idiot?' He shook his head, looking kind enough; but it didn't make him, she felt, more natural. 'My dear, it's all beyond me.'

'I mean,' she said with a shade of uncertainty, 'about poor dear Beadel.'

'So do I. So does everyone. No one now, at any moment, means anything about anyone else. But I've lost intellectual control – of the extraordinary case. I flattered myself I still had a certain amount. But the situation at last escapes me. I break down. Non comprenny? I give it up.'

She continued to look at him hard. 'Then what's the matter with you?'

'Why, just *that*, probably – that I feel like a clever man "done", and that your tone with me adds to the feeling. Or, putting it otherwise, it's perhaps only just one of the ways in which I'm so interesting; that, with the life we lead and the age we live in, there's *always* something the matter with me – there can't help being: some rage, some disgust, some fresh amazement against which one hasn't, for all one's experience, been proof. That sense – of having been sold again – produces emotions that may well, on occasion, be reflected in the countenance. There you are.'

Well, he might say that, 'There you are,' as often as he liked without, at the pass they had come to, making her in the least see where she was. She was only just where she stood, a little apart in the lobby, listening to his words, which she found eminently characteristic of him, struck with an odd impression of his talking against time, and, most of all, tormented to recognize that she could fairly do nothing better, at such a moment, than feel he was awfully nice. The moment – that of his most blandly (she would have said in the case of another most impudently) failing, all round, to satisfy her – was appropriate only to some emotion consonant with her dignity. It was all crowded and covered, hustled and interrupted now; but what really happened in this brief passage, and with her finding no words to reply to him, was that dignity quite appeared to collapse and drop from her, to sink to the floor, under the feet of people visibly bristling with 'paper', where the young man's extravagant offer of an arm, to put an end and help her in, had the effect of an invitation to leave it lying to be trampled on.

Within, once seated, they kept their places through two intervals, but at the end of the third act – there were to be no less than five – they fell in with a movement that carried half the audience to the outer air. Howard Bight desired to smoke, and Maud offered to accompany him, for the purpose, to the portico, where, somehow, for both of them, the sense was immediately strong that *this*, the squalid Strand, damp yet incandescent, ugly yet eloquent, familiar yet fresh, was life, palpable, ponderable, possible, much more than the stuff, neither scenic nor cosmic, they had quitted. The difference came to them, from the street, in a moist mild blast, which they simply took in, at first, in a long draught, as more amusing than their play, and which, for the moment, kept them conscious of the voices of the air as of something mixed and vague. The next thing, of course, however, was that they heard the hoarse newsmen, though with the special sense of the sound not standing out – which, so far as it did come, made them exchange a look. There was no hawker just then within call.

'What are they crying?'

'Blessed if I care!' Bight said while he got his light – which he had but just done when they saw themselves closely approached. The Papers had come into sight in the form of a small boy bawling the 'Winner' of something, and at the same moment they recognized their reprieve they recognized also the presence of Mortimer Marshal.

He had no shame about it. 'I fully believed I should find you.'

'But you haven't been,' Bight asked, 'inside?'

'Not at today's performance – I only just thought I'd pass. But at each of the others,' Mortimer Marshal confessed.

'Oh, you're a devotee,' said Bight, whose reception of the poor man contended, for Maud's attention, with this extravagance of the poor man's own importunity. Their friend had sat through the piece three times on the chance of her being there for one or other of the acts, and if he had given that up in discouragement he still hovered and waited. Who now, moreover, was to say he wasn't rewarded? To find her companion as well as at last to find herself gave the reward a character that it took, somehow, for her eye, the whole of this misguided person's curiously large and flat, but distinctly bland, sweet, solicitous countenance to express. It came over the girl with horror that here was a material object – the incandescence, on the edge of the street, didn't spare it – which she had had perverse moments of seeing fixed before her for life. She asked herself, in this agitation, what she would have likened it to; more than anything perhaps to a large clean china plate, with a neat 'pattern', suspended, to the exposure of hapless heads, from the centre of the domestic ceiling. Truly she was, as by the education of the strain undergone, learning something every hour – it seemed so to be the case that a strain enlarged the mind, formed the taste, enriched, even, the imagination. Yet in spite of this last fact, it must be added, she continued rather mystified by the actual pitch of her comrade's manner, Bight really behaving as if he enjoyed their visitor's 'note'. He treated him so decently, as they said, that he might suddenly have taken to liking his company; which was an odd appearance till Maud understood it – whereupon it became for her a slightly sinister one. For the effect of the honest gentleman, she by that time saw, was to make her friend nervous and vicious, and the form taken by his irritation was just this dangerous candour, which encouraged the candour of the victim. She had for the latter a residuum of pity, whereas Bight, she felt, had none, and she didn't want him, the poor man, absolutely to pay with his life.

It was clear, however, within a few minutes, that this was what he was bent on doing, and she found herself helpless before his smug insistence. She had taken his measure; he was *made* incorrigibly to try, irredeemably to fail – to be, in short, eternally defeated and eternally unaware. He wouldn't rage – he *couldn't*, for the citadel might, in that case, have been carried by his assault; he would only spend his life in walking round and round it, asking everyone he met how in the name of goodness one did get in. And everyone would make a fool of him – though no one so much as her companion now – and everything would fall from him but the perfection of his temper, of his tailor, of his manners, of his mediocrity. He evidently rejoiced at the happy chance which had presented him again to Bight, and he lost as little time as possible in proposing, the play ended, an adjournment again to tea. The spirit of malice in her comrade, now inordinately excited, met this suggestion with an amendment that fairly made her anxious; Bight threw out, in a word, the idea that he himself surely, this time, should entertain Mr Marshal.

'Only I'm afraid I can take you but to a small pothouse that we poor journalists haunt.'

'They're just the places I delight in – it would be of an extraordinary interest. I sometimes venture into them – feeling awfully strange and wondering, I do assure you, who people are. But to go there with *you* –!' And he looked from Bight to Maud and from Maud back again with such abysses of appreciation that she knew him as lost indeed.

6

IT was demonic of Bight, who immediately answered that he would tell him with pleasure who everyone was, and she felt this the more when her friend, making light of the rest of the entertainment they had quitted, advised their sacrificing it and proceeding to the other scene. He was really too eager for his victim – she wondered what he wanted to do with him. He could only play him at the most a practical joke – invent appetizing identities, once they were at table, for the dull consumers around. No one, at the place they most frequented had an identity in the least appetizing, no one was anyone or anything. It was apparently of the essence of existence on such terms – the terms, at any rate, to which *she* was reduced – that people comprised in it couldn't even minister to each other's curiosity, let alone to envy or awe. She would have wished therefore, for their pursuer, to intervene a little, to warn him against beguilement; but they had moved together along the Strand and then out of it, up a near cross street, without her opening her mouth. Bight, as she felt, was acting to prevent this; his easy talk redoubled, and he led his lamb to the shambles. The talk had jumped to poor Beadel – her friend had startled her by causing it, almost with violence, at a given moment, to take that direction, and he thus quite sufficiently stayed her speech. The people she lived with mightn't make you curious, but there was of course always a sharp exception for *him*. She kept still, in fine, with the wonder of what he wanted; though indeed she might, in the presence of their guest's response, have felt he was already getting it. He was getting, that is – and *she* was, into the bargain – the fullest illustration of the ravage of a passion; so sublimely Marshal rose to the proposition, infernally thrown off, that, in whatever queer box or tight place Beadel might have found himself, it was something, after all, to have so powerfully interested the public. The insidious artless way in which Bight made his point! – 'I don't know that I've ever known the public (and I watch it, as in my trade we have to, day and night) *so* consummately interested.' They had that phenomenon – the present consummate interest – well before them while they sat at their homely meal, served with accessories so different from those of the sweet Chippendale (another chord on which the young man played with just the right effect!), and it would have been hard to say if the guest were, for the first moments, more under the spell of the marvellous 'hold' on the town achieved by the great absentee, or of that of the delicious coarse tablecloth, the extraordinary form of the saltcellars, and the fact that he had within range of sight, at the other end of the room, in the person of the little quiet man with blue spectacles and an obvious wig, the greatest authority in London about the inner life of the criminal classes. Beadel, none the less, came up again and stayed up – would clearly so have been *kept* up, had there been need, by their host, that the girl couldn't at last fail to see how much it was for herself that his intention worked. What *was* it, all the same – since it couldn't be anything so simple as to expose their hapless visitor? What had she to learn about *him*? – especially at the hour of seeing what there was still to learn about Bight. She ended by deciding – for his appearance bore her out – that his explosion was but the form taken by an inward fever. The fever, on this theory, was the result of the final pang of responsibility. The mystery of Beadel had grown too dark to be borne – which they would presently feel; and he was meanwhile in the phase of bluffing it off, precisely because it was to overwhelm him.

'And do you mean you too would pay with your *life*?' He put the question, agreeably, across the table to his guest; agreeably of course in spite of his eye's dry glitter.

His guest's expression, at this, fairly became beautiful. 'Well, it's an awfully nice point. Certainly one would like to *feel* the great murmur surrounding one's name, to *be* there, more or less, so as not to lose the sense of it, and as I really think, you know, the pleasure; the great city, the great empire, the world itself for the moment, hanging literally on one's personality and giving a start, in its suspense, whenever one is mentioned. Big sensation, you know, that,' Mr Marshal pleadingly smiled, 'and of course if one were dead one wouldn't enjoy it. One would have to come to life for that.'

'Naturally,' Bight rejoined – 'only that's what the dead don't do. You can't eat your cake and have it. The question is,' he good-naturedly explained, 'whether you'd be willing, for the certitude of the great murmur you speak of, to part with your life under circumstances of extraordinary mystery.'

His guest earnestly fixed it. 'Whether *I* would be willing?'

'Mr Marshal wonders,' Maud said to Bight, 'if you are, as a person interested in his reputation, definitely proposing to him some such possibility.'

He looked at her, on this, with mild, round eyes, and she felt, wonderfully, that he didn't quite see her as joking. He smiled – he always smiled, but his anxiety showed, and he turned it again to their companion. 'You mean – a – the knowing how it might be *going* to be felt?'

'Well yes – call it that. The consciousness of what one's un-explained extinction – given, to start with, one's high position – would mean, wouldn't be able to *help* meaning, for millions and millions of people. The point is – and I admit it's, as you call it, a 'nice' one – if you can think of the impression so made as worth the purchase. *Naturally*, naturally, there's but the impression you make. You don't receive any. You can't. You've only your confidence – so far as that's an impression. Oh, it *is* indeed a nice point; and I only put it to you,' Bight wound up, 'because, you know, you do like to be recognized.'

Mr Marshal was bewildered, but he was not so bewildered as

not to be able, a trifle coyly, but still quite bravely, to confess to
that. Maud, with her eyes on her friend, found herself thinking of
him as of some plump, innocent animal, more or less of the pink-
eyed rabbit or sleek guinea-pig order, involved in the slow spell of
a serpent of shining scales. Bight's scales, truly, had never so
shone as this evening, and he used to admiration – which was just
a part of the lustre – the right shade of gravity. He was neither so
light as to fail of the air of an attractive offer, nor yet so earnest as
to betray a gibe. He might conceivably have been, as an under-
taker of improvements in defective notorieties, placing before his
guest a practical scheme. It was really quite as if he were ready to
guarantee the 'murmur' if Mr Marshal was ready to pay the
price. And the price wouldn't of course be only Mr Marshal's
existence. All this, at least, if Mr Marshal felt moved to take it so.
The prodigious thing, next, was that Mr Marshal *was* so moved –
though, clearly, as was to be expected, with important qualifica-
tions. 'Do you really mean,' he asked, 'that one would excite *this*
delightful interest?'

'You allude to the charged state of the air on the subject of
Beadel?' Bight considered, looking volumes. 'It would depend a
good deal upon who one *is*.'

He turned, Mr Marshal, again to Maud Blandy and his eyes
seemed to suggest to her that she should put his question for him.
They forgave her, she judged, for having so oddly forsaken him,
but they appealed to her now not to leave him to struggle alone.
Her own difficulty was, however, meanwhile, that she feared to
serve him as he suggested without too much, by way of return,
turning his case to the comic; whereby she only looked at him
hard and let him revert to their friend. 'Oh,' he said, with a rich
wistfulness from which the comic was not absent, 'of course
everyone can't pretend to be Beadel.'

'Perfectly. But we're speaking, after all, of those who do count.'

There was quite a hush, for the minute, while the poor man
faltered. 'Should you say that *I* – in any appreciable way – count?'

Howard Bight distilled honey. 'Isn't it a little a question of how
much we should find you *did*, or, for that matter, might as it were,
be made to, in the event of a real catastrophe?'

Mr Marshal turned pale, yet he met it too with sweetness. 'I like the way' – and he had a glance for Maud – 'you talk of catastrophes!'

His host did the comment justice. 'Oh, it's only because, you see, we're so peculiarly in the presence of one. Beadel shows so tremendously what a catastrophe does for the right person. His absence, you may say, doubles, quintuples, his presence.'

'I see, I see!' Mr Marshal was all there. 'It's awfully interesting to be so present. And yet it's rather dreadful to be so absent.' It had set him fairly musing; for couldn't the opposites be reconciled? 'If he *is*,' he threw out, 'absent –!'

'Why, he's absent, of course,' said Bight, 'if he's dead.'

'And really dead is what you believe him to be?'

He breathed it with a strange break, as from a mind too full. It was on the one hand a grim vision for his own case, but was on the other a kind of clearance of the field. With Beadel out of the way his own case could live, and he was obviously thinking what it might be to be as dead as that and yet as much alive. What his demand first did, at any rate, was to make Howard Bight look straight at Maud. Her own look met him, but she asked nothing now. She felt him somehow fathomless, and his practice with their infatuated guest created a new suspense. He might indeed have been looking at her to learn how to reply, but even were this the case she had still nothing to answer. So in a moment he had spoken without her. 'I've quite given him up.'

It sank into Marshal, after which it produced something. 'He ought then to come back. I mean,' he explained, 'to see for himself – to *have* the impression.'

'Of the noise he has made? Yes' – Bight weighed it – 'that would be the ideal.'

'And it would, if one must call it "noise",' Marshal limpidly pursued, 'make – a – more.'

'Oh, but if you *can't*!'

'Can't, you mean, through having already made so much, add to the quantity?'

'Can't' – Bight was a wee bit sharp – 'come back, confound it, at all. Can't return from the dead!'

Poor Marshal had to take it. 'No – not if you *are* dead.'

'Well, that's what we're talking about.'

Maud, at this, for pity, held out a perch. 'Mr Marshal, I think is talking a little on the basis of the possibility of your not being!' He threw her an instant glance of gratitude, and it gave her a push. 'So long as you're not quite too utterly, you *can* come back.'

'Oh,' said Bight, 'in time for the fuss?'

'Before' – Marshal met it – 'the interest has subsided. It naturally then *wouldn't* – would it? – subside!'

'No,' Bight granted; 'not if it hadn't, through wearing out – I mean your being lost too long – already died out.'

'Oh, of course,' his guest agreed, 'you mustn't be lost *too* long.' A vista had plainly opened to him, and the subject led him on. He had, before its extent, another pause. 'About how long, do you think –?'

Well, Bight *had* to think. 'I should say Beadel had rather overdone it.'

The poor gentleman stared. 'But if he can't help himself –?'

Bight gave a laugh. 'Yes; but in case he could.'

Maud again intervened, and, as her question was for their host, Marshal was all attention. 'Do you consider Beadel has overdone it?'

Well, once more, it took consideration. The issue of Bight's, however, was not of the clearest. 'I don't think we can tell unless he *were* to. I don't think that, without seeing it, and judging by the special case, one can quite know how it would be taken. He might, on the one side, have spoiled, so to speak, his market; and he might, on the other, have scored as never before.'

'It might be,' Maud threw in, 'just the making of him.'

'Surely' – Marshal glowed – 'there's just that chance.'

'What a pity then,' Bight laughed, 'that there isn't someone to take it! For the light it would throw, I mean, on the laws – so mysterious, so curious, so interesting – that govern the great currents of public attention. They're not wholly whimsical – wayward and wild; they have their strange logic, their obscure reason – if one could only get *at* it! The man who does, you see – and who can keep his discovery to himself! – will make his everlasting fortune, as well, no doubt, as that of a few others. It's *our* branch, *our* preoccupation, in fact, Miss Blandy's and mine – this pursuit of the incalculable, this study, to that end, of the great forces of publicity. Only, of course, it must be remembered,' Bight went on, 'that in the case we're speaking of – the man disappearing as Beadel has now disappeared, and supplanting for the time every other topic – must have someone on the spot for him, to keep the pot boiling, someone acting, with real intelligence, in his interest. I mean if he's to get the good of it when he does turn up. It would never do, you see, that *that* should be flat!'

'Oh no, not *flat*, never!' Marshal quailed at the thought. Held as in a vice by his host's high lucidity, he exhaled his interest at every pore. 'It wouldn't be flat for Beadel, would it? – I mean if he *were* to come.'

'Not much! It wouldn't be flat for Beadel – I think I can undertake.' And Bight undertook so well that he threw himself back in his chair with his thumbs in the armholes of his waistcoat and his head very much up. 'The only thing is that for poor Beadel it's a luxury, so to speak, wasted – and so dreadfully, upon my word, that one quite regrets there's no one to step in.'

'To step in?' His visitor hung upon his lips.

'To do the thing better, so to speak – to do it right; to – having raised the whirlwind – really *ride* the storm. To seize the psychological hour.'

Marshal met it, yet he wondered. 'You speak of the reappearance? I see. But the man of the reappearance would have, wouldn't he? – or perhaps I don't follow? – to be the same as the man of the *dis*appearance. It wouldn't do as well – would it? for *somebody else* to turn up?'

Bight considered him with attention – as if there were fine possibilities. 'No; unless such a person should turn up, say – well, with news of him.'

'But what news?'

'With lights – the more lurid the better – *on* the darkness. With the facts, don't you see, *of* the disappearance.'

Marshal, on his side, threw himself back. 'But he'd have to know them!'

'Oh,' said Bight, with prompt portentousness, 'that could be managed.'

It was too much, by this time, for his victim, who simply turned on Maud a dilated eye and a flushed cheek. 'Mr Marshal,' it made her say – 'Mr Marshal would like to turn up.'

Her hand was on the table, and the effect of her words, combined with this, was to cause him, before responsive speech could come, to cover it respectfully but expressively with his own. 'Do you mean,' he panted to Bight, 'that you have, amid the general collapse of speculation, facts to give?'

'I've always facts to give.'

It begot in the poor man a large hot smile. 'But – how shall I say? – authentic, or as I believe you clever people say, "inspired" ones?'

'If I should undertake such a case as we're supposing, I would of course by that circumstance undertake that my facts should be – well, worthy of it. I would take,' Bight on his own part modestly smiled, 'pains with them.'

It finished the business. 'Would you take pains for *me*?'

Bight looked at him now hard. 'Would you like to appear?'

'Oh, "appear"!' Marshal weakly murmured.

'Is it, Mr Marshal, a real proposal? I mean are you prepared–?'

Wonderment sat in his eyes – an anguish of doubt and desire. 'But wouldn't you prepare me –?'

'Would you prepare *me* – that's the point,' Bight laughed – '*to* prepare you?'

There was a minute's mutual gaze, but Marshal took it in. 'I don't know what you're making me say; I don't know what you're making me *feel*. When one is with people so up in these things –' and he turned to his companions, alternately, a look as of conscious doom lighted with suspicion, a look that was like a cry for mercy – 'one feels a little as if one ought to be saved from one's self. For I dare say one's foolish enough with one's poor little wish –'

'The little wish, my dear sir' – Bight took him up – 'to stand out in the world! Your wish is the wish of all high spirits.'

'It's dear of you to say it.' Mr Marshal was all response. 'I shouldn't want, even if it *were* weak or vain, to have lived wholly unknown. And if what you ask is whether I understand you to speak, as it were, professionally –'

'You *do* understand me?' Bight pushed back his chair.

'Oh, but so well! – when I've already seen what you can do. I need scarcely say, that having seen it, I shan't bargain.'

'Ah, then, *I* shall,' Bight smiled. 'I mean with the Papers. It must be half profits.'

'"Profits"?' His guest was vague.

'Our friend,' Maud explained to Bight, 'simply wants the position.'

Bight threw her a look. 'Ah, he must take what I give him.'

'But what you give me,' their friend handsomely contended, '*is* the position.'

'Yes; but the terms that I shall get! I don't produce you, of course,' Bight went on, 'till I've prepared you. But when I do produce you it will be as a value.'

'You'll get so much for me?' the poor gentleman quavered.

'I shall be able to get, I think, anything I ask. So we divide.' And Bight jumped up.

Marshal did the same, and, while, with his hands on the back of his chair, he steadied himself from the vertiginous view, they faced each other across the table. 'Oh, it's too wonderful!'

'You're not afraid?'

He looked at a card on the wall, framed, suspended and marked with the word 'Soups'. He looked at Maud, who had not moved. 'I don't know; I may be; I must feel. What I *should* fear,' he added, 'would be his coming back.'

'Beadel's? Yes, that would dish you. But since he can't –!'

'I place myself,' said Mortimer Marshal, 'in your hands.'

Maud Blandy still hadn't moved; she stared before her at the cloth. A small sharp sound, unheard, she saw, by the others, had reached her from the street, and with her mind instinctively catching at it, she waited, dissimulating a little, for its repetition or its effect. It was the howl of the Strand, it was news of the absent, and it would have a bearing. She had a hesitation, for she winced even now with the sense of Marshal's intensest look at her. He

202

couldn't be saved from himself, but he might be, still, from Bight; though it hung of course, her chance to warn him, on what the news would be. She thought with concentration, while her friends unhooked their overcoats, and by the time these garments were donned she was on her feet. Then she spoke. 'I don't want you to be "dished".'

He allowed for her alarm. 'But how *can* I be?'

'Something has come.'

'Something –?' The men had both spoken.

They had stopped where they stood; she again caught the sound. 'Listen! They're crying.'

They waited then, and it came – came, of a sudden, with a burst and as if passing the place. A hawker, outside, with his 'extra', called by someone and hurrying, bawled it as he moved. 'Death of Beadel-Muffet – Extraordinary News!'

They all gasped, and Maud, with her eyes on Bight, saw him, to her satisfaction at first, turn pale. But his guest drank it in. 'If it's true then?' – Marshal triumphed at her – 'I'm *not* dished.'

But she only looked hard at Bight, who struck her as having, at the sound, fallen to pieces, and as having above all, on the instant, turned cold for his worried game. 'Is it true?' she austerely asked.

His white face answered. 'It's true.'

7

THE first thing, on the part of our friends – after each interlocutor, producing a penny, had plunged into the unfolded 'Latest' – was this very evidence of their dispensing with their companion's further attendance on their agitated state, and all the more that Bight was to have still, in spite of agitation, his function with him to accomplish: a result much assisted by the insufflation of wind into Mr Marshal's sails constituted by the fact before them. With Beadel publicly dead this gentleman's opportunity, on the terms just arranged, opened out; it was quite as if they had seen him, then and there, step, with a kind of spiritual splash, into the empty seat of the boat so launched, scarcely even taking time to master the essentials before he gave himself to the breeze. The essentials indeed he was, by their understanding, to receive in full from Bight at their earliest leisure; but nothing could so vividly have marked his confidence in the young man as the promptness with which he appeared now ready to leave him to his inspiration. The news moreover, as yet, was the rich, grim fact – a sharp flare from an Agency, lighting into blood-colour the locked room, finally, with the police present, forced open, of the first hotel at Frankfort-on-the-Oder; but there was enough of it, clearly, to bear scrutiny, the scrutiny represented in our young couple by the act of perusal prolonged, intensified, repeated, so repeated that it was exactly perhaps with this suggestion of doubt that poor Mr Marshal had even also a little lost patience. He vanished, at any rate, while his supporters, still planted in the side-street into which they had lately issued, stood extinguished, as to any facial communion, behind the array of printed columns. It was only after he had gone that, whether aware or not, the other lowered, on either side, the absorbing page and knew that their eyes had met. A remarkable thing, for Maud Blandy, then happened, a thing quite as remarkable at least as poor Beadel's suicide, which we recall her having so considerably discounted.

Present as they thus were at the tragedy, present in far Frankfort just where they stood, by the door of their stale pothouse and in the thick of London air, the logic of her situation, she was sharply conscious, would have been an immediate rupture with Bight. He was scared at what he had done – he looked his scare so straight out at her that she might almost have seen in it the dismay of his question of how far his responsibility, given the facts, might, if pried into, be held – and not only at the judgement-seat of mere morals – to reach. The dismay was to that degree illuminating that she had had from him no such avowal of responsibility as this amounted to, and the limit to any laxity on her own side had therefore not been set for her with any such sharpness. It put her at last in the right, his scare – quite richly in the right; and as that was naturally but where she had waited to find herself, everything that now silently passed between them had the merit, if it had none other, of simplifying. Their hour had struck, the hour

after which she was definitely not to have forgiven him. Yet what
occurred, as I say, was that, if, at the end of five minutes, she had
moved much further, it proved to be, in spite of logic, not in the
sense away from him, but in the sense nearer. He showed to her,
at these strange moments, as blood-stained and literally hunted;
the yell of the hawkers, repeated and echoing round them, was
like a cry for his life; and there was in particular a minute during
which, gazing down into the roused Strand, all equipped both
with mob and with constables, she asked herself whether she had
best get off with him through the crowd, where they would be
least noticed, or get him away through quiet Covent Garden,
empty at that hour, but with policemen to watch a furtive couple,
and with the news, more bawled at their heels in the stillness,
acquiring the sound of the very voice of justice. It was this last
sudden terror that presently determined her, and determined with
it an impulse of protection that had somehow to do with pity
without having to do with tenderness. It settled, at all events, the
question of leaving him; she couldn't leave him there and so; she
must see at least what would have come of his own sense of the
shock.

The way he took it, the shock, gave her afresh the measure of
how perversely he had played with Marshal – of how he had tried
so, on the very edge of his predicament, to cheat his fears and
beguile his want of ease. He had insisted to his victim on the truth
he had now to reckon with, but had insisted only because he
didn't believe it. Beadel, by that attitude, was but lying low; so
that he would have no promise really to redeem. At present he
had one, indeed, and Maud could ask herself if the redemption of
it, with the leading of their wretched friend a further fantastic
dance, would be what he depended on to drug the pain of remorse.
By the time she had covered as much ground as this, however, she
had also, standing before him, taken his special out of his hand
and, folding it up carefully with her own and smoothing it down,
packed the two together into such a small tight ball as she might
toss to a distance without the air, which she dreaded, of having,
by any looser proceeding, disowned or evaded the news. Howard
Bight, helpless and passive, putting on the matter no governed

face, let her do with him as she liked, let her, for the first time in their acquaintance, draw his hand into her arm as if he were an invalid or as if she were a snare. She took with him, thus guided and sustained, their second plunge; led him with decision, straight to where their shock was shared and amplified, pushed her way, guarding him, across the dense thoroughfare and through the great westward current which fairly seemed to meet and challenge them, and then, by reaching Waterloo Bridge with him and descending the granite steps, set him down at last on the Embankment. It was a fact, none the less, that she had in her eyes, all the while, and too strangely for speech, the vision of the scene in the little German city: the smashed door, the exposed horror, the wondering, insensible group, the English gentleman, in the disordered room, driven to bay among the scattered personal objects that only too floridly announced and emblazoned him, and several of which the Papers were already naming – the poor English gentleman, hunted and hiding, done to death by the thing he yet, for so long, always *would* have, and stretched on the floor with his beautiful little revolver still in his hand and the effusion of his blood, from a wound taken, with rare resolution, full in the face, extraordinary and dreadful.

She went on with her friend, eastward and beside the river, and it was as if they both, for that matter, had, in their silence, the dire material vision. Maud Blandy, however, presently stopped short – one of the connections of the picture so brought her to a stand. It had come over her, with a force she couldn't check, that the catastrophe itself would have been, with all the unfathomed that yet clung to it, just the thing for her companion's professional hand; so that, queerly but absolutely, while she looked at him again in reprobation and pity, it was as much as she could do not to feel it for him as something missed, not to wish he might have been there to snatch his chance, and not, above all, to betray to him this reflection. It had really risen to her lips – 'Why aren't *you*, old man, on the spot?' and indeed the question, had it broken forth, might well have sounded as a provocation to him to start without delay. Such was the effect, in poor Maud, for the moment, of the habit, so confirmed in her, of seeing time marked only by the dial of the Papers. She had admired in Bight the true journalist that she herself was so clearly not – though it was also not what she had *most* admired in him; and she might have felt, at this instant, the charm of putting true journalism to the proof. She might have been on the point of saying: 'Real business, you know, would be for you to start *now*, just as you are, before anyone else, sure as you can so easily be of having the pull'; and she might, after a moment, while they paused, have been looking back, through the river-mist, for a sign of the hour, at the blurred face of Big Ben. That she grazed this danger yet avoided it was partly the result in truth of her seeing for herself quickly enough that the last thing Bight could just then have thought of, even under provocation of the most positive order, was the chance thus failing him, or the train, the boat, the advantage, that the true journalist wouldn't have missed. He quite, under her eyes, while they stood together, ceased to be the true journalist; she saw him, as she felt, put off the character as definitely as she might have seen him remove his coat, his hat, or the contents of his pockets, in order to lay them on the parapet before jumping into the river. Wonderful was the difference that this transformation, marked by no word and supported by no sign, made in the man she had hitherto known. Nothing, again, could have so expressed for her his continued inward dismay. It was as if, for that matter, she couldn't have asked him a question without adding to it; and she didn't wish to add to it, since she was by this time more fully aware that she wished to be generous. When she at last uttered other words it was precisely so that she mightn't press him.

'I think of *her* – poor thing: that's what it makes me do. I think of her there at this moment – just out of the "Line" – with this stuff shrieked at her windows.' With which, having so at once contained and relieved herself, she caused him to walk on.

'Are you talking of Mrs Chorner?' he after a moment asked. And then, when he had had her quick 'Of course – of who else?' he said what she didn't expect. 'Naturally one thinks of her. But she has herself to blame. I mean she drove him –' What he meant, however, Bight suddenly dropped, taken as he was with another idea, which had brought them the next minute to a halt. 'Mightn't you, by the way, see her?'

'See her *now* –?'

'"Now" or never – for the good of it. Now's just your time.'

'But how can it be hers, in the very midst –?'

'*Because* it's in the very midst. She'll tell you things tonight that she'll never tell again. Tonight she'll be great.'

Maud gaped almost wildly. 'You want me, at such an hour, to *call* –?'

'And send up your card with the word – oh, of course the right one! – on it.'

'What do you suggest,' Maud asked, 'as the right one?'

'Well, "The world *wants* you" – that usually does. I've seldom known it, even in deeper distress than is, after all, here supposable, to fail. Try it, at any rate.'

The girl, strangely touched, intensely wondered. 'Demand of her, you mean, to let me explain for her?'

'There you are. You catch on. Write *that* – if you like – "Let me explain." She'll want to explain.'

Maud wondered at him more – he had somehow so turned the tables on her. 'But she doesn't. It's exactly *what* she doesn't; she never *has*. And that he, poor wretch, was always wanting to –'

'Was precisely what made her hold off? I grant it.' He had waked up. 'But that was before she had killed him. Trust me, she'll chatter now.'

This, for his companion, simply forced it out. 'It wasn't *she* who killed him. That, my dear, you know.'

'You mean it was I who did? Well then, my child, interview *me*.' And, with his hands in his pockets and his idea apparently genuine, he smiled at her, by the grey river and under the high lamps, with an effect strange and suggestive. '*That* would be a go!'

'You mean' – she jumped at it – 'you'll tell me what you know?'

'Yes, and even what I've done! But – if you'll take it so – for the Papers. Oh, for the Papers only!'

She stared. 'You mean you want me to get it in –?'

'I don't "want" you to do anything, but I'm ready to help you, ready to get it in for you, like a shot, myself, if it's a thing you yourself want.'

'A thing I want – to give you away?'

'Oh,' he laughed, 'I'm just now worth giving! You'd really do it, you know. And, to help you, here I am. It *would* be for you – only judge! – a leg up.'

It would indeed, she really saw; somehow, on the spot, she believed it. But his surrender made her tremble. It wasn't a joke – she *could* give him away; or rather she could sell him for money. Money, thus, was what he offered her, or the value of money, which was the same; it was what he wanted her to have. She was conscious already, however, that she could have it only as he offered it, and she said therefore, but half-heartedly, 'I'll keep your secret.'

He looked at her more gravely. 'Ah, as a secret I can't give it.' Then he hesitated. 'I'll get you a hundred pounds for it.'

'Why don't you,' she asked, 'get them for yourself?'

'Because I don't care for myself, I care only for you.'

She waited again. 'You mean for my taking you?' And then as he but looked at her: 'How should I take you if I had dealt with you that way?'

'What do I lose by it,' he said, 'if, by our understanding of the other day, since things have so turned out, you're not to take me at all? So, at least, on my proposal, you get something else.'

'And what,' Maud returned, 'do you get?'

'I *don't* "get"; I lose. I *have* lost. So I don't matter.' The eyes with which she covered him at this might have signified either that he didn't satisfy her or that his last word – *as* his word – rather imposed itself. Whether or no, at all events, she decided that he still did matter. She presently moved again, and they walked some minutes more. He had made her tremble, and she continued to tremble. So unlike anything that had ever come to her was, if seriously viewed, his proposal. The quality of it, while she walked, grew intenser with each step. It struck her as, when one came to look at it, unlike any offer any man could ever have made or any woman ever have received; and it began accordingly, on the instant, to affect her as almost inconceivably romantic, absolutely, in a manner, and quite out of the blue, *dramatic*; immeasurably more so, for example, than the sort of thing she had come out to hear in the afternoon – the sort of thing that was already so far away. If he was joking it was poor, but if he was serious it was, properly, sublime. And he wasn't joking. He was, however, after an interval, talking again, though, trembling still, she had not been attentive; so that she was unconscious of what he had said until she heard him once more sound Mrs Chorner's name. 'If you don't, you know, someone else will, and someone much worse. You told me she likes you.' She had at first no answer for him, but it presently made her stop again. It was beautiful, if she would, but it was odd – this pressure for *her* to push at the very hour he himself had renounced pushing. A part of the whole sublimity of his attitude, so far as she was concerned, it clearly was, since, obviously, he was not now to profit by anything she might do. She seemed to see that, as the last service he could render, he wished to launch her and leave her. And that came out the more as he kept it up. 'If she likes you, you know, she really wants you. Go to her as a friend.'

'And bruit her abroad as one?' Maud Blandy asked.

'Oh, as a friend *from* the Papers – from them and *for* them, and with just your half-hour to give her before you rush back to them. Take it even – oh, you can safely' – the young man developed – 'a little high with her. That's the way – the real way.' And he spoke the next moment as if almost losing his patience. 'You ought by this time, you know, to understand.'

There was something in her mind that it still charmed – his mastery of the horrid art. He could see, always, the superior way, and it was as if, in spite of herself, she were getting the truth from him. Only she didn't want the truth – at least not that one. 'And if she simply, for my impudence, chucks me out of window? A short way is easy for them, you know, when one doesn't scream or kick, or hang on to the furniture or the banisters. And I usually, you see' – she said it pensively – 'don't. I've always, from the first, had my retreat prepared for any occasion, and flattered myself that, whatever hand I might, or mightn't, become at getting in, no one would ever be able so beautifully to get out. Like a flash, simply. And if she does, as I say, chuck me, it's *you* who fall to the ground.'

He listened to her without expression, only saying 'If you feel for her, as you insist, it's your duty.' And then later, as if he had made an impression, 'Your duty, I mean, to try. I admit, if you will, that there's a risk, though I don't, with my experience, feel it. Nothing venture, at any rate, nothing have; and it's all, isn't it? at the worst, in the day's work. There's but one thing you can go on, but it's enough. The greatest probability.'

She resisted, but she was taking it in. 'The probability that she will throw herself on my neck?'

'It will be either one thing or the other,' he went on as if he had not heard her. 'She'll not receive you, or she will. But if she does your fortune's made, and you'll be able to look higher than the mere *common* form of donkey.' She recognized the reference to Marshal, but that was a thing she needn't mind now, and he had already continued. 'She'll keep *nothing* back. And you mustn't either.'

'Oh, won't I?' Maud murmured.

'Then you'll break faith with her.'

And, as if to emphasize it, he went on, though without leaving her an infinite time to decide, for he looked at his watch as they proceeded, and when they came, in their spacious walk, abreast of another issue, where the breadth of the avenue, the expanses of stone, the stretch of the river, the dimness of the distance, seemed to isolate them, he appeared, by renewing their halt and looking up afresh towards the town, to desire to speed her on her way. Many things meanwhile had worked within her, but it was not till she had kept him on past the Temple Station of the Underground that she fairly faced her opportunity. Even then too there were still other things, under the assault of which she dropped, for the moment, Mrs Chorner. 'Did you really,' she asked, 'believe he'd turn up alive?'

With his hands in his pockets he continued to gloom at her. 'Up there, just now, with Marshal – what did you take me as believing?'

'I gave you up. And I do give you. You're beyond me. Only,'

211

she added, 'I seem to have made you out since then as really staggered. Though I don't say it,' she ended, 'to bear hard upon you.'

'Don't bear hard,' said Howard Bight very simply.

It moved her, for all she could have said; so that she had for a moment to wonder if it were bearing hard to mention some features of the rest of her thought. If she was to have him, certainly, it couldn't be without knowing, as she said to herself, something – something she might perhaps mitigate a little the solitude of his penance by possessing. 'There were moments when I even imagined that, up to a certain point, you were still in communication with him. Then I seemed to see that you lost touch – though you braved it out for me; that you had begun to be really uneasy and were giving him up. I seemed to see,' she pursued after a hesitation, 'that it was coming home to you that you had worked him up too high – that you were feeling, if I may say it, that you had better have stopped short. I mean short of *this*.'

'You may say it,' Bight answered. 'I *had* better.'

She looked at him a moment. 'There was more of him than you believed.'

'There was more of him. And now,' Bight added, looking across the river, 'here's *all* of him.'

'Which you feel you have on your heart?'

'I don't know where I have it.' He turned his eyes to her. 'I must wait.'

'For more facts?'

'Well,' he returned after a pause, 'hardly perhaps for "more" if – with what we have – this *is* all. But I've things to think out. I must wait to see how I feel. I did nothing but what he wanted. But we were behind a bolting horse – whom neither of us could have stopped.'

'And *he*,' said Maud, 'is the one dashed to pieces.'

He had his grave eyes on her. 'Would you like it to have been me?'

'Of course not. But you enjoyed it – the bolt; everything up to the smash. Then, with that ahead, you were nervous.'

'I'm nervous still,' said Howard Bight.

Even in his unexpected softness there was something that escaped her, and it made in her, just a little, for irritation. 'What I mean is that you enjoyed his terror. That was what led you on.'

'No doubt – it was so grand a case. But do you call charging me with it,' the young man asked, '*not* bearing hard –?'

'No' – she pulled herself up – 'it *is*. I don't charge you. Only I feel how little – about what has been, all the while, *behind* – you tell me. Nothing explains.'

'Explains what?'

'Why, his act.'

He gave a sign of impatience. 'Isn't the explanation what I offered a moment ago to give you?'

It came, in effect, back to her. 'For use?'

'For use.'

'Only?'

'Only.' It was sharp.

They stood a little, on this, face to face; at the end of which she turned away. 'I'll go to Mrs Chorner.' And she was off while he called after her to take a cab. It was quite as if she were to come upon him, in his strange insistence, for the fare.

8

IF she kept to herself, from the morrow on, for three days, her adoption of that course was helped, as she thankfully felt, by the great other circumstance and the great public commotion under cover of which it so little mattered what became of private persons. It was not simply that she had her reasons, but she couldn't during this time have descended again to Fleet Street even had she wished, though she said to herself often enough that her behaviour was rank cowardice. She left her friend alone with what he had to face, since, as she found, she could in absence from him a little recover herself. In his presence, the night of the news, she knew she had gone to pieces, had yielded, all too vulgarly, to a weakness proscribed by her original view. Her original view had been that if poor Beadel, worked up, as she inveterately kept

213

seeing him, *should* embrace the tragic remedy, Howard Bight wouldn't be able not to show as practically compromised. He wouldn't be able not to smell of the wretched man's blood, morally speaking, too strongly for condonations or complacencies. There were other things, truly, that, during their minutes on the Embankment, he *had* been able to do, but they constituted just the sinister subtlety to which it was well that she should not again, yet awhile, be exposed. They were of the order – from the safe summit of Maida Hill she could make it out – that had proved corrosive to the muddled mind of the Frankfort fugitive, deprived, in the midst of them, of any honest issue. Bight, of course, rare youth, had *meant* no harm; but what was precisely queerer, what, when you came to judge, less human, than to be formed for offence, for injury, by the mere inherent play of the spirit of observation, of criticism, by the inextinguishable flame, in fine, of the ironic passion? The ironic passion, in such a world as surrounded one, might assert itself as half the dignity, the decency, of life; yet, none the less, in cases where one had seen it prove gruesomely fatal (and not to one's self, which was nothing, but to others, even the stupid and the vulgar) one was plainly admonished to – well, stand off a little and think.

This was what Maud Blandy, while the Papers roared and resounded more than ever with the new meat flung to them, tried to consider that she was doing; so that the attitude held her fast during the freshness of the event. The event grew, as she had felt it would, with every further fact from Frankfort and with every extra-special, and reached its maximum, inevitably, in the light of comment and correspondence. These features, before the catastrophe, had indubitably, at the last, flagged a little, but they revived so prodigiously, under the well-timed shock, that, for the period we speak of, the poor gentleman seemed, with a continuance, with indeed an enhancement, of his fine old knack, to have the successive editions *all* to himself. They had been always of course, the Papers, very largely about him, but it was not too much to say that at this crisis they were about nothing else worth speaking of; so that our young woman could but groan in spirit at the direful example set to the emulous. She spared an occasional moment to the vision of Mortimer Marshal, saw him drunk as she might have said, with the mere fragrance of the wine of glory, and asked herself what art Bight would now use to furnish him forth as he had promised. The mystery of Beadel's course loomed, each hour, so much larger and darker that the plan would have to be consummate, or the private knowledge alike beyond cavil and beyond calculation, which should attempt either to sound or to mask the appearances. Strangely enough, none the less, she even now found herself thinking of her rash colleague as attached, for the benefit of his surviving victim, to this idea; she went in fact so far as to imagine him half-upheld, while the public wonder spent itself, by the prospect of the fun he might still have with Marshal. This implied, she was not unconscious, that his notion of fun was infernal, and would of course be especially so were his knowledge as real as she supposed it. He would inflate their foolish friend with knowledge that was false and so start him as a balloon for the further gape of the world. This was the image, in turn, that would yield the last sport – the droll career of the wretched man as wandering forever through space under the apprehension, in time duly gained, that the least touch of earth would involve the smash of his car. Afraid, thus, to drop, but at the same time equally out of conceit of the chill air of the upper and increasing solitudes to which he had soared, he would become such a diminishing speck, though traceably a prey to wild human gyrations, as she might conceive Bight to keep in view for future recreation.

It wasn't however the future that was actually so much in question for them all as the immediately near present, offered to her as the latter was in the haunting light of the inevitably unlimited character of any real inquiry. The inquiry of the Papers, immense and ingenious, had yet for her the saving quality that she didn't take it as real. It abounded, truly, in hypotheses, most of them lurid enough, but a certain ease of mind as to what these might lead to was perhaps one of the advantages she owed to her constant breathing of Fleet Street air. She couldn't quite have said why, but she felt it wouldn't be the Papers that, proceeding from link to link, would arrive vindictively at Bight's connection with his late client. The enjoyment of that consummation would rest in another quarter, and if the young man were as uneasy now as she thought he ought to be even while she hoped he wasn't, it would be from the fear in his eyes of such justice as was shared with the vulgar. The Papers held an inquiry, but the Authorities, as they vaguely figured to her, would hold an inquest; which was a matter – even when international, complicated and arrangeable, between Frankfort and London, only on some system unknown to her – more in tune with possibilities of exposure. It was not, as need scarce be said, from the exposure of Beadel that she averted herself; it was from the exposure of the person who had made of Beadel's danger, Beadel's dread – whatever these really represented – the use that the occurrence at Frankfort might be shown to certify. It was well before her, at all events, that if Howard Bight's reflections, so stimulated, kept pace at all with her own, he would at the worst, or even at the best, have been glad to meet her again. It was her knowing that and yet lying low that she privately qualified as cowardice; it was the instinct of watching and waiting till she should see how great the danger might become. And she had moreover another reason, which we shall presently learn. The extra-specials meanwhile were to be had in Kilburnia almost as soon as in the Strand; the little ponied and painted carts, tipped at an extraordinary angle, by which they were disseminated, had for that matter, she observed, never rattled up the Edgware Road at so furious a rate. Each evening, it was true, when the flare of Fleet Street would have begun really to smoke, she had, in resistance to old habit, a little to hold herself; but for three successive days she tided over that crisis. It was not till the fourth night that her reaction suddenly declared itself, determined as it partly was by the latest poster that dangled free at the door of a small shop just out of her own street. The establishment dealt in buttons, pins, tape, and silver bracelets, but the branch of its industry she patronized was that of telegrams, stamps, stationery, and the 'Edinburgh rock' offered to the appetite of the several small children of her next-door neighbour but one. 'The Beadel-Muffet Mystery, Startling Disclosures, Action of the Treasury' – at these words she anxiously gazed;

after which she decided. It was as if from her hilltop, from her very housetop, to which the window of her little room was contiguous, she had seen the red light in the east. It *had*, this time, its colour. She went on, she went far, till she met a cab, which she hailed, 'regardless', she felt, as she had hailed one after leaving Bight by the river. 'To Fleet Street' she simply said, and it took her – that she felt too – back into life.

Yes, it was life again, bitter, doubtless, but with a taste, when, having stopped her cab, short of her indication, in Covent Garden, she walked across southward and to the top of the street in which she and her friend had last parted with Mortimer Marshal. She came down to their favoured pothouse, the scene of Bight's high compact with that worthy, and here, hesitating, she paused, uncertain as to where she had best look out. Her conviction, on her way, had but grown; Howard Bight would be looking out – *that* to a certainty; something more, something portentous, had happened (by her evening paper, scanned in the light of her little shop window, she had taken instant possession of it), and this would have made him know that she couldn't keep up what he would naturally call her 'game'. There were places where they often met, and the diversity of these – not too far apart, however – would be his only difficulty. He was on the prowl, in fine, with his hat over his eyes; and she hadn't known, till this vision of him came, what seeds of romance were in her soul. Romance, the other night, by the river, had brushed them with a wing that was like the blind bump of a bat, but that had been something on *his* part, whereas this thought of bringing him succour as to a Russian anarchist, to some victim of society or subject of extradition, was all her own, and was of this special moment. She *saw* him with his hat over his eyes; she saw him with his overcoat collar turned up; she saw him as a hunted hero cleverly drawn in one of the serializing weeklies or, as they said, in some popular 'ply', and the effect of it was to open to her on the spot a sort of happy sense of all her possible immorality. That was the romantic sense, and everything vanished but the richness of her thrill. She knew little enough what she might have to do for him, but her hope, as sharp as a pang, was that, if anything, it would put her in danger too.

The hope, as it happened then, was crowned on the very spot; she had never so felt in danger as when, just now, turning to the glazed door of their cookshop, she saw a man, within, close behind the glass, still, stiff and ominous, looking at her hard. The light of the place was behind him, so that his face, in the dusk of the side-street, was dark, but it was visible that she showed for him as an object of interest. The next thing, of course, she had seen more – seen she could be such an object, in such a degree, only to her friend himself, and that Bight had been thus sure of her; and the next thing after that had passed straight in and been met by him, as he stepped aside to admit her, in silence. He *had* his hat pulled down and, quite forgetfully, in spite of the warmth within, the collar of his mackintosh up.

It was his silence that completed the perfection of these things – the perfection that came out most of all, oddly, after he had corrected them by removal and was seated with her, in their common corner, at tea, with the room almost to themselves and no one to consider but Marshal's little man in the obvious wig and the blue spectacles, the great authority on the inner life of the criminal classes. Strangest of all, nearly, was it, that, though now essentially belonging, as Maud felt, to this order, they were not conscious of the danger of his presence. What she had wanted most immediately to learn was how Bight had known; but he made, and scarce to her surprise, short work of that. 'I've known every evening – known, that is, that you've wanted to come; and I've been here every evening, waiting just there till I should see you. It was but a question of time. Tonight, however, I was sure – for there's, after all, *something* of me left. Besides, besides –!' He had, in short, another certitude. 'You've been ashamed – I knew, when I saw nothing come, that you would be. But also that that would pass.'

Maud found him, as she would have said, all there. 'I've been ashamed, you mean, of being afraid?'

'You've been ashamed about Mrs Chorner; that is, about *me*. For that you did go to her I know.'

'Have you been then yourself?'

'For what do you take me?' He seemed to wonder. 'What had

218

I to do with her – except *for* you?' And then before she could say: 'Didn't she receive you?'

'Yes, as you said, she "wanted" me.'

'She jumped at you?'

'Jumped at me. She gave me an hour.'

He flushed with an interest that, the next moment, had flared in spite of everything into amusement. 'So that I was right, in my perfect wisdom, up to the hilt?'

'Up to the hilt. She took it from me.'

'That the public wants her?'

'That it won't take a refusal. So she opened up.'

'Overflowed?'

'Prattled.'

'Gushed?'

'Well, recognized and embraced her opportunity. Kept me there till midnight. Told me, as she called it, everything about everything.'

They looked at each other long on it, and it determined in Bight at last a brave clatter of his crockery. 'They're stupendous!'

'It's *you* that are,' Maud replied, 'to have found it out so. You know them down to the ground.'

'Oh, what I've found out –!' But it was more than he could talk of then. 'If I hadn't really felt sure, I wouldn't so have urged you. Only now, if you please, I don't understand your having apparently but kept her in your pocket.'

'Of course you don't,' said Maud Blandy. To which she added, 'And I don't quite myself. I only know that now that I have her there nothing will induce me to take her out.'

'Then you potted her, permit me to say,' he answered, 'on absolutely false pretences.'

'Absolutely; which is precisely why I've been ashamed. I made for home with the whole thing,' she explained, 'and there, that night, in the hours till morning, when, turning it over, I saw all it really was, I knew that I *couldn't* – that I would rather choose *that* shame, that of not doing for her what I had offered, than the hideous honesty of bringing it out. Because, you see,' Maud declared, 'it was – well, it was too much.'

Bight followed her with a sharpness! 'It was so good?'

'Quite beautiful! Awful!'

He wondered. 'Really charming?'

'Charming, interesting, horrible. It was *true* – and it was the whole thing. It was herself – and it was *him*, all of him too. Not a bit made up, but just the poor woman melted and overflowing, yet at the same time raging – like the hot-water tap when it boils. I never saw anything like it; everything, as you guaranteed, came out; it has made me know things. So, to have come down here with it, to have begun to hawk it, either through you, as you kindly proposed, or in my own brazen person, to the highest bidder – well, I felt that I didn't *have* to, after all, if I didn't want to, and that if it's the only way I can get money I would much rather starve.'

'I see.' Howard Bight saw all. 'And that's why you're ashamed?'

She hesitated – she was both so remiss and so firm. 'I knew that by my not coming back to you, you would have guessed, have found me wanting; just, for that matter, as *she* has found me. And I couldn't explain. I can't – I can't to *her*. So that,' the girl went on, 'I shall have done, so far as her attitude to me was to be concerned, something more indelicate, something more indecent, than if I had passed her on. I shall have wormed it all out of her, and then, by not having carried it to market, disappointed and cheated her. She was to have heard it cried like fresh herring.'

Bight was immensely taken. 'Oh, beyond all doubt. You're in a fix. You've played, you see, a most unusual game. The code allows everything *but* that.'

'Precisely. So I must take the consequences. I'm dishonoured, but I shall have to bear it. And I shall bear it by getting *out*. Out I mean, of the whole thing. I shall chuck them.'

'Chuck the *Papers*?' he asked in his simplicity.

But his wonder, she saw, was overdone – their eyes too frankly met. 'Damn the Papers!' said Maud Blandy.

It produced in his sadness and weariness the sweetest smile that had yet broken through. 'We *shall*, between us, if we keep it up, ruin them! And you make nothing,' he went on, 'of one's having at last so beautifully started you? Your complaint,' he developed, 'was that you couldn't get in. Then suddenly, with a splendid jump, you *are* in. Only, however, to look round you and say with disgust "Oh, *here*?" Where the devil do you *want* to be?'

'Ah, that's another question. At least,' she said, 'I can scrub floors. I can take it out perhaps – my swindle of Mrs Chorner,' she pursued – 'in scrubbing *hers*.'

He only, after this, looked at her a little. 'She has written to you?'

'Oh, in high dudgeon. I was to have attended to the "press-cutting" people as well, and she was to have seen herself, at the furthest, by the second morning (that was day-before-yesterday) all over the place. She wants to know what I mean.'

'And what do you answer?'

'That it's hard, of course, to make her understand, but that I've felt her, since parting with her, simply to be too good.'

'Signifying by it, naturally,' Bight amended, 'that you've felt yourself to be so.'

'Well, that too if you like. But she was exquisite.'

He considered. 'Would she do for a ply?'

'Oh God, no!'

'Then for a tile?'

'Perhaps,' said Maud Blandy at last.

He understood, visibly, the shade, as well as the pause; which, together, held him a moment. But it was of something else he spoke. 'And you who had found they would never bite!'

'Oh, I was wrong,' she simply answered. 'Once they've *tasted* blood –!'

'They want to devour,' her friend laughed, 'not only the bait and the hook, but the line and the rod and the poor fisherman himself? Except,' he continued, 'that poor Mrs Chorner hasn't yet even "tasted". However,' he added, 'she obviously will.'

Maud's assent was full. 'She'll find others. She'll appear.'

He waited a moment – his eye had turned to the door of the street. 'Then she must be quick. These are things of the hour.'

'You hear something?' she asked, his expression having struck her.

He listened again, but it was nothing. 'No – but it's somehow in the air.'

'What is?'

'Well, that she must hurry. She must get in. She must get out.' He had his arms on the table, and, locking his hands and inclining a little, he brought his face nearer to her. 'My sense tonight's of an openness –! I don't know what's the matter. Except, that is, that you're great.'

She looked at him, not drawing back. 'You know everything – so immeasurably more than you admit or than you tell me. You mortally perplex and worry me.'

It made him smile. 'You're great, you're great,' he only repeated. 'You know it's quite awfully swagger, what you've done.'

'What I haven't, you mean; what I never shall. Yes,' she added, but now sinking back – 'of course you see that too. What *don't* you see, and what, with such ways, is to be the end of you?'

'You're great, you're great' – he kept it up. 'And I like you. That's to be the end of me.'

So, for a minute, they left it, while she came to the thing that, for the last half-hour, had most been with her. 'What *is* the "action", announced tonight, of the Treasury?'

'Oh, they've sent somebody out, partly, it would seem, at the request of the German authorities, to take possession.'

'Possession, you mean, of his effects?'

'Yes, and legally, administratively, of the whole matter.'

'Seeing, you mean, that there's still more in it –?'

'Than meets the eye,' said Bight, 'precisely. But it won't be till the case is transferred, as it presently will be, to this country, that they *will* see. Then it will be funny.'

'Funny?' Maud Blandy asked.

'Oh, lovely.'

'Lovely for *you*?'

'Why not? The bigger the whole thing grows, the lovelier.'

'You've odd notions,' she said, 'of loveliness. Do you expect his situation won't be traced to you? Don't you suppose you'll be forced to speak?'

'To "speak" –?'

'Why, if it *is* traced. What do you make, otherwise, of the facts tonight?'

'Do you call them facts?' the young man asked.

'I mean the Astounding Disclosures.'

'Well, do you only read your headlines? "The most astounding disclosures are expected" – *that's* the valuable text. Is *it*,' he went on, 'what fetched you?'

His answer was so little of one that she made her own scant. 'What fetched me is that I can't rest.'

'No more can I,' he returned. 'But in what danger do you think me?'

'In any in which you think yourself. Why not, if I don't mean in danger of hanging?'

He looked at her so that she presently took him for serious at last – which was different from his having been either worried or perverse. 'Of public discredit, you mean – for having so unmercifully baited him? Yes,' he conceded with a straightness that now surprised her, 'I've thought of that. But how can the baiting be proved?'

'If they take possession of his effects won't his effects be partly his papers, and won't they, among them, find letters from you, and won't your letters show it?'

'Well, show what?'

'Why, the frenzy to which you worked him – and thereby your connection.'

'They won't show it to dunderheads.'

'And are they all dunderheads?'

'Every mother's son of them – where anything so beautiful is concerned.'

'Beautiful?' Maud murmured.

'Beautiful, my letters are – gems of the purest ray. I'm covered.'

She let herself go – she looked at him long. 'You're a wonder. But all the same,' she added, 'you don't like it.'

'Well, I'm not sure.' Which clearly meant, however, that he almost *was*, from the way in which, the next moment, he had exchanged the question for another. 'You haven't anything to tell me of Mrs Chorner's explanation?'

Oh, as to this, she had already considered and chosen. 'What do you want of it when you know so much more? So much more, I mean, than even she has known.'

'Then she *hasn't* known –?'

'There you are! What,' asked Maud, 'are you talking about?'

She had made him smile, even though his smile was perceptibly pale; and he continued. 'Of what was behind. Behind any game of mine. Behind everything.'

'So am I then talking of that. No,' said Maud, 'she hasn't known, and she doesn't know I judge, to this hour. Her explanation therefore doesn't bear upon that. It bears upon something else.'

'Well, my dear, on what?'

He was not, however, to find out by simply calling her his dear; for she had not sacrificed the reward of her interview in order to present the fine flower of it, unbribed, even to *him*. 'You know how little you've ever told me, and you see how, at this instant, even while you press me to gratify you, you give me nothing. I give,' she smiled – yet not a little flushed – 'nothing *for* nothing.'

He showed her he felt baffled, but also that she was perverse. 'What you want of me is what, originally, you wouldn't hear of: anything so dreadful, that is, as his predicament must be. You saw that to make him want to keep quiet he must have something to be ashamed of, and that was just what, in pity, you positively objected to learning. You've grown,' Bight smiled, 'more interested since.'

'If I have,' said Maud, 'it's because *you* have. Now, at any rate, I'm not afraid.'

He waited a moment. 'Are you very sure?'

'Yes, for my mystification is greater at last than my delicacy. I don't know till I do know' – and she expressed this even with difficulty – 'what it has been, all the while, that it was a question of, and what, consequently, all the while, we've been talking about.'

'Ah, but why should you know?' the young man inquired. 'I can understand your needing to, or somebody's needing to, if we were in a ply, or even, though in a less degree, if we were in a tile.

But since, my poor child, we're only in the delicious muddle of life itself –!'

'You may have all the plums of the pudding, and I nothing but a mouthful of cold suet?' Maud pushed back her chair; she had taken up her old gloves; but while she put them on she kept in view both her friend and her grievance. 'I don't believe,' she at last brought out, 'that there *is*, or that there ever was, anything.'

'Oh, oh, oh!' Bight laughed.

'There's nothing,' she continued, '"behind". There's no horror.'

'You hold, by that,' said Bight, 'that the poor man's deed is *all* me? That does make it, you see, bad for me.'

She got up and, there before him, finished smoothing her creased gloves. 'Then we *are* – if there's such richness – in a ply.'

'Well, we are not, at all events – so far as we ourselves are concerned – the spectators.' And he also got up. 'The spectators must look out for themselves.'

'Evidently, poor things!' Maud sighed. And as he still stood as if there might be something for him to come from her, she made her attitude clear – which was quite the attitude now of tormenting him a little. 'If you know something about him which she doesn't, and also which *I* don't, she knows something about him – as I do too – which *you* don't.'

'Surely: when it's exactly what I'm trying to get out of you. Are you afraid *I'll* sell it?'

But even this taunt, which she took moreover at its worth, didn't move her. 'You definitely then won't tell me?'

'You mean that if I will you'll tell *me*?'

She thought again. 'Well – yes. But on that condition alone.'

'Then you're safe,' said Howard Bight. 'I *can't*, really, my dear, tell you. Besides, if it's to come out –!'

'I'll wait in that case till it does. But I must warn you,' she added, 'that *my* facts *won't* come out.'

He considered. 'Why not, since the rush at her is probably even now being made? Why not, if she receives others?'

Well, Maud could think too. 'She'll receive them, but they won't receive *her*. Others are like *your* people – dunderheads.

Others won't understand, won't count, won't exist.' And she moved to the door. 'There *are* no others.' Opening the door, she had reached the street with it, even while he replied, overtaking her, that there were certainly none such as herself; but they had scarce passed out before her last remark was, to their somewhat disconcerted sense, sharply enough refuted. There was still the other they had forgotten, and that neglected quantity, plainly in search of them and happy in his instinct of the chase, now stayed their steps in the form of Mortimer Marshal.

9

HE was coming in as they came out; and his 'I *hoped* I might find you,' an exhalation of cool candour that they took full in the face, had the effect, the next moment, of a great soft carpet, all flowers and figures, suddenly unrolled for them to walk upon and before which they felt a scruple. Their ejaculation, Maud was conscious, couldn't have passed for a welcome, and it wasn't till she saw the poor gentleman checked a little, in turn, by their blankness, that she fully perceived how interesting they had just become to themselves. His face, however, while, in their arrest, they neither proposed to re-enter the shop with him nor invited him to proceed with them anywhere else – his face, gaping there, for Bight's promised instructions, like a fair receptacle, shallow but with all the capacity of its flatness, brought back so to our young woman the fond fancy her companion had last excited in him that he profited just a little – and for sympathy in spite of his folly – by her sense that with her too the latter had somehow amused himself. This placed her, for the brief instant, in a strange fellowship with their visitor's plea, under the impulse of which, without more thought, she had turned to Bight. 'Your eager claimant,' she, however, simply said, 'for the opportunity now so beautifully created.'

'I've ventured,' Mr Marshal glowed back, 'to come and remind you that the hours are fleeting.'

Bight had surveyed him with eyes perhaps equivocal. 'You're afraid someone else will step in?'

'Well, with the place so tempting and so empty –!'

Maud made herself again his voice. 'Mr Marshal sees it empty itself perhaps too fast.'

He acknowledged, in his large, bright way, the help afforded him by her easy lightness. 'I do want to get in, you know, before anything happens.'

'And what,' Bight inquired, 'are you afraid *may* happen?'

'Well, to make sure,' he smiled, 'I want myself, don't you see, to happen first.'

Our young woman, at this, fairly fell, for her friend, into his sweetness. '*Do* let him happen!'

'*Do* let me happen!' Mr Marshal followed it up.

They stood there together, where they had paused, in their strange council of three, and their extraordinary tone, in connection with their number, might have marked them, for some passer catching it, as persons not only discussing questions supposedly reserved for the Fates, but absolutely enacting some encounter of these portentous forces. 'Let you – let you?' Bight gravely echoed, while on the sound, for the moment, immensities might have hung. It was as far, however, as he was to have time to speak, for even while his voice was in the air another, at first remote and vague, joined it there on an ominous note and hushed all else to stillness. It came, through the roar of thoroughfares, from the direction of Fleet Street, and it made our interlocutors exchange an altered look. They recognized it, the next thing, as the howl, again, of the Strand, and then but an instant elapsed before it flared into the night. 'Return of Beadel-Muffet! Tremenjous Sensation!'

Tremenjous indeed, so tremenjous that, each really turning as pale with it as they had turned, on the same spot, the other time and with the other news, they stood long enough stricken and still for the cry, multiplied in a flash, again to reach them. They couldn't have said afterwards who first took it up. 'Return –?'

'From the *Dead* – I *say*!' poor Marshal piercingly quavered.

'Then he *hasn't* been –?' Maud gasped it with him at Bight.

But that genius, clearly, was not less deeply affected. 'He's alive?' he breathed in a long, soft wail in which admiration appeared at first to contend with amazement and then the sense of the comic to triumph over both. Howard Bight uncontrollably – it might have struck them as almost hysterically – laughed.

The others could indeed but stare. 'Then who's dead?' piped Mortimer Marshal.

'I'm afraid, Mr Marshal, that *you* are,' the young man returned, more gravely, after a minute. He spoke as if he saw *how* dead.

Poor Marshal was lost. 'But someone was killed –!'

'Someone undoubtedly was, but Beadel somehow has survived it.'

'Has he, then, been playing the game –?' It baffled comprehension.

Yet it wasn't even that what Maud most wondered. 'Have you all the while really known?' she asked of Howard Bight.

He met it with a look that puzzled her for the instant, but that she then saw to mean, half with amusement, half with sadness, that his genius was, after all, simpler. 'I wish I had. I really believed.'

'All along?'

'No; but after Frankfort.'

She remembered things. 'You haven't had a notion this evening?'

'Only from the state of my nerves.'

'Yes, your nerves must be in a state!' And somehow now she had no pity for him. It was almost as if she were, frankly, disappointed. '*I*,' she then boldly said, 'didn't believe.'

'If you had mentioned that then,' Marshal observed to her, 'you would have saved me an awkwardness.'

But Bight took him up. 'She did believe – so that she might punish me.'

'Punish you –?'

Maud raised her hand at her friend. 'He doesn't understand.'

He was indeed, Mr Marshal, fully pathetic now. 'No, I don't understand. Not a wee bit.'

'Well,' said Bight kindly, 'we none of us do. We must give it up.'

'You think *I* really must –?'

'You, sir,' Bight smiled, 'most of all. The places seem so taken.'

His client, however, clung. 'He won't die again –?'

'If he does he'll again come to life. He'll never die. Only *we* shall die. He's immortal.'

He looked up and down, this inquirer; he listened to the howl of the Strand, not yet, as happened, brought nearer to them by one of the hawkers. And yet it was as if, overwhelmed by his lost chance, he knew himself too weak even for *their* fond aid. He still therefore appealed. 'Will *this* be a boom for him?'

'His return? Colossal. For – fancy! – it was exactly what we talked of, you remember, the other day, as the ideal. I mean,' Bight smiled, 'for a man to be lost, and yet at the same time –'

'To be found?' poor Marshal too hungrily mused.

'To be boomed,' Bight continued, 'by his smash and yet never to have been too smashed to know how he was booming.'

It was wonderful for Maud too. 'To have given it all up, and yet to have it all.'

'Oh, better than that,' said her friend: 'to have *more* than all, and more than you gave up. Beadel,' he was careful to explain to their companion, 'will have more.'

Mr Marshal struggled with it. 'More than if he were dead?'

'More,' Bight laughed, 'than if he weren't! It's what *you* would have liked, as I understand you, isn't it? and what you would have got. It's what *I* would have helped you to.'

'But who then,' wailed Marshal, 'helps *him*?'

'Nobody. His star. His genius.'

Mortimer Marshal glared about him as for some sign of such aids in his own sphere. It embraced, his own sphere too, the roaring Strand, yet – mystification and madness! – it was with Beadel the Strand was roaring. A hawker, from afar, at sight of the group, was already scaling the slope. 'Ah, but *how* the devil –?'

Bight pointed to this resource. 'Go and see.'

'But don't *you* want them?' poor Marshal asked as the others retreated.

'The Papers?' They stopped to answer. 'No, never again. We've done with them. We give it up.'

'I mayn't again see you?'

Dismay and a last clutch were in Marshal's face, but Maud, who had taken her friend's meaning in a flash, found the word to meet them. 'We retire from business.'

With which they turned again to move in the other sense, presenting their backs to Fleet Street. They moved together up the rest of the hill, going on in silence, not arrested by another little shrieking boy, not diverted by another extra-special, not pausing again till, at the end of a few minutes, they found themselves in the comparative solitude of Covent Garden, encumbered with the traces of its traffic, but now given over to peace. The howl of the Strand had ceased, their client had vanished forever, and from the centre of the empty space they could look up and see stars. One of these was of course Beadel-Muffet's, and the consciousness of that, for the moment, kept down any arrogance of triumph. He still hung above them, he ruled, immortal, the night; they were far beneath, and he now transcended their world; but a sense of relief, of escape, of the light, still unquenched, of their old irony, made them stand there face to face. There was more between them now than there had ever been, but it had ceased to separate them, it sustained them in fact like a deep water on which they floated closer. Still, however, there was something Maud needed. 'It had been all the while worked?'

'Ah, not, before God – since I lost sight of him – by *me*.'

'Then by himself?'

'I dare say. But there are plenty for him. He's beyond me.'

'But you thought,' she said, 'it *would* be so. You thought,' she declared, 'something.'

Bight hesitated. 'I thought it would be great if he *could*. And *as* he could – why, it *is* great. But all the same I too was sold. I *am* sold. That's why I give up.'

'Then it's why *I* do. We must do something,' she smiled at him, 'that requires less cleverness.'

'We must love each other,' said Howard Bight.

'But can we live by that?'

He thought again; then he decided. 'Yes.'

'Ah,' Maud amended, 'we must be "littery". We've now got stuff.'

'For the dear old ply, for the rattling good tile? Ah, they take better stuff than this – though this too is good.'

'Yes,' she granted on reflection, 'this is good, but it has bad holes. *Who was the dead man in the locked hotel room?*'

'Oh, I don't mean that. *That*,' said Bight, 'he'll splendidly explain.'

'But how?'

'Why, in the Papers. Tomorrow.'

Maud wondered. 'So soon?'

'If he returned tonight, and it's not yet ten o'clock, there's plenty of time. It will be in *all* of them – while the universe waits. He'll hold us in the hollow of his hand. His chance is just there. And there,' said the young man, 'will be his greatness.'

'Greater than ever then?'

'Quadrupled.'

She followed; then it made her seize his arm. '*Go* to him!'

Bight frowned. '"Go" –?'

'This instant. *You* explain!'

He understood, but only to shake his head. 'Never again. I bow to him.'

Well, she after a little understood; but she thought again. 'You mean that the great hole is that he really had no reason, no funk –?'

'I've wondered,' said Howard Bight.

'Whether he *had* done anything to make publicity embarrassing?'

'I've wondered,' the young man repeated.

'But I thought you knew!'

'So did I. But I thought also I knew he was dead. However,' Bight added, 'he'll explain that too.'

'Tomorrow?'

'No – as a different branch. Say day after.'

'Ah, then,' said Maud, 'if he explains –!'

'There's no hole? I don't know!' – and it forced from him at last a sigh. He was impatient of it, for he had done with it; it would soon bore him. So fast they lived. 'It will take,' he only dropped, 'much explaining.'

His detachment was logical, but she looked a moment at his sudden weariness. 'There's always, remember, Mrs Chorner.'

'Oh yes, Mrs Chorner; we luckily invented *her*.'

'Well, if she drove him to his death –?'

Bight, with a laugh, caught at it. 'Is that it? *Did* she drive him?'

It pulled her up, and, though she smiled, they stood again, a little, as on their guard. 'Now, at any rate,' Maud simply said at last, 'she'll marry him. So you see how right I was.'

With a preoccupation that had grown in him, however, he had already lost the thread. 'How right –?'

'Not to sell my Talk.'

'Oh yes,' – he remembered. 'Quite right.' But it all came to something else. 'Whom will *you* marry?'

She only, at first, for answer, kept her eyes on him. Then she turned them about the place and saw no hindrance, and then, further, bending with a tenderness in which she felt so transformed, so won to something she had never been before, that she might even, to other eyes, well have looked so, she gravely kissed him. After which, as he took her arm, they walked on together. 'That, at least,' she said, 'we'll put in the Papers.'

MORE ABOUT PENGUINS
AND PELICANS

Penguinews, which appears every month, contains details of all the new books issued by Penguins as they are published. From time to time it is supplemented by *Penguins in Print*, which is our complete list of almost 5,000 titles.

A specimen copy of *Penguinews* will be sent to you free on request. Please write to Dept EP, Penguin Books Ltd, Harmondsworth, Middlesex, for your copy.

In the U.S.A.: For a complete list of books available from Penguins in the United States write to Dept CS, Penguin Books, 625 Madison Avenue, New York, New York 10022.

In Canada: For a complete list of books available from Penguins in Canada write to Penguin Books Canada Ltd, 41 Steelcase Road West, Markham, Ontario.

Arnold Bennett

THE GRAND BABYLON HOTEL

Arnold Bennett's reputation has revived suddenly and remarkably over recent years. His status as a 'Penguin Modern Classics author' is assured, though not all his work reaches the high standard of such novels as *Anna of the Five Towns*.

The Grand Babylon Hotel is in this category. Written 'for a lark' and sold as a serial for £100, the novel was intended by its author to be 'absolutely sublime in those qualities that should characterize a sensational serial'. And it is.

As action crowds on action (with cliff-hangers to close every chapter) crowned heads, petty princelings, and pluto-crats jostle with international conspirators and murderers in the public rooms and corridors of the greatest hotel in Europe.

When Theodore Racksole, New York railroad millionaire, buys the Grand Babylon on a whim, he is warned by the vendor, M. Félix Babylon: 'You will regret the purchase.' Returning to his table in the *salle à manger*, he imparts the news to his beautiful daughter, Nella.

And now read on.

Arnold Bennett

THE CLAYHANGER TRILOGY

CLAYHANGER

Arnold Bennett's careful evocation of a boy growing to manhood during the last quarter of the nineteenth century, with its superb portrait of an autocratic father, stands on a literary level with *The Old Wives' Tale*.

HILDA LESSWAYS

Relating the early life of Hilda Lessways, before her marriage to Edwin Clayhanger. Her involvement with the enigmatic, self-made man, George Cannon, and his enterprises take her from the offices of an embryo newspaper in the Five Towns to a venture into the guest house business in Brighton.

THESE TWAIN

In what is in many ways the most accomplished novel of the trilogy, Bennett achieves a remarkably subtle and biting portrait of a marriage. Hilda and Edwin Clayhanger are living in Bursley, with Hilda's son by her disastrous 'marriage' to George Cannon. As they cope with immediate tensions and old wounds, they are forced continually to reassess their relationship.

Joseph Conrad

'Conrad is among the very greatest novelists in the language – or any other language' – F. R. Leavis in *The Great Tradition*.

LORD JIM

The novel by which Conrad is most often remembered; it tells of the enigmatic and impressive sailor once condemned for cowardice.

THE NIGGER OF THE NARCISSUS, TYPHOON, and Other Stories

Conrad's first sea novel, together with 'Typhoon', 'Falk', 'Amy Foster', and 'Tomorrow'.

Also published in Penguins:

HEART OF DARKNESS
NOSTROMO
AN OUTCAST OF THE ISLANDS
YOUTH *and* THE END OF THE TETHER

Henry James

'He is as solitary in the history of the novel as Shakespeare in the history of poetry' – Graham Greene in *The Lost Childhood*.

THE BOSTONIANS

Intending to write 'a very American tale', Henry James drew attention, in *The Bostonians*, to 'the situation of women, the decline of the sentiment of sex, the agitation in their behalf'.

THE EUROPEANS

'This small book, written so early in James's career, is a masterpiece of major quality' – F. R. Leavis in *The Great Tradition*.

WASHINGTON SQUARE

Set in New York, this closely constructed novel studies the plight of an innocent heiress, deceived by the good looks and charm of a worthless suitor.

SELECTED SHORT STORIES

The four stories in this volume provide excellent introductions to the themes and styles of the author's three periods.

Henry James

THE WINGS OF THE DOVE

Milly Theale, the 'dove' of the title, knows when she visits Europe that she is shortly to die, which lends urgency to her eager search for happiness.

WHAT MAISIE KNEW

'One of the most remarkable technical achievements in fiction. We are shown corruption through the eyes of innocence that will not be corrupted' – Walter Allen in *The English Novel*.

THE AWKWARD AGE

Thrust suddenly into the immoral circle gathered round her mother, Nanda Brookenham finds herself in competition with Mrs Brookenham for the affection of a man she admires.

THE GOLDEN BOWL

Henry James's last, most controversial novel in which Walter Allen has found 'a classical perfection never before achieved in English'.

THE TURN OF THE SCREW AND OTHER STORIES

For James the whole world of Americans, Cockneys, upper-class snobs, writers, dilettanti and intriguers allowed him to indulge his greatest obsession: observation.

and
THE PORTRAIT OF A LADY

Henry James

THE AMBASSADORS

The Ambassadors, though it was the author's own favourite among his novels, is one of those (his last three) which have abruptly divided modern critics. In them Walter Allen finds 'the final splendid flowering of James's genius' and Graham Greene groups them together as his 'three poetic master-pieces'.

On the other hand: 'We are asked to admire *The Ambassa-dors*,' writes F. R. Leavis: 'and *The Ambassadors* seems to me not only *not* one of his great books, but to be a bad one.'

Paris provides the brilliant, compelling focal point for this story of a Young American whose wealthy mother dispatches from the States two successive embassies to bring him home; but the 'fine central intelligence' of the novel resides in the character of Strether, the first ambassador, who falls prey to the charms of Europe.

E. M. Forster, at any rate, detected a peculiar symmetry in the novel – 'the shape of an hour-glass ... Everything is planned, everything fits; none of the minor characters are just decorative ... they elaborate on the main theme, they work.'